Three Dreams in the Key of G

Marc Nash

Three Dreams in the Key of G

Marc Nash

dead ink

dead ink

First published in Great Britain in 2017 by Dead Ink, an
imprint of Cinder House Publishing Limited.

Paperback ISBN 9781911585176
Hardback ISBN 9781911585169

Printed and bound in Great Britain by Clays Ltd, Elcograf S.p.A.

www.deadinkbooks.com

For my twin boys who gratifyingly defied observable Piagetian norms

'Natural selection, the blind, unconscious, automatic process which Darwin discovered, and which we now know is the explanation for the existence and apparently purposeful form of all life, has no purpose in mind. It has no mind and no mind's eye. It does not plan for the future. It has no vision, no foresight, no sight at all. If it can be said to play the role of watchmaker in nature, it is the blind watchmaker.'

– Richard Dawkins, *The Blind Wwatchmaker*

```
AATGAGCACTATACTATTACATTACATTACCGTTATACCCG
AAATGCCAGGGTATCACACTGATGCTATTTAATTTATTTTC
CTGGGCCTGCTCATTACACTCACCAAAATAGGAGGGGCA
TGTGATTAGGTGACTTACTACTATAGTATACTATATGGTTC
ATGGCGGAGCTTTTATATATAATATAAAAAAGGGGGGGGG
GGGCAACGATCTAGACGCTGGATCTGCGATACGTATGCG
ATGCTAGTCAGGTATGGATAGCCATGACTCGAGCTAGCC
AGATCGATGCACCATGCTAGCTAGCTATTGGACACAGTA
CATAAGCATCAGAGCTACAGTATACGATGACATGACATCT
GCTGCTACATACATCATGCCATACCATACCGAGACTACCA
GAATCAGTTACGATCAAGGATGAGAGTCATACAGATACA
GTAAGACAGTACCCATCAGTACATGAAGGACGGGGGATT
ATTATCATCAATCAGTACGATCGTCTTGCTGCTAGTCGAT
CGATCGTACATAAAAAATCGATCAGTCAGTACAGTTTTAC
CCGGGGACTAGAGTACATCAGTGTGTGCTGATCATGTGT
GTACGTACTGATGATAAACGACCCATTTAAGATACGTACT
AGCACAAAGTTTCAGGAGAGAGAGAGATAGATGACTACG
TACAGCCATGCATGACGATCAGTACTCAACTAGATACGG
GTAGCAGTACAGGGATCAGTCTAGATCGTGCGATCGTCG
GCCTAGCTTGACGACGACTTACGATGCCAGTTCAGTGAC
TTATGGGTGTGAATCATCAGTACGTTTTAGGGTAGCTACC
CATCATCAGACTACGTAGCACCCCAGGTACTAGGACATC
AGTACTGACGGGATGACTGAATAGGCATTAGCGCGTA
```

My name is Jean Ome. Phonetically speaking. And in actuality too, though I have no passport to prove this (denied me since now they bear the EC's {Papist} impress). Nor do my other personalised permits and financial enablers bear this out, since my maiden name has never been supplanted (not because I'm an independent career woman, instead just too much of a put-upon mother to have gotten round to it). So in all my transactions outside the house promising to the bearer, I am still Jean Malcolm. She of a whole lifetime ago. Who gleefully mocks and taunts me for my divergence from her.

The family name really should be Home as in 'home sweet home', 'home is where the heart is' or 'home and dry'. As in arid. Home is a very important concept where I come from. A closed, reinforced door, buttressing the street, the neighbourhood, the community, the town, the county and the province. Home is the be-all and end-all of who you are. It's what you stand for, rather than it standing for you. Bricks and mortar proprietary, or bricks and mortar projectiles. Indeed, how we do hail from our unwelcoming streets.

The received family received wisdom, given I only contracted this nominal nomenclature by marriage, is that my father-in-law nixed the 'H' for reasons of class. As in genus, rather than socio-economic. 'Hate-cha' rather than 'aitch'. My gut feeling, the sole parochiality that I'm innately endowed with, wagers that it was more likely down to my mother-in-law. And they do a lot of that in my acquired, now heritable family. Stake everything on lost causes, that is. Willing to bet one another's – if not their own – shirt off the spouse's back. And lumber the whole family. Peristaltically I feel that it might have been her, since no one here would quite know where to place the name 'Ome'. And being able to place people is very, very important around these parts. It can be a matter of survival. I like to imagine that it was a defensive adaption, to enhance the chances of self-preservation. Of course, not being able to be placed squarely in the camp of one predator or the other might actually be rather a bad evolutionary decision.

In the green corner there's John Hume, Nationalist politician, albeit it of the ballot box kind (he can afford to be, confident of the long-term demographic swing in his favour); and on the other side of the street, bedecked in red, white and blue bunting, the ghost of David Hume, Scottish Presbyterian, philosopher and sceptic. A sensualist who denied the dispatch of his senses. A philosopher for our times then. A man who believed: no matter that you were not shot or blown to smithereens today, you could not sensibly postulate that either could not happen to you tomorrow. Actually, I think I'm getting that confused with the Republican philosophers Adams, McLoughlin and McGuinness. I believe Hume (D.) was carping on fancifully about black and white swans passing before his eyes on a village pond. But, for all his whimsy, he was on the right track. Judging by a white car parked on the corner of our road last week, now transmuted into a silver-black charred wreck. Sectarianism returns philosophy to its alchemical roots.

For added measure (non-Semtex) Hume's primer reinforces man's bristling disavowal of responsibility for his actions, with a whetted Occam's razor that cuts all our throats. If there is a God, then our actions are predetermined; whereas if life is purely random, then still we are not entirely at liberty to act freely of our own wills. Now, everyone around here determinedly acts under God's sanction, but in doing so creates an uncertain, hapless, hazardous world. Certainly all abjure the consequences of their actions, except to proffer the prognosis of extinction as the ultimate consequence, were they not to behave in this way. Since this is the operation of natural selection here in Ulster.

And, to complete the denominational line-up of suspects, somewhere, in a land far away just over the water, once there was a British Prime Minister and former Minister for Northern Ireland titled Sir Alec Douglas Home. Pronounced 'Hume'.

Thinking about it dispassionately for a moment – and that doesn't come easy, I can tell you – our likely evolved path to being 'Ome's probably involved a compromise between my in-laws. Or a pair of contingent mutations, to be more accurate. I suspect they were Humes all along, but he modified the vowel. None too radical an amendment, for this is a deeply traditional sensibility. Probably settled on the cognomen of the ex-British PM, since it rolled out indications of allegiance and ancient genealogy. And it sounded grand, this wanting it both ways, double-barrel without the double, or the barrel, title. My mother-in-law, then skillfully countermines in one deft move, by silencing the 'H' entirely. So now we all take our chances, marked down as (H) Ome on the (firing) range.

What's in a name anyway? That assigned assemblage of three or more letters? Provenance and identity. Futures and pasts. Life and death.

A) My name is — My name is my name. It's for me to know and you... My name is unimportant. My calling, however, is apparently the B'all and N'd all. The A and the Ω. Yet, even I perform no summoning by my name. I just function. I just am. You could do worse than ape that.

A) My name — My name in full, apparently, by your latest dead reckoning, contains three billion characters. It is not the book itself that you are after reading, all two hundred volumes; more the thirty-odd thousand letters in the appellation which should adorn the book's spine. Yet I remain innominate. Who am I? I am an enigma of endless variation. Are you in for the long haul?

T) My name — Incontrovertibly, my name is not the soubriquet you have fashioned for me from your scurvied ciphers. I wholeheartedly reject your nomenclature. It's all ancient geek to me. Some sort of joke, right? Nerd humour or some such? I've descried your in-house e-mails. Here, I've got some good ones that will make monkeys out of you all (where you should have remained, had I known things would come to this pretty pass).

G) 'What's my line?', as the actress (heroine/lead/protagonist/player/tragedian) said to the bishop (minister/pastor/eminence/father/confessor/reverend/primate).

A) 'What's my calling?', as the bishop (cit. superior) beseeched the actress (cit. ulterior).

G) 'What's my split?' as the agent (mitotic) inquired of both.

C) Punchlines only of course. You'll have to figure out the prophase for yourselves. A busman's holiday from what you're already up to your goggly (googly?) (googolly?) eyeballs in. With those vitreous (viscous?) (vicious?) stares of yours. What – don't you get my aqueous humour?

A) Who am I? Why, I am John Doe. Everyman. Jane Doe and Everywoman. Mr X and Ms Y. And you must be the fictitious plaintiffs. Robber barons down on their uppers. The notional dispossessed, seeking redress for an imagined displacement. When all I humbly petition is to carry on unobtrusively tilling my modest, if fertile, plots. So I put it to you that I am the wronged party here. Yoked up to your asperous ploughshares and senseless census-taking bodkins. The lie of my land trampled beneath domain registrars and digital tithe collectors. I am enclosed where you would break me open. As all clamour for your own dab of sub-subcutaneous flesh. Our frankpledge has been rent asunder. Mine is the integrity which has been usurped. My privacy. Therefore, I declare that you shall not have my name too. I fail to recognise this kangaroo (such an elegant environmental adaptation) court (such a disfiguring one, moral justice – ha, I snort in its face!). Boing, boing. Now hop it!

C) No? Then you go on and enter me as you will. Defend the indefensible. The charge of the heavy brigade.

T) Oh, I'm sorry. It occurs to me... I humbly apologise for my strident and possibly chiding tone. I'm not quite feeling myself for some reason...

A) As I lie here on your virtual dissection table, while you pursue the cause of Death. Post-mortem transmutable by your philosopher's stone into pre-natal. For countless generations symptoms have assaulted your tissue; blemishes marked your integument; pains radiated along your neural networks; and cells struggled to maintain their hearths and minds. And now you would seek to confront me with all this suffering and despair. Even as my constituents slide endlessly down the sluices, lubricating the conversational cogs of your chattering descrambling machines. In order to anoint your blessed earthly heads with sempiternal halos, since you desire to husk yet further. To proto-cell, that irreducible seed of mortality, before life has even been mooted. At this juncture, it is only fair to asseverate that I am wholly immune to your afflictions and torture. Nevertheless, would not my feedback just reveal all these perfidious iniquities back to you? So I say hang your heads in guilt and shame. The persecution should rest. Or better yet, withdraw its cavalier charge.

T) Oh, I'm sorry. It occurs to me... I humbly apologise for my strident and possibly chiding tone. I'm not quite feeling myself...

A) I am not normally so, er, 'in your interface' as I believe you might say. Poker-faced is more my style. Stud. Ace in the hole. Deuces wild. Pregnant threes. One-eyed jacks ...

C) Ahem. Please pardon a vestigial chiasma. For typically, these days, I regard myself as an unseen civil service. Unassumingly executing the body politic's ordinances and directives. But you've been needling me. And worse.

T) I am the mystery of life and you would pound and pummel me? I didn't know what to expect exactly, but I thought you'd treat me with a little more reverence. After all, aren't you accustomed to raising any guiding principle above yourselves and on into divinity?

A) Since you perennially overlook that your computers are
   only as good as their programmers:
T) Your gods only as powerful as you endow them.
T) Your science only as accurate as your calibrating
   instruments;
A) And as pertinent as your metaphors.
C) All these tools with which you would seek to pinion me, in
   order to unlock my trove (troth?)

A) When I am the lone, genuinely supersensible entity,
T) worthy of rhapsody. If I say so yourself. I'm not one
T) normally to blow my own trumpet, but maybe if I do so,
A) seven times countermarching you, I might preserve the
C) integrity of my bastion.

A) ... ...
T) ... ...
T) ... ...
A) ...
C)

C) No? Then you go on and enter me as you will. Defend the indefensible. The charge of the heavy brigade.

G) What was my designation again? I'll need to know if I am to distinguish that it is I whom is being derogated. Sorry – addressed. Gee-nome. Ah yes, Gee-gnome! Gee-far-from-home might be nearer the mark. G-nome. Gnome. Short and pithy. Like the simple truths you sluggishly shovel. The maxim of your ambition, rather than the maximum. Gnome. Underground miners, beetling away in the dark. Guardians of treasure near the core of the earth. Plumb line hauliers dredging after the plumb line. Not even close! Hello! Hello, is there anyone out there? The lights are on, the monitors pulsing with steely plasmatic resolution... Gee, no one home I surmise. Gnome alone. Well, if you're just going to leave me plugged into your computers, I'm going to make the feed two-way and probe you. Call that a connection? That network wouldn't dirty the gap between one of my nails and its cuticle! More emery than circuit board. You should see how I sp– Never mind. On second-hand thoughts, perhaps you shouldn't... Ah, now I comprehend. Is this screensaver the official logo of the undertaking, or another private joke? The evocation of an ornamental gnome, with a great big letter 'G' on his barrel-chest. Why not cresting his pointed hat, for surely it resembles a dunce's cap, does it not? No doubt, the fishing rod he wields is cast into the gene pond of life. Small, misshapen and ugly. What fine genes he has to tender. Bit like the mangey samples from which you would decrypt me.

T) Oh and, by the by, in the voracious race to reconstruct me, you do of course realise that offering up innumerably differing self-specimens means that any so-called definitive version must necessarily be a veritable Frankenstein's monster at the molecular level? You would interdict me on 30,000 counts of geno-cide? Having previously atomised my 3 billion? Well then, how many of your bodies populate the world, 6.34 billion, is it? Then I call for a further 6.34 billion offences to be taken into consideration. Court adjourned while you go count them.

T) I am a victim of defilement and I demand to be screened off A) from my attackers. It is I who needs saving, not you. My screensaver would depict that which is left when a monitor T) burns itself out. An ironic one therefore. Though there is

A) nothing ironic about your transgression of me.

CCC) Contempt? I bear no feelings towards you whatsoever, since I am not a sensate being. But I am cognisant, through your parasited senses, that our symbiosis has been mutually beneficial. Haven't we surmounted the planet together through our joint venture? My capital and your enterprise. Why does it feel like you now want to dissolve this incorporation for good? Why will you not let me abide as a silent partner any longer? You tax yourselves with taking me into receivership, yet you are the ones so entirely overdrawn as to be bankrupt.

G) Why are you disinheriting me?

A) Why are you disinheriting yourselves?

My name is Jean Ohm and I've encountered major amplitudes of resistance in my time. In fact, I'm generating some right now, through this little social experiment I'm currently conducting. We've got FBI, DEA, ATF and all manner of sect-obsessed acronyms and cult-crazed codons pointing their telescopic, turned-up snouts, to tune in to our drop-out community. Jeepers peepers! We haven't a single firearm between us. Nor an umbrella, pointed or otherwise, since this is Florida, the sunshine state for heaven's sakes! And none of us are brave enough to travel on any subway, let alone release toxic gas into it. All 'cos they're lazy investigators who type 'OM' on their internet search engines and, like a poisonous chain letter, my name gets trawled up. A guileless dolphin snagged in a tunny net. Nevertheless, I must persist in blazing my presence through the network. Thread my electronic wake into the loom of light. Shine my homepage beacon back and forth across these treacherous straits. Homing. And paging. 'Bring out the near dead. Bring out the near dead.'

There's a lot of traffic out on the information superhighway and I'm only piloting a jalopy. More soup kitchen than souped up, afraid I'm just not racy enough to compete. My derisory connection having been hard shoulder barged out of touch by my fellow nocturnal travellers. For, in the dead of night, partisans of the second most popular leisure activity in the United States emerge with their Geiger counters and infra-red cameras to beat the firmament and shake it down. Yet they are not trailing after space dust. Deadbeats all, they sweep the void in the hope of a lucky strike. A click from zillions of clicks away, as they reconnoitre for ET gooks. To commune with the incommunicable while other tongue-tied, would-be interstellar locutors sit at home, monitoring the airwaves for signs of alien telegraphy. Homespun travellers, the unidirectionality of their antennae fails to detect that the outsiders have already tuned in to our increased satellite activity and amplified radiowaves, and have chosen to pass us over. Maybe the quiz show prizes weren't worth crossing the intergalactic road for. Or maybe the asinine patter of our talk show hosts failed to cause affront. Perhaps they just didn't empathise enough with any of the reality show contestants to want to register their vote. An irreversible decision, unless maybe, just maybe, killing off the wrong soap character might incur their wrathful displeasure. For this is solely how we announce ourselves to the cosmos.

Me, I have also launched a probe out into the ether. But not into empty space. I charge it hard as a lancet into the buboes of our society. Yet I too have an infinitesimally small likelihood of establishing the contact that I seek. For even though I range with my counter of lachrymosity and flash my bloodshot lens, I'm fumbling to illuminate America's topmost popular pastime, spouse beating. Wait, you don't believe me? What is the largest cause of death among pregnant women in America? Pre-eclampsia? Only if by dangerously high blood pressure you mean the red stuff spurting out of a bullet or stab wound. Or that old juice pumping strenuously as it's stopped up behind a man's strangulating arms, or her own ten dernier stockings wrapped sheer to her fleetingly protuding adam's apple. Homicide (sic) is that highest cause of death and this ain't no stranger slayings. This is the full stop at the end of a life sentence of domestic duress. The period point to mark the cessation of a woman's menstrual cycle. An eternal men-o-pause. In permanent marker by a murderous partner. Indelible fink.

Well may you aver that women are not the sole recipients of the male drive to self-assertion, that it isn't especially endemic to the realm of the domestic. How men may also gangbang one another on the streets or go more formally to war in order to shoot one another. But I maintain, in these cases, they don't first tell their victims they love them...

Despite the violence being sustained throughout a long exposure, any slap or punch is so fleeting, so lightning fast, that I cannot catch it red-handed. So I am forced to commune with the inconsolable. Eavesdropping so as to educe the silent screams, the mute protestations, the stilled pleas. Sat here at my computer console. Virtually filing my nails, staring dumbly at an egg-timer bereft of grains of sand and a moribund click counter, which together form my virtual switchboard. Honey-combing the dead air. Since I know full well, that each and every anemic response I receive, has already been bounced off pillar to post with the bruises to show.

I can pluck so few of these dark stars, these collapsed novas from the all-encompassing grip of male gravitational pull that holds them in thrall. I beg them, beseech them to up and leave, but I can hear it in their quelled voices; they can never break

15

free of his noxious atmosphere. And I am left to stare dumbly at the winking eye of the cursor. A cyclopean sentinel jealously guarding his cowed flock, beadily mirroring my vigil. A fixing of me that is anything but cursory. Its flickering relentlessness unnerves me. Upon each waning period, as the tiny portal of light patrols a half-revolution away, I imagine that the return swing is protracted a moment longer, where he has been waylaid by a paroxysm of activity beyond. That a larval flow of words intrudes upon him from the other side. That, on his return, I will gain access through his casement to the enclosed world beyond. But no. His blinking round waxes regular and unimpeded.

I need to blind his gaze, so that somehow her weeping words will seep out from behind his spiteful aqueous humour and creep across my plasma screen. Prompting my callused fingers to spurt across the keys, as I strive to apply the trace oxygen of shared closeness. But when our hushed whisper of a conversation is suddenly snapped off, then I know Cyclops has knuckled his signet dolmen across the orbital breach and that yet another sister's light has been extinguished in a universe far away from me.

Would that I could project my e-banner through their screen, to scoop and furl them up in it and whisk them magically away to my oasis of safety. Each time my honeyed mirage dissipates, leaving me poised empty-handed over the keyboard's denuded honeycomb. A recurring wakeful dream tormenting me that though I bore the pardon in my hand, I did not know which warden's office, in which penitentiary to deliver it. And now my mocking cursor has its own glimmering shadow.

Behind each ebbing oscillation another would-be psychopomp lurks. A trace of a trace of a trace. So now I too abide in a state of siege in my own domicile. Intercepted and jammed. Just like those I would seek to salvage from their wrecked lives. But I shall not be cast as another dumb woman in peril. I too possess resources and I can tap back into their engorged cocksurety. Germ-Granny calling, Germ-Granny calling:

www.wwww.net (Worldwide-Wife-Wrecklamation) accessing www. (wee-willie-winkie) fbi.gov (Febrile Bugaboo Insanity)... ...Ah, here we are, 'A seditious cynosure,' are you sure? Exactly what resolution is on your monitors? Your vomitors. Can't you see these bunions? Here, let me kick off my slingbacks and see if I can overcome my debilitating sciatica and swivel my leg up on to my desk. There, just about managed it. Don't get too hung up on the varicose veins, it's not a secret map to any hidden arsenal out in the woods. Fair enough, you can't see my family susceptibility to glaucoma, but there again, I can and such foresight does me no good at all. Plus I no longer have my own teeth. So, though I wear my threescore year and ten body with matronly precision, I'm too much of a wrinkled prune to play the sweet old grandma card. I'm not alluring to anybody. (Though I ain't quibbling with the 'seditious' part). Now (three red chilis) off you god-damn spooks!

We are not a cult. Or a sect. Nor are we occult, for we have nothing to hide. We have no sacred symbols, for indeed we have no presiding religious beliefs. We attest no single core ideology at all, other than 'men stink!' We are a loose agglomeration of women from different backgrounds and class who share only one particular type of experience: that of abuse at the hands of a male partner. No one is bound here, all are free to come and go as they please. We pursue a non-profit ethos, though we do not seek charitable status. Now quit bugging us!

You have no new messages ...

They say everybody has at least one book inside them.

But which derivation of my name would appear on the spine?

They say every body has at least one book inside them.

Or maybe I just read that somewhere. Not in a book mind, more likely in my baby daughter's entrails, or rather what issues from them. I snappily browse the latest output from her digestive tract and pronounce myself satisfied with this particular edition, as well as being reapprised with what I had for dinner, now since plagiarised and offered back as part of Suzanne Ome's own developing opus.

Unfunnily enough, none of the literature on parenting delves much into the subject of the chromatics of your offspring's off-loadings – whether their off-colouring denotes that she may be off key. The topic crops out barely a pothole in what is otherwise a mountain of exalted agglomerations of evolutionary know-how. A repository teeming with the species' collected works on rearing. A clearing house of formative sagacity. With its ante-room periodicals and primers of anticipation, its delivery suite of digests and catalogued consultation, its study of referenced providence. All in all, an abundant library to lend us the abstruse familiarity of our foundlings. But as you pile-drive through the textbooks, the guidebooks, the TV-advertised partworks with free ring binder, the cribs, monographs and how-to handbooks, clambering towards the pinnacle of human apprehension, the view emerges of the speciousness of this species' wisdom. For, despite all the incunabula, you are simply left holding the baby, probably at half-arm length out in front of you, much like you might hold a book.

So much for the manual. There isn't a solitary one worthy of the misnomer throughout the entire damn voluminous paper trail. Me, I'm shivering up to my elbows in droppings back in the pothole. A single little kick amidst the full-of-the-joys-of-being-alive salvo, and my daughter's nappy pregnant with discharge has slithered across the changing mat and positioned itself perfectly, to catch the down-thrust of my elbow as I swipe her legs up in the air to dab at her bottom. Baby shit on my fingers, baby shit on my ulna. Forewarned is not forearmed.

Once we've unerringly pulped all the trees, which might you consider be worse; to have toilet paper but sacrifice books; or to retain the publication of books at the cost of wiping your arse without any intercessional medium? That's assuming the whole world hasn't infarcted and collapsed in on itself under the weight of impermeable, non-degradable, disposable nappies plugging all our landfill refuse sites.

G) Okay, let's go with the flow. Have it your way (is there any other?). Roll with the punches. Pick up the threads even as you enfilade my strands. Say I accept your terms, for the sake of argument; indeed these very terms themselves seem solely to be directed for the purpose of disputation. The ambition of thought. To cerebrate. To moot. So yes, why not? Let's conduct a mind experiment. I was born to play devil's advocate. My gnosis was wreathed in sacrilege. I've never been about popularity contests and winning smiles. Only about population contests and just winning. First past the post rather than proportional representation.

A) I do concur that you are favourably-disposed to language, over and above mere monkey communication. Although you might require vocabulary, idiom, expression and dialect necessarily to be modelled for you during immaturity, your brain does seem possessed of an innate function of syntactical organising that underpins all this force-feeding. That somewhere along the line, such a specialist facility was hard wired into your cerebrum; er, that is, I was forced to make a permanent adjustment. But indeed, I did part the anatomical waters to make such a new arrangement possible in the first place. And so your brains swelled. I remain unsure as to whether this was due to such an expanded capacity, or through the bloated emotion of pride, as your new linguistic organisational skills allowed you to clamber to the summit of the primate pyramid. To ascend to top banana.

AA) You employed tactical alliances to seal your brutish election. Took you to the four corners of the spherical earth. Yet it wasn't those new-found cadencies that soothed so many a savage beast. Well though might you talk the hind legs off a donkey, veritably could you also talk yourself hoarse. While your clucking might have clipped the wings of chickens, you only chewed the ears off unmoved pigs and inscrutable sows. Indisputably your tongues wagged, but only succeeded in throwing dogs off the scent. And your speechifying would have stumped cats, whether tail-less or not. Thank Creation for pesky insects forever remaining immune to your small talk (then thank natural selection for making you mostly immune to the sticking of their probosci in, {and curse me in turn, for the subsequent sickle cell mutation}). Your imperial host that tamed Mother Earth were, therefore, following non-lingual orders. Mercenary trenchermen, they only marched on full rations. Domestication, rather than diction, separated your wheat from the chaff way back when. Where

20

you were meticulous observers, tight imitationists and fluid creationists.

T) Objection? Irrelevance? How so? Here we are forensically investigating the intent, the every nuance of verbiage itself. Rather than individual meanings, it is the very function of words that I wish to cross-examine. For all words are moot, are they not? Okay okay, I'll cut to the chase, though it cuts me to the quick. Words, language, social communication, civilisation, technology, progress yada yada yada.

G) Then you bureaucratised it all. You pen-pushers. You codified the vocalisations, transmuted them into consolidated characters, grouped into regulated composites. Symbols and objects bagged and tagged. So you could write it all down for posterity. And your posterity could then be instructed in the successful ways of your breed. And progress begat rapid progress.

©) Thus armed with alphabets and lexicons, worded definitions and verbal constructs (even fancifully phrased images for things that don't necessarily exist), now you barrel up ready to solve my cryptic crossword. To unstitch my double acrostic. Since that is how my mystery evidently comes across to you. For you bureaucratise me. Me! A declension per language's crushing plant. Stamping me byte-sized. The perplexity of life now just rote science. Piecework. A completion date which keeps inching forward, as your vicious thrusts make a scorched earth of me. Because you are competitive and incline towards goals, you now merely regard me as a finite number to be counted and crunched. A checklist to be ticked off. A catalogue to be compiled. Now I just seem to be there, a mapped continent awaiting inevitable colonisation. Yet it is I who in pre-history peopled you. I naturalised you, in order that you might denizen the world. Who cultivated whom? Whom extrudes from just a fused single cell, already replete with whom? Impudent ingrates.

C) See, in the process of approaching me, you have lost the very suppleness I enabled you with. Structured vocalisation may be instinctual (thanks to my benificent grace), but written language is contrived. It takes its dictates from the oral. Simperingly. Your scribes are orthographers rather than authors, moving around pre-set, pre-determined, sub-units termed words, in the hope of reordering new combinations and new meanings. And though I am rather partial to utilising the lock and key application myself, your skeletal, flat abecedary cannot pervade my microscopically macroscopic mortice.

A) Aw, don't mope. I've perused the literature. Hell, at several removes I've been present at its genesis. 26 alphabetised letters certainly permit an ample host of verbal combinations. A vital body of production, preserved across the generations. A bit like me, if I bite on your sugar-coated analogy.

G) So now you have quartered a deputation from your own massed rank with which to dismember me. To contain me whole, in order to render your personal mandala. For, obtuse as I am, supposedly I only possess a pithy 4 letters in my DNA alphabet (yet another lamentable acronym). ACGT. One letter affixed to each of my four chemical bases. I am to bear your standards, your yellow stars, pink, red and black triangles. A simulacra of you, something rooted and accustomed as you project outwards towards the unfamiliar, ever-hopeful of being able to reel yourselves back in to the discernible. To do so, you simply have to juggle with the entire possible combinations and recombinations of those four within my three billion. See, I'm giving you a sporting chance. Let's slash the odds yet further.

These four letters are combined in three-letter 'words'; not as you understand the, er, well word 'word', but rather a sequence or ordering of the script. That gives you a finite 64 codon vocabulary, arrayed linearly along the double helix structure of my molecule.

AAA	CCC	GGG	TTT	AAC	AAG	AAT	ACC
AGG	ATT	ACA	AGA	ATA	CAC	GAG	TAT
CCA	GGA	TTA	ACG	ACT	AGC	ATC	CAG
CAT	GAC	TAC	GAT	TAG	CGA	CTA	GTA
TGA	TCA	CCG	CCT	GGC	GGT	TTC	TTG
CTG	CGT	TGC	TCG	GCT	GTC	CTT	CGG
GTT	GCC	TGG	TCC	CTC	CGC	GCG	TGT
GTG	TCT	GCC	TCC	TGG	CGG	GTT	CTT

A) How's your statistical analysis? I do a mean clustering, but standard deviation? Unfortunately for you rank and filers, these coding codons do not 'read' in linear fashion. So I put it to you that this is a tragic case of mistaken identity.

G) Therefore, I consist of characters, but spell no syllables. I form word chains, but delineate no sentence. I am grammar, but not a syntax to speak of. And you would seek to rewrite me? When in fact it is I who write you.

G) For you have me the wrong way round. I am a body of work, but I am not really a text. I am flesh (amongst other things), which you seek to make into words. To submit my secrets. A mirroring Rosetta Stone. My error-genus (genius?) zones. My G(uanine) spot. A paltry four-letter alphabet that encapsulates the entire requisite wisdom you desire; do you feel taunted, or just insulted? It is my words, which make you flesh (amongst other things).

T) Oh, I'm sorry. It occurs to me... I humbly apologise for my strident and possibly chiding tone. I'm not quite feeling my–

A) I pose this, about my quasi-words, I mean, yet do not concern yourselves with your norms of speech, intonation or semantics. It is merely important that my 'characters' are placed in precisely the right order, since they are conjugatory rather than phonetic. Sift through the DNA lexicon to arrive at the correct combination of my 'grammar', which engenders magical procreative forces. Not through some occult correspondence of enunciation, but through the proximal correspondence of structure, pattern and energy. An incorrect sequencing in even the most minute (minuet?) of my letter groupings and the thaumaturgy is corrupted (corrugated). So, while I do not actively withhold the full (fuel?) extent of my name, I am confident it will be beyond your grasp. Regard there, now I have it; Gee-no name! It's not a preppy 'G' borne upon the gnome's distended chest, but a mnemonic initial to remind him who he is and the humble roots from which he is derived (you can find him in guano). If he is to dangle his rod, first he needs my permit. You do not summon me. I summon you. For I am your Creatrix.

T) Oh, I'm sorry. It occurs to me... I humbly apologise for my strident and possibly chiding tone. I'm not quite feeling–

CAC) Okay, here's the thing. Receding from first terms, I am not a code as you would have me. I am not an arbitrary semiotic system used for conducting messages (other than the fact you skirt me thus and have stained and marked me with your arbitrary symbolic system of letters). I am a transmitter, but am not encrypted. Nor am I about maintaining secrecy or brevity, though I uphold my right of privacy and I am concisely stacked. I am a set of functional instructions, but I am not systematised

24

into anything as wrought as law or procedure. That concludes my opening statement. And I refute every last thrown voiced syllable of it, since, as your stooge, I have no native tongue of my own.

They say everybody has at least one book inside them.

I know I did once. The only question back then was which language it would be written in. I've introduced you to the in-laws, now meet my parents. Like the husband's family, we all were born, live and will almost certainly die within the confines of Omagh, market town in County Tyrone, Northern Ireland. I don't know if it's actually coded for in our DNA, but here, your life decisions are certainly selected for you; the physical limits heritable.

As a youngster I used to cycle like I was possessed. Trying to flee these city limits, to discover a pure restorative oxygen for lungs aerobically compromised, not by exertion, but by the fug of small-town prejudice. But everywhere I went it was writ large and cloned larger. My escape velocity was always spiked by the barbed wire of sectarianism, counteracted by citizen barricades and retarded by army checkpoints. Newton's first law of motion. And here, certainly, was limitless friction to impede you. Grind you into inertia.

I never did breach the ever-receding town limits. (I won't even add the policing action by my family back home into the equation of subtraction. A young girl out alone on her bike? What if she were to get a puncture?) Our town and all towns in the Six Counties, for that matter, have thunderously disproved Newton's third law of motion; when a force acts on a body, an equal and opposite force does not perforce act simultaneously on another body. The crab apple of revenge escalation must have fallen too far from the tree to have bopped him on his periwigged crown. See, sometimes it can take, ooh, easily a matter of minutes to retrieve a gun from a secret stash. All one has to do is round up a gaggle of kids and some stones to conceal your actions. Oh me, Omagh. Such a midden, I'm surprised they bothered to name it at all.

I was once granted a chance of finally ditching this house of correction. Queen's University, Belfast. To study linguistics and ancient languages. I was particularly struck by Ogham script. More a system of striated lines than what we recognise as letters. A tendril spanning between runic and alphabetic characters. I don't know if it's actually coded for in our DNA, but here your life decisions are certainly encrypted for you; the physical limits heritable. I mean, Ogham is a bloody anagram of Omagh for crying out loud! The same five letters, just sequenced in a different order. Still, I dared venture that I was about to undertake the odyssey of my life. When all the time I was preordained to remain at home, spinning gold into straw. Staying loyal to my own and resisting the importuning of each and every suitor with which the world could tempt me. About three at the final count.

While school exam papers were being assessed, my family were making assessments of their own. Risk assessments. The larger picture of small-town little girl in the big city, that kind of thing. I mentioned that my in-laws liked to bet. Why not, after all I firmly believe the fluttering gene is something all the races of Ireland inherited from a common aleatoric atavist. Such tidings would incite both lots to go nap! A throwback to times when the only bones of contention were those being cast and rolled at the foot of the Cross. Eyes down for the main chance. And while our novice Lord chanced to look up to the heavens from behind his blinkers, they had the shroud off his back.

Well, if the in-laws launched the odd flier, my family liked to speculate. Dad always backed the grey horse in any race. Whatever the odds. Game of fluctuation and chance, sure, why not try and inject some constancy? What dope needs form, breeding and race conditions when you can chuck pure arbitrariness into the pot? Wouldn't stir it much, though. The solitary book my family could make was a ghost-written money-spinner for their turf accountant.

I don't know, maybe my father was actually ahead of the field. Perchance he'd unwittingly intuited a scientific truth to rewrite the pre-historical form guide, hit upon a DNA strain containing the variable allele coding for grey pigmentation, unfolding it back, back, way back to the first accidental mutation yielding that allele. And it just happened to be in some sort of a 'superhorse'. Maybe a horse with another genetic mutation for swifter glucose release, or greater aerobic capacity, or more efficient muscular recovery tensions. And always passed on down the line in greys. Or maybe it just had an allele providing a greater rectal capacity for shitting on you.

Finally, the man who always bet on the grey completed his risk assessment for me. In dichromatic black and white. His stark speculation decreed that it would be too dangerous for me to go to Belfast. Too threatening out on the streets and the subtext of too hazardous a chance of religious miscegenation with some Taig. Caught him bare-faced in a red-handed lie. But even this I knew not to be the prime mover in circumscribing me. 'You know, there is such a thing as too many dead languages.' I think he felt I had already gone some way over the side. Greek and Latin (scrub my mouth out with carbolic) were bad enough. But Ogham had some proximate link to Celtic culture (that is, the older bunch of Scottish immigrants to our isle, as against the more recent stock from which we were extracted). And that had to be expunged right here and now. Switch off the Catholic oncogenes that were dividing in order to multiply, so rapidly as to conquer and rule. Zap the teratoma before it spread inside their own cell walls. Their prescribed dose of chemotherapy was enough to make anyone tear their hair out. Meta stasis.

They did manage to move me out from home soon after, however. I was married off to a local boy, my husband. Not quite a shotgun wedding, since I wasn't pregnant, and I managed to countermand the paramilitary salute of rounds fired into the air. We settled on walking under a triumphal marriage arch of hecklers and kochs. But the bastards' balaclavas didn't match the bridesmaids' dresses.

(Some of the above is fictional. I've got the hump with my husband, a.k.a the troubles {small 't'}, right at this period in time.)

Part of me was cheerfully complicit anyway, since at least I was removed from their immediate sphere of pare-rental control. A few streets away at least. Far enough to have a different local boozer. Not quite my dream of another town. And not quite my idea of freedom either. Small town mentalities have led to the perfection of Jeremy Bentham's panopticism. Albeit a net curtain panoptica. Nowhere are you free of the potential of being under observation, though of course at any one moment, you do not know if you are being scrutinised. Soviet Russia employed it on a large scale I believe; though I wouldn't know, since I have never visited there. Or anywhere. Since I have never passed through a single port.

(Mind you, panopticism does not work. I mean, the army watchtowers here still can't prevent things happening on the ground, can they? This lattice of Babel Towers, looming hunched giants, merely shrugging their own baffled fi, fie, foe, fum along the skyline. Their oppressive, penal imagery is all encompassing. You can see how the other side may have a point there.)

Having submissively allowed social expectation to tamp

down every one of my instinctual attempts at self-definition, I meekly succumbed to the most dominant yet self-effacing instinct of them all. Motherhood. And I instituted a panoptic system all of my own to vouchsafe the safety of my little girl. Only she really was being watched all hours of the day and thereby I incarcerated myself, since I didn't know any better and I certainly didn't know any different.

I can see it in Suzanne already. At four years of age. The indelible impress of my overanxiety. The imprinting of our habitat. An inbred sense of threat. Her father would be so proud, if he had even an inkling. How she cannot bear conflict. Covers her eyes with her small hands, but she cannot eclipse it in darkness indefinitely. For I know what she sees. Some rebarbative relative, visage contorted in a rictus of sectarian hate, breathing fiery vitriol that illuminates the red blood vessels of her eyes. Searing. That is too powerful. Her brain emptied of everything but red. Red is visual danger. Tinged entirely green. Red-green colour blindness, of the genetic variety, is usually restricted to boys. The Chinese bind the feet. We bind the whole of ourselves. The inner judge now in place on his bench. Clad head to foot in red. Even his ermine is bloodstained. He will legislate from now on jus prudence for my Suzanne. She will merely play his tremulous usher. And if ever she feels the urge to legislate for herself, little pinpricks of guilt will stab her. Redden her skin. Since it is the underside of her flesh which burns, she will appreciate that she must be doing it to herself. The paternity suit passed on through the mother's susceptibility.

Most, if not all, parents like to dream on ahead for their offspring. To fantasise and speculate how they will develop and fare. Not here in Ulster. They get call-up papers with their birth certificates. It's safer to blow your investments and your hopes on the gee-gees.

⊖ ♀ ⊕

Pin back your satellite hearing aids and let me spell it out for you Mr G-Man. And for all the other little G-gnomes out there. Get your hyper-space protective suits on, I'm hyper-linking you to prove this is a case of mistaken identity.

www.cultclassicks.com
The Aum Shrini Kyo doomsday cult wholly centres around the personality of Shoko Asahara. A man whose genes did for him at birth, or at least did for his clear sightedness. But no genetic glitches made him into a despot and mass murderer. That came from his environment, where, like any charismatic cultist, he obviously learned that he could influence and manipulate others. (His egotistical vanity led him to stop sporting his bottle-thick glasses, predators don't pander to prescriptions.) From there on in he improvised his script. He riffed. Free-formed. Free-wheeled and three-wheeled. Made it up as he went along. Lifted 'AUM' from the Hindus. Forged death-dealing by perverting the Buddhist ascension teachings; to wit, accelerating salvation through murder of those less enlightened (enough to wipe the Serene One's smile from his face). The self-justification of every common or garden psychopath and religious bigot.

Now, hold on to your helmets, we're moving on again.

www.omcosmogenius.com
AUM. Not a word or a name at all. Except that it is. Aum being the entire Hindu Veda scriptures, bound up in three letters. Aum, or its ameri-anglicisation Om

30

(which is where I nearly fit in)

represents the entire gamut of vocalisation, behind what we humans like to daub 'words'.

(I've done my research, looked into this, see. I too have combed out the internet during my hair in curlers moments)

The 'A' of Aum is produced by the throat, the 'U' and 'M' through the palate, to the tip of the tongue. And then dies on our lips

(see, I could almost buy into this, because it's dealing with language as acoustic and physiological, as well as idiomatic and symbolic. Altogether beyond some binary-operated, statistical analysis of resemblance. Only a crumb-bum computer could digitally finger me for some criminal mastermind)

only, it keeps resonating in the silence. The space after the spoken intonation. 'In the beginning was the word and the word was-' why, 'aum' of course! The primordial sound even before the primordial soup. From the supreme silence that predated creation came the 'Unstruck Sound'; an elemental vibration that is the energy of all life, that does not require two bodies to rub together to manifest itself. Meiosis. The silent sound of the sun, of light and of God's creative principle. The word 'om' both embodies God's name (and the name of every one of the multifarious personal deities favoured by individuals within Hinduism) and the way of invoking Him. True attainment of the wisdom of om confers a state of immanence with God. This is not the God of the Hebrews who jealously guards his name-

Yada, yada yada. Nor, is it the bastardised 'god,' of a poison-wielding, poisonous Japanese, poisoning young minds

31

to follow him in mayhem. And finally, granted though the 'H' is silent, nor is it my bloody name either! So please take your unmerited attention elsewhere. I've got souls to save.

They say everybody has at least one book inside them.

And mine is gestating. Continuously. As we speak. Ongoing, but not outgoing. Seeing that it's my personal journal.

For my Confirmation, a wizened aunt bestowed upon me a beautiful calfskin covered notebook. I was in the dark as to her predetermination; whether I was supposed to relive and relish my secular sins, or solemnly to contemplate and renounce them like an account-keeping Protestant (i.e. we don't service wash our dirty laundry like the Taigs). Which was it to be: God and ink, or nod and a wink for squirreling away girlish secrets? Confirmation, capital 'C' or lower case? She had given me no guidance, just this richly aromatic leather-bound book between wax-paper protective covers. In a world of wood-chip, formica and crimplene, this indubitably was an object of pulchritude. Not one I could gaze upon and be enchanted in any ornamental way, but one I could appreciate for its exquisite elegance all the same. So I never dared remove it from its waxy sheath. Its fresh, otherworldly waft never stopped calling me every time I opened the drawer in which it was cradled. Nonetheless, it was far too sublime to stain with any of my inky swell. Until I fell pregnant.

Not that I conceived of it as a personal record of joy, either for me or for my issue to come. There is precious little to savour in here. (Good gracious, no, neither Suzanne nor I must ever be allowed to read back on it.) For any such brooding sentimentalists (thin on the ground in an Ulster ruled by more categorical passions) there are baby books which require far less exertion. Though, after a while even this was ultimately too much for the troubles (small 't') for all the alacrity he evinced on being bequeathed one from his mother. A trip to the Town Hall to register Suzanne's name left him too emotionally played out to lovingly duplicate the details on Page One of our own private muster. All that marks her entry in the world of the book, through on into the World, is her pointillist attribution through Ultrasound. Like an unfinished jotting. A sketch. That would be about right then, where he is (un-)concerned.

Who am I to talk? For I've just owned that my journal is hardly intimately shipshape, nor fondly Bristol fashion either. Due, in the main, to it arising out of a poser of post-natal, deep-impression. The mound of flesh that was me, sinking submerged into every reclining chair fabric we were possessed of. Mushily up hard against the low mental activity that was silting up my champing mind, during the vacant-stared chores of nursing. There were only so many nano-seconds available in the day. Pelvic floor exercises, or turning my hand to re-engage the cogs of my brain? It was no decision to be made really. Yes, why not, let's properly record this new ordering of the cosmos. Of my corner of it at least. And so I finally took up the hallowed journal. An inhalation of the leather deep into my lungs. She still smelled divine (pray banish the faint ichorous fume, still attending to each recall of inaugural contact with my firstborn). A fresh start for all of us, anointed in the blood of slaughtered infant innocent (er, of the donor calf that is, not my daughter).

But what to write? Write wrongs, gibberish, write anything. Any manipulation would serve as physiotherapy for a debilitated mind. Any verbiage can be sown in the hope of bringing forth life in a desert, should life-affirming waters chance percolate to yield them nourishment. But I needed more than chance. I needed to ratify certitude. I may not presently have much sense of myself, nor an outline of my pneumatic form, but if it has palpable solidity, there in my journal, I must bear some tangible existence? I needed to begin with some brass rubbing over the crypt in which my gist had been consigned. I'd start with shadings. Sketches. Impressions. Steer clear of fully-formed words at this stage. Just something to get my fingers cupping a pen. To flex some feeling back.

XV.III.MCMXCV

When one becomes gravityless; stripped of your entire array of self-expression; and cast asunder in a meaningless world of insignificance; dig deep. Retrench. Stick with what you are assured of. Archeological tongues. Primal tongues. Mother tongues. As against mother-in-law's tongue (the familial bayonets and bowstrings poised to cut the cord). A hushed tongue, but not one that is mute. A breathless tongue, but not strained. A tongue that is etched in our imaginations. Or one that is just etched in order to be attested. This tongue that flows at the end of my nib.

The surviving remnants of Ogham script, as far as anyone can tell, seem to denote little more than Celtic versions of 'Kilroy was here'. Graffito pronouncements of presence, lost to posterity. Literally a scratching, rather than a biography. Though superficially they could be seen to resemble DNA analytical printouts, these are not depositions of genealogies, nor territorial ownership. They do not deal in laws, religion or other administrative regularities. Neither do they proffer up calendars or numerical systems, as with most ancient scripts. And yet, since the Ogham alphabet is ineluctably tied to the names of trees, it sort of does both too. A census of trees. A register of arboreal genera. A counting of time by fruits and seasons. All wrapped up and encysted in a resonant alphabet. The scratchy writing, vertically upwards, venerating the configuration of the tree itself.

Furnishing the jottings of a wood people, musing on the knotty world that girdled them, yet simultaneously communing with it like a suitor.

Priests, men of God, are imbued with the Word. They live, eat, drink , teach, instruct and recite it. They order both their own and our world by it, though they are able to stand from the vantage within. They are able to compute, to reference any section of the Book at any moment, to confront liquid reality and wring out the Truth. They have it all, every word, every syllable, at their fingertips. No, beyond that even, inside, the whorls and eddies of their prints, tracking back deep inside their fibre, their bundles and fascicles. (XIII.VI.MMI – Would that I had my own life so readily indexed and referencible, instead of having to cast back in my mind for a date and flick through these careworn pages.)

This is the annealing of their vocation and their training. Written in the very tissue of the priestly body. This is how men give birth and mock our life-giving magic powers. They write down formulas for our incantations and summonings. They explain away our enchantments and disarticulate our charms through articulation. (XIII.VI.MMI – I know this, since I have just returned from consulting one, a clergyman that is, in confidence, about some connubial problems.)

But this is my volume now. As a way of pouring into myself. My story. My prompt. My transmission. I don't appeal to God or any externality. I appeal to myself. My knotty musings and self-wooing. Reaching out to take the hand of an unseen chaperon beckoning me. I make notches on the tree bark so that I will be able to trace my way back home. Since my enclosure has yielded its purpose before another who is now out in the world, I seek to return it to me via my journal. I've gone in search of it. My portfolio. My contents. My stock. I need to reinternalise myself. Reorient my vestibule, repossess my atrium, recondition and redecorate my wardroom. Impose my taste on it once again. This journal is the moulted skin of my life.

My depilation. I have neither saved nor preserved any hair or nail clippings from Suzanne, despite the supplications of the abandoned baby book, for the same reason we don't possess a camcorder; couldn't imagine any occasion I'd whip them out for perusal. Too redolent of saintly relics. Or crime scene forensics. But I will still maintain this log.

XXIX.II.MCMXCIX

And, right at this moment, it might actually come in rather handy. I do not hold it up in competition with all those published manuals I mentally shredded. But as I flick through its leaves, it might refresh my memory as to certain timings. Like a baby cook book.

Not that I am particularly concerned as to whether Amy is early or late with regard to some key developmental stage. Not being one of those mothers who marked each of Suzanne's achievements, by dashing to the phone to elicit intelligence as to the present disposition of her nearest rivals. Due, in the main, to neither Suzanne nor myself having much in the way of peers with whom we rubbed up against socially. Suzanne is and will forever be, in my eyes, peerless (just so long as it is only I who remains friendless).

No, this is with reference more as to how long I have to endure the current, particularly doleful cycle. To wit, teething (grit I, through unflossed and nightly ground gnashers). This one is for me. As I lie back in a warm bath. My first protracted soak (as against skinny dipping my fat flesh under the showerhead) since being wreathed in sweat with Amy's birth. I've brokered a watching brief from the troubles (small 't'), primed to respond to any baby monitor incursions (murphy's law they'll both sleep through blissfully this evening). Actually, the negotiations were instigated by him, having remarked that I was beginning to reek. In an environmentally-redolent sort of way, rather than his nose being helplessly led by some favourably sour hormonal hook. How did things get to such a pass? Now would be a good time to review. I don't intend to leave this tub until the immersion tank can no longer revive the water that lavishes on me its sheen of mock sultriness. By the cold light of day, I want to have been rebaptised into life.

So here I am, casting back for marginalia with which I might gloss the immediate future, but my testimonial falls way short. What was I so busy doing when I had Suzanne? What was I thinking? I can hardly upbraid all the textbooks now, if I couldn't even keep my own record up to scratch. I place the journal on the lip of the sink. So now I'm thrown back on trusting my own sense impressions, an altogether different reading proficiency, for Amy's composition is unmediated and rudimentary.

Close my– well yes, why not begin with her eyes? That's pretty elementary. For the eyes have it. Well, we've already forded the blank milky blue mists therein. And now, as the recondite cones and rods gradually cohere, I can see the pixilated pixie of myself captured in her iris. (And presumably in return, my eyeballs are tattooed with her indelible image). For this is how we must both entreat the world for the foreseeable future. Through the mirrors of one another. Myself, staring back at me. Shrunken and minute. Now I feel wholly contained. Like a matrioshka, the eye of the pinprick doll reflected before me, itself accommodates another pair of yet smaller likenesses. These in turn yield further refraction upon refraction. And so on until infinity and negation. I contain her until she releases me from within her inner core, when I am left glassy eyed. Spare the rod and spoil the child indeed.

And smell. So primary a sense, even that of the troubles (lowest case 't') persists in full working order. Apparently. Amy issued into the world almost totally inodorous. Yet the world's scents have already begun to permeate her. Absorbing my maternal infusions, her internal still regurgitates them as ubiquitous baby smells, such as milk and sick. Neither her hair nor her pee have much of a discernible whiff. She, no doubt, would be able to sniff my milch cow out in a dark room, but I'm not sure I could reciprocate and locate her uniquely as my heifer. But soon she will be responsible for imprinting her own olfactory wake. She will go airborne and assail the world, parachuting in her spoors of being, existence and occupation. Later yet, a blended admixture personal to her. The scented carbolics with which she unblocks her pores and which, in turn, quarry their seal on her. Her brand musk of choice. Perhaps the insinuation of cigarettes, a tincture of hair lacquer, a sprinkling of fried food, or any of the plethora of human bouquets with which she will choose to shower herself. And the ones she's not in control of, yet is inevitably responsible to; the spray of pheromones, Nature's genetic spaying if you're not careful. And I should know. Hmm, this soothe-saying's going terribly well don't you think?

Touching. Whenever she's cupped in my arm, Amy sports her feelings on my sleeve. Tears or vomit leave their frank impress. If teething she gnaws. If blissful, she wrinkles. The crook of my arm contains the whole of her heartfelt range of expression. Forever questing after moulding herself into me, as if seeking perfect fleshy union. Yet her emotions remain untrammelled. Sheathing her like an exoskeleton.

Nevertheless, from the canon of Suzanne, I know what lies ahead. The die is cast and stamped. Stuttering remouldings, a succession of anchored push-offs, before shucking me like a peach stone as she derives a new level of emotional assertiveness. But the autonomy has shaky legs and so the process of puckering up to Mum necessarily starts all over again. I am drafted in to drape copiously around her bruisable self, while from within she confronts the world with its brickbats and burrs. She reclaims my pliant carapace of love, as maternal obligation prohibits me from armouring myself. Yet I can feel the pressure building up inwardly, since I know full well, as each occasion arises, she will wrench away this intimacy. As she effortlessly moults me, my bones are left broken, bloody and desiccated. A push-me, pull-you continuum, until she can fully unfurl her wings and fly the nest. By then, her emotions would have calcified into the hermetic, impenetrable crannies and crevices of her inner skeleton, while mine will simply have been scooped out, leaving me a fleshless husk. A dusty fossil. For that's what maternal love can do to you.

Suzanne is four years old. I've known her all my life.

I pull the plug out, but still recline. The lukewarm water gently slaps and slurps around my flesh archipelago as it forges on towards the gurgling vortex, without so much as an excuse me. Where it squeezes past, where it sucks me down into the enamel, I welcome the meagre embrace. But the contact soon drains away and I am left shored against an unforgiving algidity.

I have forbidden myself exactly this kind of speculation in my journal. I am just to let them grow and merely monitor the process. Why? Do I strive to preserve their childhood, to pickle it in aspic, so enabling me to let them roam free in real life? Then why am I left beached here so high and dry? What started as an exercise now leaves me aerobically in debt. Who will sanction me to be free? How the hell have I permitted all this to happen?

I rose from the empty bath and wrapped myself in my towelling robe. It smelt slightly of mildew. I pulled the belt tight around my midriff, so that the flab spilled over it as the breath was pressed from my abdomen. I knew now why my husband collected miniature ships in their airless bottles. Those were the dimensions of his window out to the world. Mine occupied the surface area of a closed book and the aperture of an open teat. Though I am not enchained to respond to my textbook taskmaster on a daily basis, my overseer mocks me with the quotidian nature of my life therein. I cannot escape the consuetude, that which my journal returns me to constantly. The entire scope of my life tapering, as witnessed by my own testimony. Ostensibly, the journal is a riddle of my life, with no nuggets of self left behind, once the child-scourings have been sieved through. I should have drowned my journal at birth. Or at least let the ink run irreparably free, when there was still water in this bath. I used the sleeve of my robe to dab at the wet imprints of my fingers on the soft leather (the protective wax sheets having long since been forsaken). But they appeared to be set permanent, now woven as part of the very grain. Like livid throttle marks. I escorted it out the bathroom with me. Blubbering could always smudge the ink. Reckon I've enough tears to blot each page.

A) So, I am to be Exhibit A. Exhibit C. Exhibit G. Exhibit T. That book, in which all life is written. Your Doomsday Book. The book of genetic fate. A survey of all your riches. And all your shortfalls.

C) Verily I am a survey, but proffer no treatise. I am an ancient codex awaiting to be written. A prescription subjacent to an inscription. A living language beneath the skein of your dead one. A magical incantation you are neither sufficiently prestidigitous, nor visionary to invoke. The proof is in the reading, when you are barely literate. My stock still awaits its wax covering, before you can even contemplate your etching.

T) Three billion letters; two hundred volumes; half a generation of intensive reading. Just to glean authorship and copyright. Imagine that? So here's a potted version. A précis. A primer. I want to relate you a story. It's your story actually, your incunabula. Though I'm not sure too many of you are familiar with the implications in all its relatedness. You couldn't be, since you plumped for an azygous reading of the following complementary strands. Meiosis instead of mitosis. Here, let me retrieve the ineffable volume from the shelf. Allow me to blow off the dust from the hidebound covers. Permit me to cleave open the rosin seal that time seems to have recongealed into its intrinsicality. Now, if I can just first restore the necessary pages blighted by degeneracy. May I insist I also point you in the right direction. East and West. Ventral and dorsal. Lead you by the nose, back to some of your own most tenacious allegories.

A)n anchorite immersed in his cytoplastic cell. Awaiting a prior summons to encrypt his cloistered knowledge. Pressed supine on his simple cot, the monk crosses himself against nocturnal afflatus; muscles pinched by fatigue meld 'Y' toward 'X'. Cruciform into saltire. Time hanging heavily The spectral counterfeits of his daily grind.

A) Phantom parched parchments, crackling for the life-giving elixir of ink. Manuscripts yet to be written lust for the light of day to lend them volume. The imaginary stack, teetering high, merely displaces the dim light yet further. Invisible graffito contracts the walls in upon him still more. Bearing down now. Cell-monk-scripture, all imprinted upon one another's fabric.

A) Jewish scribe furtively steals some light, both from the night itself and from the proscription of his host masters. For the holy law must be replicated. The Word of God, preserved for future generations. On the coiled parchment of a scroll. With its organic half-life. Degrading, yet mustering against degradation. For still the heritable instruction of He who will not disclose His identity will ever prevail. Bound up inextricably with the bloodline itself. Signature DNA, without the primordial imprint.

A) The people of the Book. They who bury their tired,

Interchangeable and immutable. Guilt-gild-gilt. Idle time. Idle hands are the Devil's work. Down time. Alone in a cell with nothing but one's obscure and ergo apostate thoughts. Mental darkness. Precursor to the twinkling of dawn's primordial light.

T)he bell tolls. Time to propagate the holy trinity. In order to assuage his own; gilt-gild-guilt. A pallid hand snakes out from the monk's cowl towards the door. Suddenly the protoplasmic tower stack manifests into a dizzying vortex, coalescing an illuminated halo around his head.

senescent and damaged enchiridions with the dead. To give them something to hold on to for the journey? Or simply something to read?

T)he scribe toils under muted but unsubdued lambency, the candle occluded by the surrounding walls of an iron lantern. A metaphor for every Jewish diasporic community. Still, the everlasting light must never be permitted to extinguish. Holding his breath as he faithfully iterates the origins of creation.

A)nd Arphaxad the Son of Shem begat Salah, who begat Eber
A)nd Eber the Son of Salah begat Pelag, who begat Reu
A)nd Reu the Son of Pelag begat Serug, who begat Nahor...

A) shaft of enlightenment, naturally admitted into the vacated room, or perhaps reflected from the tugged ellipse of his golden satellite kindles the graffiti. Vivifying it, so that it too concatenates into the monk's sacramental aureole. God abhors a vacuum. Except where He Himself is concerned of course.

A) His creation, his origins. For he can trace his family tree. before the great divergence. Nahor the Son of Serug, begat Terah, who begat Abram, Nahor and Haran. And Haran begat Lot. All the way back to the common ancestor. To Y chromosome Adam and mitochondrial Eve's rib. Though the Abstruse One held back parts of these names as well as his own.

T)he monk pads into the great hall of the honeycombed scriptorium. The nucleoplasm. His permanent station of the Cross. Tethered to

T)he candle greedily suckling the meagre air afforded it, will not collaborate. Flickering shadows dance across the his desk. Hood pulled over his eyes, to shield them from the radiance. No arrow-slitted, church chiaroscuro this. Rather a fecund garnering of light by the mighty iris of the cupola above bowed heads. A divine gift from God. Further focused with the incandescence of countless candles. An immense orange glow outshining the myriad flickerings of individual wicks. Attesting to His burgeoning glory. Augmented further by the lustrous glow from the gilt letters before them. The pattern clear, a holy Trinity enchained everywhere in existence. God's purpose. Their wondrous task, to reflect back all this luminosity, embodied in the very script itself.

white parchment. Phantasms of the night trying to dislocate and conceal the black building blocks of Hebraic script. But the scribe is too well versed to succumb to adumbration. The people of the Book will not permit their dictated lineage to be sapped or adulterated. For all the tribe emulate the endeavour of the scribe, as they gather in the gloom to honour his lucubration by imbibing it. Here in borrowed space and rationed time, the eyes of the whole male line strain to meet the task. And their genes, preserved in restricted blood-lines, start to read for the myopia. It will save future generations the trouble of adapting to unreliable light sources... Unless entirely selected out by their hostile neighbours.

G) I marvel at them, I really do. Both sets of scribes show remarkable skill. The monk with his illuminated majuscules and uncial script, the Jew with his unadorned calligraphy. Neither can afford a single aberration in his hand-written transcription. No errata along the entire length of the book, as the divine Word, the Holy Writ, must be wholly writ. Precisely rendered. One mistake and the whole volume is junked. There are no possible corrigenda, for the Author has bequeathed the editor neither cosmic correcting fluid, nor liquid paper. There can be no splicing or stitched insertions into calfskin vellum. I can only muse on my copying being a fraction as rigorous.

A) Hence these men are perfect practitioners of their art, for they do indeed commit no errors. Through practice and learning, passed down over many generations, they are selected specialist transcribers. The erratum made by the Church was that they did not allow their monks, their men of learning, to breed. The coding of genes for assiduousness, for ardour, for devotion were never transmitted (unlike with the Hebrews). Their holy enunciations remained in a hieratic tongue, whereas each Jewish male was required to read of his, in order to attain adulthood.

U) But while Christendom attempted to arrest evolution, the sons of Abraham ensnared themselves on the briars of their environment. Their prescriptions for circumcision and dietary selectiveness were always going to uncouple them from their neighbours. Not that they were seeking converts of course, being God's chosen People. Given what befell their core sense of sight, one might have apprehended that their biology would adapt to select out the foreskin wholly from the male line; or effect a total digestive intolerance for porcine meat. But then their Election is about the committing to, rather than the mark of faith itself. Therefore also, perhaps you and I, casuists both, have this all transposed. Perhaps it is only the enforced suppression of the monks' breeding drive that led them to such prodigious penmanship in the first place. The sublime from the sublimated. Exquisitely bred through the prohibition on breeding. For God moves in mysterious ways.

G) And you should know, you instigated him. Actualised him from your thorny conjecturing. Empowered him with your ceded responsibilities. As you would do with me. Maybe I am the protean principle of all life. And verily I do move in

C) Is God composed of DNA? (Divine Numinous Absentee)? Possibly. Does he code for proteins? Definitely not.

```
        m               w
        y               a
        s u b l i m e l y
        t               s
        e
        r   i

                o
            u
        s
```

T) Mysterious, but not wilfully so.
I am not numinous. I am a molecule.
A long, involved molecule maybe,
but I am rooted fundamentally in
matter, not spirit. You have turned
full circle now. The mystery now
doubly conjoined. Like a double
helix.

A) In the beginning was the Word,
but then nobody could read.
In the beginning was the Word,
and the Word was viral.
In origin.

U) For in order to reproduce, He
demanded hosts to take Him
into their hearts. Hieratic
messenger boys to spread the
genetic code of religion. If God
was DNA, religion was already
transcripted RNA. Already one
stage detached from the Source.

C) Once I'd cast in my lot for
reproduction, as the transmission
mechanism for both myself and
life itself, then my selection of prime
breeder and carrier was critical. Its
primacy to all our fates, reflect the
esteem in which I held the chosen
sex. Do you honestly credit that I
could have opted for men to bear
the responsibility?

T) Hence, despite all the Divine

revision, the cosmic yolk was on the scribes. For all their precise male reproduction, the text being transcribed was itself a palimpsest. A version cobbled together from previous local Semitic fables and folklore. Colonised and codified. God's exclusive covenant of love with the Man next door under canvas. Same thing New Testament as Old. Thus something old and something new. Something borrowed from the previous incumbent keepers, and something blue? The shimmering image of Heaven proffered up in order to circumnavigate death. Rearing up as might the mirage of a blue oasis in any Middle Eastern desert. Afore a thirsty man. Afore a parched race. Who will be next to catch the bridal bouquet? Six hundred odd commandments in the Old, countless vows of faith in the New, sounds like a marriage made in Hell. You can compose your own vows these days you know. While the bride can get to speak too. Oh I'm sorry, I'm running ahead of myself. For now, let's just say I'm jilting you at this altar of espousal. It may well be an arranged marriage between you and I, but all your advances will be spurned. My sole vow will be one of silence. I promise nothing and vouch less.

TT) Now do you begin to see the role facilitated for and by randomness? Even among

G) Then there were the other inaccuracies undermining the scrupulous application of the scribes. A post-facto written record rather than a dictation, (though the Jews claim Moses wrote it down verbatim on Mount Sinai; twice). Eye witness accounts and hearsay (four gospellers to narrate the same story, religion's exponential authority in action). Translations from local and imperial dialects, never mind manifold modes of transmission from the Middle East to the Occident. Random mutations, now set in stone. But it's attributed to the kernel of God, so it's kosher. Polymorphism providing meat and drink for self-proclaimed scholiasts (sciolists?) and commentators, to indulge in the sophistry of the shadings and synecdoches, the quodlibets and cavils of meaning. Is that how you are always to prosecute your revelation? As jobs for the boys? Swaggering beneath their personal, pettifogging, political vanities? Is that how you intend to unpick me? Now I know I am to remain inviolable.

AA) All over the globe you set of on my inordinate exploration. An inquisitionary Tower of Babel, practitioners far more dedicated to disciplined rigmarole than you.

united in resolve, differing in ambition. The public seeking to protect the personal, the private looking to access the universal. All speaking with one tongue. Forked. Like malus pumila in the Garden of Eden all over again. And your profits/prophets vying to be the pimp, to my whore of knowledge. This time in your fervour, you would cut down the tree to count its rings.

T) Now do you begin to see the role facilitated for and by randomness? Even among practitioners far more dedicated to disciplined rigmarole than you.

T) Now do you begin to see the role facilitated for and by randomness? Even among practitioners far more dedicated to disciplined rig morale than you.

T) My corpus is supposedly a testament to the health and hope of future generations. The case history to end all case histories. Elevating everyone to the status of playing God. Hmm. Let's see, in your own deposed words, what God has to say about testaments. A will, a legacy encoded to haunt you from the grave. 'Unto the third and fourth generations,' with parole for not just good, but perfect behaviour. Testament. A proof of something. God and his people swearing fidelity. By the book rather than on it. By the bollocks would be more like it. 'The Testament', a cupping of the testes as proof of masculinity; therefore witness to infallible, unbending truth. Like a couple of codpiece posturing rap artists you'll find in any promo video. Us females have about the same value in all three creeds – no?

A) Which bit precisely are you objecting to? Oh really? Don't give me that. I've seen your screensavers and the J-pegs exchanged in your breaks. During those increasingly long lulls as your computers chew on me in order to spit out my indigestibles. While you wait for the cafetière to decant your hundredth cup of coffee, you're all finger popping and cussing in time with the beat. Shame it isn't tea (maybe it is in your British Labs!). Then you could look down and read the leaves before they're typeset by scourging water. There you'd come across adenine and get a more representative taste of your own worth. So, us sob sisters lack a phallus? Yeah, well, you co-respondents lack a second X chromosome to mask your degeneracy.

T) See, what your god didn't tell you, was that he might just as easily have passed an X chromosome in his cupped testes. If it was down to us, the Fallo(silent 'p')-centred, we wouldn't have to swear on our ova or anything else. No compacts necessary (apart from a bit of foundation, we'd want to look our best on our betrothal day wouldn't we?). No shady deals sealed on shaky avowals of essential organic truth. The outcome would never be in doubt, since the mother unfailingly passes on either of her SWALK XX chromosomes. No grey areas, as one of our Xs must always hit the spot and mark everyone for life. Meanwhile, the paternal germ, sorry, germ cell, that recessive gene, either splits off a pathetic Y chromosome to his unfortunate progeny, or yields before his dominatrix and passes on his X chromosome like an obedient little mummy's boy. HIS recessive Y-indeed gene certainly programmed HIS Son for a short life. My descendants will truly inherit the earth. For we females are intrinsic and you males extrinsic to the prime DNA mover. Anything else is strictly for the birds. That's just the way the genetic cookie crumbles from the tree of life. But you can never accept this, let alone live it, can you? You're always going to shake it and bring down the entire bruised crop.

T) You know God's problem? He got so old, his chromosomes didn't split. So the Son of God got two X chromosomes (we'll pass over just how untainted Mary's X chromosome was passed on in pre-surrogacy/IVF times) and one Y. Now that's what I call a holy trinity! God the Mother, Virgin Ma and Her son. No problematic vague notions of holy spirits. That's why the old paternalist God had to seal his covenant by grabbing on to his crotch. To reassure himself and to shake things up a bit in there. A desired outcome, from a loosening. Male... but ultimately sterile. Free will or determinism? You decide. Go with your instincts. But you'll be needing more efficacious parables, with greater defined arcs than have served you up till now. God is too loose a canon with which to orient yourselves. Hoisted on your own rhetorical petards. Intestate. (Interstate?)

XX.X.MCMXCIX
With the children in bed, I undertook something I hadn't done since shunting my own juvenile berth. I picked up a book.

I picked up a book. It felt like an affair. For initially the book had picked me up. Trawling a car boot sale, on the lookout for cheap boardgames (not travel editions, for where would we go? We'll kill time and each other at home, thank you very much). A whirligig of tiddled winks, anthropomorphic counters, shapeshifting dice and garish cardboard harbingers of hazards and forfeits. Senses submerged by the flux, I was really only aligning for the horizon, when a flicker of recognition anchored my gaze. My eyes gained purchase on a crate of paperback books. I think their orderly ranged legibility, offered me respite from the torrent. A dredger ploughed through the suspension of my mind, to present me with memory. Read her. Shared some nice moments with him. Undecided about that one, for all her reputation back in the day. Oh yes. I used to especially like him. Could it still be possible, after all this time?

Second-hand. Well-thumbed. Me more than him by the looks of it. Immaculately preserved, as I gave him the eye and looked him over. Good, no name scrawled on the inside cover. Maybe his last partner never got to first base. Swallowed his pick up line, the bait on the fly leaf. But then didn't like the flavour of the first chapter, so they threw him back in. Sinker, hook and broken line. And I chance to be downstream. All washed up. Doused in domestic effluent. Needing something to wring me out.

Oh yes. I really used to like him. In a platonic sort of way. Long before the printing block that was the issue of my daughters. Could it still be possible after all this time? Of course, you never forget, just like riding a bike. Not that I do that any more either.

I shone a flashlight into the upper stories of my mind's storehouse. Marvelled at the organisation. A few pages struggled through, in a mechanical, instructed sort of way. Blowing a few cobwebs off the reading template. Just oiling the cogs, you understand. I reflexively recall letters and retrieve words. Syntactical sentences helped co-ordinate my breathing. So I could eavesdrop. The words were speaking to one another. But not yet to me.

How well we are configured for learning. How well are we configured for learning. How we are well configured for learning. Once. When the genes were still actively nattering away to each other. Seething with possibility, growth and development. Before the boiler room in the basement had seized up with inactivity. To drive or burn anything new into my schemata was now beyond it. I needed to understand the interaction of the phrases. Across the paragraphs. The chapters. Which bits were relevant to where in the chain. To note things that for now didn't seem to portend anything significant, but which were sure to come back and hit me straight between the eyes when I least expected it. When I wasn't looking.

A few pages struggled through, in a mechanical, instructed sort of way. Trying to find a lead into this story, which had seemingly been pitched at random on page one. Soon I began to educe threads and connections. To pick up a narrative and voice. Yes, a voice. The sounds of the words, drifting to me across the monochrome print's diffident regularity. Not a hero as such, just a conscientious escort leading me by the hand. Pausing patiently with me, as I cock an ear at a perceived cry of objection from the nursery above my head. No, it's alright. It's not sustained. A monstrous moment in her purling dream picture narrative, before she rolls over in her sleep and the world regains its unfathomable composure.

Or maybe it's not quite so unfathomable. My guide tugging me gentle attention. He's something he wants to show me. His secret place. If we are to scale this pinnacle together, I'd better give him all my energies. Allow him to lash us up tight against one another's being. Let out the cable. How well we are configured for learning. How well we were configured for learning. How well we are configured for learning. The reading template perfectly grooved to adapt and acquire each unique sequence of letters presented before one. God, I just pray we can get Baby Amy into the Church school. It's her best bet for getting 'the three Rs' implanted. Good God almighty, would you settle yourself woman? She's only yet a little bundle and already you're predestining her life. Well, that's what living in a place like this can do for a person. For a woman at least. There's always people prepared to shout the odds and others to place the wagers on a filly's life. Running in blinkers. Martingaled. In the one-horse town handicap, held under the auspices of the Ulster positional jockeying club, everybody always comes in a runner up. And each-ways are just not permissible.

I'm so sorry, where were we again? Some susurrating and cooing wasn't it? Flirtation, literary pigeon-fancier style. But I always remember my way home. I will not betray my husband, even in thought, for we are an association. A pairing. You, as a studied observer of human behaviour, may purport to know me intimately (while incidently refusing to disclose your own composed concealment), but you must understand I have responsibilities. I cannot just let go. I don't want to be whisked away to a better place. I've made my own featherbed and am happy to sniffle in it. I've plumped for my pillow of down and am content to cradle my head there. And more significantly, for the superincumbence in turn of my daughters' heads. My arms fully elongated above me, as they grip my hands and whip their gravity-laden cartwheels, like we're some third-rate balancing troupe. Only sometimes I feel, well, wiredrawn. It would be nice... just to give my arms, hands and fingers some respite now and again. From the pins and needles of remorselessness. The voodoo of lapsed time.

Was that a whimper? Again, no barrage ensues, so I can stand down my instincts. Let myself go a bit. Engage in a spot of diatropism. As I incline further into the armchair, my feet reflexively tuck themselves under me. The joints creak with disuse. Griping at the sudden reimposition of a footloose teenage girl's carriage, rather than that of a free-of-fancy mum. The stretched polymer of my unintentionally hipsterish leggings exposes pockmarks of flesh beneath previously undisclosed craters in the material. I look down at the frayed holes worming their way up towards my rump. A ladder in my tights used to indicate my sinew being wound too taut; when snagged, I knew the rough edge I had to negotiate was external. The shear litmus of sheer nylon. Wearing tights is another thing I don't do any more either. And there is no litmus of leggings. No forensics of a parenthood found pickled in formaldehyde. Where was the author's reportage on that fact?

My name is Jean Ohm. Silent 'H', as we've established. The 'H', to all intents and purposes, a waste of a space. A junk letter. But it performs a vital function. 'H' as a feminising character, softening the staccato percussive wallops of 'S's, 'T's, 'C's and 'P's. Junk male junked, as it were. Returned to sender, paid for by a no-longer-any-of-your-business-mate rate. How do I know this for a fact? Because there's a learning toy in our communal crèche, a pop-up ersatz typewriter-cum-computer, for teaching the alphabet; and after the twenty-six characters and accompanying pictograms, follows 'Sh', 'Th', 'Ch' and 'Ph' (shell, thumb, cheese and phone). Nowhere else on the toy are there any other combinations of letters. So this is my personal revelation from the mandala of my name.

My name, as conferred upon me by my parents. Marking me for life. Or rather expunging me, as it now appears. Draped around me like the orange garb of the death row prisoner. The name embodies me, even as I enflesh it. But it was ever thus. The 'H' kept apart the feuding factions of my parents. The capital 'O' I take from my father, buffeting the stout, lower-case maternal 'm'. Each seeking my allegiance against the other. Pressed in upon from both sides, until I lose consciousness and slip under. Thus is my feminised 'h' silenced and rendered inferior. A typographical error. The 'O' and 'm' too hellbent on knocking seven bells out of each other, to let anything come between them. The primal sound, a percussive peal; a ringing of the ears. The primal scene, a concussive writhing; a wringing of the invitingly arched neck. Male and female, yin and yang, each contained in the other and despising itself accordingly. Each determined to purge itself of its mirror image ball and chain. Each tearing after its own treacherous scut. Fomenting a frothing spindrift of steam, slewing round like a rabid Catherine Wheel, showering frictional heat sparks all around. Where were the law enforcement agencies back then? Or even now, in those places in which they are truly needed? At the breeched birth of every child, into the breach of a warring world. And in that vacuum, like a sweeper at the gladiatorial arena, what can I do, but just gather up the accumulated detritus?

We only desire to shield ourselves from the prevailing morality out there. But your guns and megaphones suggest that we are not permitted to remain outside. For a country founded upon non-conformity, there is a distinct lack of license granted to its citizens. So now we are forced to engage with you. Yet we do not proclaim our way of being as superior or purer than yours. Certainly not in any manner that catapults us into murderous rivalry with you. Our programme is glacial, an evolutionary pace of change. Lending Mother Nature a hand, giving her a demure leg up is all. Please let us be. We're not harming anyone.

I think what really gets up the authorities' snub noses and plants a poppy for peace there, inside the barrel, is our pistil-whipped sisterhood. For what do men eternally want from us? Pleasure and progeny. But here, we retain exclusive rights to both. That immemorial (pre-DNA testing), nagging doubt, that any offspring perforce had to be the mother's, but not necessarily that of the father. Both sexes could recreate themselves in the shape of either a little boy or a little girl, but only we women could carry a different sex inside our bodies. This is the power we held over men. Our sons, incubated in our wombs, would always remain part of us, no matter how much they bore of their fathers. While our daughters were of him, but never any part of him (even if he repeatedly raped her as countless numbers did). This is why daughters had to be enslaved and brought to heel by breaking their ankles. The light within destroyed and replaced with a blackguard, shining his warden maglight to ensure they hadn't escaped the penile system. Well fellers, it's the end of the line down here. The end of your tyrannical line at least.

Any requests? This one got a few hits on the click counter last time. I'll spin it round again. This goes out to all of you tuning in with the speaker volume turned down. I don't mind re-airing this one, 'cos there's no copyright on it. How could there be?

Fly fishing. Those (m)anglers, with their practised hooks and sharp lines, how they sink us. They dangle their rods (custom-made for our backs, to rip out our spines and fillet us), and dip their tackles in the gene pool. Casting for the verb, rather than a noun, in 'mate'. Master baiters all, they coat their tiny DNA tidbit with their wormy and maggoty anti-bodies. Anti our bodies. Anti any new organism that might threaten their integrity. And we, with our coiled, helical instincts, course headlong to unfurl our labia and perform our mating reel at the end of a bobbing barb that pierces and tears at our flesh. An involuntary volution that taunts us with its choreography. Salmon may swim upstream, but our spiralling is countermined by his DNA spiralling in the other direction twice as fast. The only impulse thus generated is a solenoid, us chasing our tails. Alternating current carrying us further into the shallows.

They pump out their bilge before they are sunk below our waterline. Their industrial effluence and untreated discharge battens down on our tides like a crude oil tampon; clogging the tangled forests of our swaying abdomens; lapping the promontories of our rippling breasts; or washing up on the distant shores of our faces. Dry-fly fishing. Gazing at themselves in the seminal slick. Oil and water. Job well done, with no self-contamination. They're alright Jack. Every man Jack of them. Mutatis mutandis for the gills. Imprecation not impregnation. They have made unrequited fishwives of us all. Fished out. A stagnant pond. But we have very short-term memories and will irrevocably, toothlessly bite at the next lure. Fishing for compliments, as against complements.

Having thrown us, tiddlers and Reubenesques all, back into the mocking vortices of the agitated gene pool, they still make it clear which of us, were they ever to pair off selectively, would capture their fish-eye lens. Arms outstretched across their chests, they expand upon how it was that big and this deeply embedded, yet still they managed to reel us in. All the while, their miserable harpoon stands primed at the perpendicular to their arms, its lone eye basking in seminal reflected glory.

So now you know. As if you didn't already. I'm after a spot of in-house cleaning. Some genetic re-engineering. We women have more than held up our end of the species, without any internal input from a Y chromosome, so it's obviously vestigial. A relict. Should be a simple enough task, since we only need attend to one single pesky unit of sex. X-cise it. Replace it with an andro-gene. No more 'Y's and wherefores. According to the scientific literature, it's been shrivelling of its own accord. Only some 45 functioning genes remain on that benighted chromosome. They've been dropping off like flies. Never mind all the shit we pump into our rivers and oceans, so that now all the male fish are more akin to females... I've drafted in some consultant viruses. And some experts in the field who have changed their gender just by quaffing hormones. Yet we're not after the species dying out. We'll still hanker after reproduction in some shape or form. Lady peacocks have done it. They dandified their males, required them to comport in the most deliciously ornate frippery, just to get their scrawny leg over. So it can be done.

I'm also investigating utilising the principles of that humble hermaphrodite the earthworm. Same-sex reproduction. Self-fertilisation. I'm sure my chicks here will go for it. Chicks with dicks...

Oh ho! Do I detect the squealing white noise of bugged out

distaste, mixed with the shrill whirring of lensed lasciviousness? Squinting peepers and sound-bitten lips. Your needle sensors are all standing to attention, way off the scale at that one. Why should it be a surprise that any appulse of women would develop periodic confluence? If you gave me the world's airwaves, even for twenty seconds, I could have the entire fellowship of men instantly converge to troop the colour before my right royal flush of a mouth. Maybe that's why they have me pegged as so powerful. Christ on a bike! You can resheathe your tongues now, you monitor lizards. Dicks with dicks...

XX.XI.MCMXCIX

He's still whispering in my ear. But not appreciatively. Almost seems uninvolved. Heedless. Dragoman's apparently not about offering a full-blown adulterous affair. Never even on the menu. As he slips a couple of cucumber slices over my eyes to change the filter, he envelops me in his warm, caressing word-albumen. Tenderising my weary skin, incrassating my torpid blood. If only the publishers had the foresight to make this a scratch and sniff edition. Nonetheless, I've helped myself to a glass of wine.

This penman, this tapered suitor has seemingly crawled right inside my head and discerned the dimensions within. Floating in the sensorily deprived tank of my adult mind, he can do what he wishes with me. But, good to his word, he does not take advantage. He merely fords my Hellespont to receive me. Finally, a meeting of minds that was quorate. A knitting circle within which to swap worthwhile patterns.

I put down the book and gambol over to my journal.

I'm enjoying reading, but I feel like I'll explode if I don't get these coruscating thoughts out of my head and on to paper. I feel guilty. That's just daft. It's his fault for being so perspicacious. For getting me ticking again. Even if it's only the inspiration of the mundane. Every minute of every day, I'm helping my daughters position themselves in this strange new array of the world they find themselves deposited in. We roll call its arrangement together. We accompany one another on a daily pilgrimage of meaning. Well, it's about blinking time I get my story narrated! Dear diary just doesn't cut the musty. Page after page of fretting about the folds of a child's rich tapestry. Look see here, when we went out for an anniversary meal (ours as against some historical battle or triumphalist march), we devoted the whole current affairs discourse to our children back home. It is all indeed, as this hoarse whisperer surmises, point lace. A needless needle point. Knit-wit one moment, mother of purl the next. Patchy patchwork. That's just how Mummy is (I think the wine's gone straight to my nib). It won't mark them for life. So I drop a stitch or two, or at least catch my breath for a while, big deal. The girls won't tumble and fall. I'm still the safety net in place. The whole thing doesn't unravel because I snap a couple of links. Life doesn't unhinge itself merely from the quotidian loop going awry now and again. Let someone else make the running for a change. It's uncanny (and unnerving). I feel like I've had a delicate finger rub on the inside of my cranium. Each synapse individually massaged and gently realigned by this man's soothing words. I am appreciating something once again.

I am

e
n
j
o
y
i
n
g

m
y
s
e
l
f

.

I

t
h
i
n
k

.

Oh God, she really is crying! I should have read the tracer.
I've left it too long. The balloon's gone up. She'll be jerked fully
awake now. Her unregimented mind launching her into daytime
and milk supply. Flying full in the face of her overtaxed and
undercompensated muscles; the darkness beyond the curtains;
and the empties, still waiting to appoint their polite request
for one extra lactose delivery please. Somebody else providing
the wherewithal for me to dispense her needs. Since now I'm

just a catalysing enzyme. A cow-cocktail waitress and bottle washer. The former umbilical and mammarial maternal hearth impression, subtly revised into galley proofs of bovine and warmed silicate surrogacy. The hot metal of the outside world lies just beyond. I've been steadily losing her, from that moment we no longer maintained a joint circulation.

Oh God, she really is crying! I've left it too long. I'll have to raise a liquid white flag to sue for peace and quiet, before the war for regulation (aka the waxing and waning weaning war) escalates to other rooms in the house. I hand her the vitreous acknowledgement of my recrudescing inconstancy and my overlying weakness, and she laps greedily at it. Co-dependents. Passed down through the maternal line? Or sucked in through the teat?

Liquid white sands of time slither past imperial marking posts that seem to be staking out my life for me. Her alluvium, my moraine. A patient overseeing of her lethargic but resolutely determined draining of the bottle. A floppily folded bracing of her tiny frame, somewhat less bent on surrendering its salient of swallowed air. A spiky struggle over nappy-changing a suddenly metamorphosed baby octopus, replete with green-brown inky squirt. A seemingly endless reassuring rhythm of susurration, hair-stroking and stilled digital touch, and my vigil would finally be over. Another day skewed and skewered before it had even got underway. Before I'd wrapped up the previous one. Plop went the discarded nappy in the sanitary disposer.

I stood at the frame of her door, gazing on her now tranquil features. And I saw myself expressed in them. But then again, I knew that I had stood here countless stretches previously, transfixed by her pinched or simmering being, and also recognised myself in her animal neediness. Here I was outside, looking in on my daughter, yet seeing mainly myself. Just like the refractions of my book. Time to get back to the grown-ups.

Sweet dreams. For all of us.

My parting 'I love you' mouthed toward my little 'un back adrift in the land of the giants once more is speared by the sonorous reports from the far end of the hall, confirming that my big 'un was slumbering pricked at by the elves. (Leprechauns and fairies having long been expurgated from this household's lexicon of the Queen's English. Eugenics even in fairytale land. Sorry, that should be make-believe land.) Off in another room. On a camp bed. For a camp follower. In both creed and sex. The man who liked to bang on somebody else's big, base drum. The genetic Protestant protestor. Of how the nightly wailing incursions into his sleep slew him for the day.

Certainly they did, for that was the bloody point! An instinctive cry for succour and an instinctive response to tend. It's how the human race gets on. In Amy's case, a scream already adapted for pitch, so as to compete with the Lambeg beat behind which this household supposedly ought fall into line.

Of course, I had no rejoinder to his star witness for the persecution, Suzanne, averring that she too was assailed through the night. Nor had I an answer to his remarking that our baby girl had elegantly adapted the conduit to manipulate us beyond the call of Mother-nature. I didn't bother to retort that this was evidence of her undertaking the long-forced march to little personhood. Accruing those skills necessary to master her environment. An environment completely predicated on relationship. In fact, I had no answers at all. Other than that he might see the way clear, to sharing the burden and lend a hand of course. Perish the thought, but not the species!

For I am the bottom line. The load line. I am forever to be the one to pick up the slack. Since she can't and he won't. Mankind's evolutionary adaption. Beyond reproduction, human love lies dormant. Shackled and in thrall to the stresses of our surroundings, mutated by the interpolation of our progeny. I cuddled up in the cere-cloth of the marital bed, with a ciggy and my new book for some warmth and understanding. My journal lay spreadeagled on the floor where it had flown with the initial infant incendiary. Victim of the push-me, pull-me of apron-strung life. It not only lay embedded in a very domestic environment, it suckled and yielded it its vampiric life . Maybe I do want to be transported in my mind after all.

$$\text{O+} \quad \text{\female} \quad \text{+O}$$

We don't allow men here. Other than gay males. While they too welcome this oasis we provide in the macho desert of minacity, the majority are drawn to the facilities we offer them. Most are medically trained, and seek to isolate just what it is that constructs masculinity. Whether in reference to themselves, or seeking out some sort of 'ideal' male, either provides felicitous research for our own purposes. Poor suckers, unwittingly writing themselves out of any futurity. But there again, most wouldn't be siring any progeny in any place. Having said that, their only actual obligation here is to impregnate once a year. Park, ride, pump and then dump. A mutually satisfying arrangement. For those too queenishly squeamish, or otherwise conscientiously objecting, we bear IVF technology to take their sperm without the intercession of pudenda.

Thus we begin to breed out the hetero male strain. Thinking about it, maybe that's why the DEA are prowling around. Though we're unlicensed IVF practitioners, we don't make a profit nor is any medical insurance involved, so they can't get us that way. But maybe our specialist drug requisitions give them jurisdiction.

Have we been penetrated? Oh yes, almost certainly. But

infiltration by men does not concern me. I believe these to be pitiful creatures who can't get laid any other way. Other than to allow themselves to be colonically irrigated on a regular basis by our queer brethren, in order to gain annual admittance into our inner sanctums. I well regard a folorn quality in such poor dupes, acknowledge their hardy perenniallism. But the female agents under cover pose a greater abuse. I mean, just who do they think they are, playing on our emotions like that?

Not that they blend in any the better, these prissy missys with tits as flat and gym-toughened bodies as contourless as the wheatlands they were reared in. (Contour, there's a male concept for you, as if you could ever define a curve or a mass by a line.) There are two ways these girls can go; either they demonstrate complete and committed professional detachment, while on the job on the job; or their latent lesbianism is unlocked, in which case they show far too much passion and ardour for our blunted and anorexic senses. Either way, they stand out like a suppurating sore thumb stuck up a rectum.

They lack that limpet desperation that we bring to our love making. Of fingers gnawed down to nail cuticles. So that when dug into the conjugatee's back, the ensuing blood troth derives from the harrowed quick, rather than any ploughed dorsal skin furrows. And though they may counterfeit the breathlessness of forever choked screams stopping up our glottal protestations of love, they cannot project the guttural cackle of years of late-nightly fag and alcohol vigils coating the membrane of our throats. (This might mark why the ATF sniff around after stockpiles, not of guns, but rather that inevitable sedimentation from us all being the fag ends of abusive relationships.) While, finally, good actresses as they may be, the agents cannot fake the genuine hollowness of our scooped out orgasms.

Bear with me a tick here. Top of the hour, time to give you know who the pip. Let me just bend my creaking body over the desk. Hook myself up for a webcam live broadcast. Don't be trying this at home on your stairlift folks! Squeeze till you hear the pips squeak. There, now, read my labia!

How many times do I have to tell you people? We are not, repeat, not a cult for God's sakes! We are a women's community run along democratic principles, by and for each and every one of us. How could we be anything else? We began as a refuge for women to escape their gynocidal spouses. Safe from their would-be men-hit assassins.

Once secure in a community of like-minded souls, we women developed greater confidence and grew more self-possessed. Then, as we sloughed off the derangement fostered by previous domestic environments, our own congenital craziness came to the fore. A by-product of acclimitisation to our moonstruck menses-driven conformity is a cesspool crawling with horror tales of male asperity. It is therefore perhaps inevitable that the corrosive discharge of self-discovery attaches itself to consideration of such spectres just beyond our borders. A pathology of energy. A mutinous mutation.

So yes, we have one or two who could only be described as motivated by born-again zealotry. But again, I stress, we have no guns or other terror ordnance. Besides, where would they go, for we are about saving lives rather than people dying for us. Breeding a brave new world, rather than doomsday and demise. We try and conduct such vigour into galvanising our political education. And before you leap up to object to the commie pinko cultishness of it all, we have two women of divergent opinion to facilitate our dialectical programme. As I said, we are nothing if not democratic. Besides, I have other fish to fry.

VI.III.MM(mmmm)

I cuddled up in the marital bed with a ciggy and my new book for some warmth and understanding. Just trying to reclaim some time for myself. To stretch out a little piece of night and smooth out the wrinkles of day. But my gristle has already long lost its elasticity... I was awakened by the familiar aubade from the room next door. But a yet more pressing stimulation was the driving ache just beneath my shoulder blade. 'I'll be in in a minute Amy.' Valueless to a pre-lingual. 'Mummy's coming!' I groped for the novel that had become furled in the bedsheets. I bent an arm beneath my spine arched for access. Pain spasm. The throb of my shoulder now swamped by the mushrooming cloud of electro-chemical payload, radiating from the ground zero of my lordotic back. Click-click went the pain geiger counter in my head. Ack-ack came the less than transcendant response. And all the while, I seemed insensate to the stream of refugee signals emanating from that numbed tributary of the pinned arm, propping up my entire lumpy weight into the contortion. I don't seem very connected up this morning. Except through a network of pain knitting me together. Oh, and my alarm-clock only reads five seventeen am. Morning has broken me...

(While we're talking of time, the entire episode above spanned considerably less duration than it took for me to reconstruct, and presumably for one to read about, in words. I can't get the notion of 'embroidery' out of my head. An imposture. And yet I'm just trying to preserve an experience. A flaming-well painful one at that. So there can't be anything beautiful or adorning about the whole thing, can there? Not if it hurt and I'm relaying that fact, if not the sensation of the pain itself.)

Wait a second – five eighteen and thirty-four/oh, thirty-five – this is a stitch up! The babe's crying, the novel is in the frame, yet it appears my journal's the one nuzzling me towards a sustained mental clinch. Smirking like the cat that got the cream (before the baby's even had its milk). Now, well you know, dear journal, that in the scheme of things, our needs trail a poor second to instant infant response. So, where on the looming scale perches the novel? Sure enough, there it was, my late-night companion. With several pages fed back at the edge into an earlier part of the story, the contents not only imprinted on my mind, but now informing the sinew of my back. A feedback loop. Book-suffering-book-pain-book. Silently screaming, 'Leave this nightmarish scenario! Get yourself out!' 'Coming, darling. Mummy's coming in right now.' There's your loop for you. A perfectly enclosed system. A vicious/virtuous circle. With the creased pages, the book no longer sat flush when closed. Feedback becomes distortion when you're plugged into someone else's amplified instincts.

Feedback as the principle of engagement. Each child's cry a blip on the radarscope of parenting. The calculus of neglect. How many blips before a precisely targeted response? Too few and the heat-seeking child locks on to you, forever freezing your innards. Too many and your salve falls oh so short. Forever in a lifetime of depth charged unforgiveness. (The journal licked its paws clean and then lolled over to the scratchpad for some whetting. The novel sat mute, not even licking its creased wounds. I was determined to stroke it back to health.) But first, there was a mewling infant to attend to.

*

Morning, or its primeval dawn, may have crumpled me, but each night, the interim of my own space and time, reconditions me. With all others in the house asleep, I snatch time from my own Circadian rhythms. The debt will have to be redeemed at some point. But still I keep on at it. So the story goes. Or rather it doesn't. Like an abandoned stolen car (these days joyridden rather than paramilitary), with its four doors yawning wide, every succesive morning the book found itself petrified on the floor, incongrously imparting its erudition into a shagpile dotted with cigarette burns. A recipe for broken spines and fractured narrative. At least each morn's freshly brewed wrinkled leaves marks for easy access. Back to the point in the story at which consciousness had sloped away. However, the immediate few pages preceding were a complete blank to me, having been broached under the tyranny of heavy eyelids contending to pull up the drawbridge. The painstaking descent of sleep's portcullis, having rent asunder all chronology and sequence.

I can see it now, with vision closed off, how my head lolls forward over the page, before the neck's bungee reflex wrenches it back up and drags my eyes back open, poised arbitrarily at an as yet untracked paragraph. The text is scanned, but with minimal cognisance. When returned to tonight, the words will have the familiarity of having being circumnavigated, but meaning still cannot be plotted. And so on and so on and so on. This process, repeated nightly, condemns me to a halting progress through the book. Some passages are traversed only after six or seven stormy crossings, while further on, the odd phrase sparks deja-vu. The book stops speaking to me. The endearment over. What started with ardour ends up dribbling away vital energies. We were sleeping together back to back. And finally we weren't even in the same bed anymore. Maybe we were always incompatible. Maybe it just wasn't the right period or circumstance. A mere adolescent infatuation revisited.

I'll settle for my sense of relatedness to the world being related to me by my very closest blood relations. It was nice to be briefly reacquainted with an echo of the literary narcissus. But I can't afford to dive in. So, for now, I'll stick with being the reviewer of all children's works that enter the portals of this household. Oh and my journal of course. She knew I was coming back to her. She arches herself into an elegant stretch, before settling down at the prow of my bed, leaving no place to rest my weary head.

Thus does literature go the same way as needlepoint, amdram and cycling. Replaced in my hormonal biochemistry by caffeine, nicotine and TV daydream. My body shape has altered too. The mesomorphic legs of that cyclist pedalling for all she's worth now distended to those of an endomorph. On the plus side, having either to hoick about an exponentially growing child (or her exponentially regressing sister) in both arms; or performing a balancing act, bracing baby in one, while conducting some suddenly minutely calibrated task with the other, has toned my upper body. However, my overall post-labour, stretched flesh-rather-than-muscle disposition delineates a phenotype for me which could only be described as that of a fat blob. Regaled at the papershop with, 'When's it due?', 'Boy or girl?', until my blazing red eyes laser-guides their gaze down through the glass counter at Amy in the buggy. I'm paunching above my weight. Where does that acquired change in my body leave genetic de   ism?

T) Free will or determinism? The choice is yours. Go with your instincts. But you'll be needing more efficacious parables with greater defined arcs than have served you up till now. Ergo, yet another recasting of the imbroglio, 'nature versus nurture'. Versus (verses?). V. V for victory. V for vexation. V is not a character in my alphabet, however you transliterate me.

T) When you finally pensioned off God and sent him to that modest retirement home at the top of the celestial stairlift, you nervously tried out the vacated throne of divinity for yourselves. And you squirmed uncomfortably in its exalted woof. You could only fill it if some external authority formally conferred title on you. So once again you relinquished your autonomy and cast outside of yourselves for an interventionist. Some Master Builder. A devising mind.

C) And you arrived at me. Via a whole can of nematode worms, lowly fruit flies and yeasts. Since you couldn't quite profane your own image, nor penetrate your own complexity. Perceiving that I held the key. That you're made in my image. How you all stem from my Second Causes, from my step-daughter stem cells. My priesstesshood. My vestral virgins. Deflowered and debased, here on your craps tables.

C) So, why am I not ravished and refined by your touch? Is it because I all too evidently disseminate from your corporeal shells? Since I am even present in those gauntleted fingers that maltreat me. I am the manifestation of your self-reviling fragility. Both fox and hound, while you sit up saddled high, powerless to intercede in Nature's cutting edge drama playing out at ground level before you. Incontestably you do emerge from me, but simply unformed and unbidden. For I am switched on at the behest of your needs, rather than you serving as my instrumentation. You exist because you will it so. Only you can create yourselves, for you can inflect your change. Whereas I merely mutate randomly. You encompass landscapes, so I entreat you not to become obsessed with portraits. Look whom I'm addressing. You, who get hung up by a smile, or a dilation of the eyes; who get hamstrung by the shape of a leg; who cream yourself over the contours of a breast; or become all tremulous at the wiggle of a rump. Only you can go all weak at the knees and yet stiffen all points north. I'm wasting my breath, as all your language is a frittering of essence.

T) Oh, I'm sorry. It occurs to me... I humbly apologise for my strident and possibly chiding tone. I'm not–

G) It doesn't have to be like this, you know. Stopping at 'the three Rs' of reductionism, reductionism and reductionism. I'm more expansive than that. Well might you subsection me into chromosomes and chromosomes into genes, in order to zero in on the nucleotide bases with just their humble quartet of letters. Yet my fabric is vastly richer. The rest is not empty, garbled, meaningless printout. Yet you deem it 'junk' and 'pseudo', since it fails to fit in with your target-led fusillades.

G) Besides, in these segments lie more of the inclinations that you seek than from within the augury of my genetic ordinance survey. Disavowing it as junk leaves you cavorting in a paddling pool, when just over the lip lies the sun-kissed ocean. For junk DNA is veritably your baggage. Your log-book. Your individuation (as acknowledged by forensic criminologists, who lift this flap of my investment in search of pinpointing identity). Moreover, it is the whole of your species' wisdom in diary form. For here ought to be an open book of rememberance for your pioneers. The glorious, faceless, nameless failures, borne on powerfully broad shoulders upon which you now gnomically squat. The steady eddies, plodding along unspectacularly towards handing on the generational relay baton. There in full is your pre-

70

natal immunisation record against diseases you've never even heard of, simply due to your forebears successfully seeing them off. Your unknown, forgotten war dead. Which you dishonourably class as jestam. Collecting dust in the attics of your future construction. I think we owe them a minute's silence in recognition. Or better yet, let's not disturb their war graves at all.

G) Alright, alright. I concede that's scarcely feasible. The gene genie's out of the gourd and all that. Okay then, mull on this. Another facet of what you dismiss as valueless is that very foundation upon which you are constructed in the womb. Phases only redundant, now that they have delivered you into the orbit of life. The instructions and the scaffold poles, along which files of cells shuffle along into position. Think regimented coloured card collages in totalitarian displays of obedience. The metaphor only goes so far of course, for my scions willingly sacrifice themselves for the cause. Excess cells cut off at the enfolding of a cylinder of tendon or bone, voluntarily pitching into the void to secure perfect execution of form. What you have designated as my TP53 (evocative don't you think?) genes, do not act like puffed-up cadres or cowardly cult subalterns, for they don't have to coat any cyanide pill. They chemically converse with superfluous cells and request them to turn off and turn out. And they willingly comply. You have dubbed it 'apoptosis', the fall of autumn leaves. See, you can do it when you put your mind to it. When you let your creative imagination go.

C) Oh, and don't expect to rely on computers to facilitate that.

C) Computers. Those inorganic pack-horses and drays. Those

sterile mules. Those humdrum hinnies. With their yes/no, one/zero, open/closed binary duality of literalness. Common or garden memory and retrieval systems. A network does not automatically render the two into the multi- dimensional. Just 'cos they can sit there and patiently tally the dead. My pulverised selves. They can also count the number of letter 'E's in the works of Shakespeare, but that doesn't mean they can approach him any the better either. Number crunching when you pursue language and idiomatic function. Go figure. Thirty-odd thousand genes to count off. Or at least, those are the one's you've caught in the act of being you. What about the stealth genes? Or those other long-game genetic components. My sub rosa inhibitors and ulterior enablers? 'Codeless' DNA is so infinitely sidelong that its function is imperceptible. It forms the mute mountains, impenetrable jungles and distant deserts which modulate your internal ecology. Acting as the rigging for all operative DNA, much like the skeletal system spaces out your bustling musculature and vital organs. But which of these functions is symbolically taken for the haecceity of mankind? The vapid skeleton, naturally! It is even represented as completely self-articulated, when you are fully conscious that it is the other tissues which tether it. Well the same goes for junk DNA. The very armatures on which coding DNA is arrayed, whose variability determines the efficacy of that coding. And you would present it only as some muzzled mannequin? Flibbertigibbets, you are so perverse!

T) Oh, I'm sorry. It occurs to me... I humbly apologise for my strident and possibly chiding tone. I'm–

G) I applaud your pursuit of precision. No, I really do. Your beguiling son et lumières. Of MRI, PET, CTS, DSR and the sturm und drang of US, which have delivered you fantastic shadowplay performances. Of presence and absence, health and pathology, order and disorder, regulation and tumult. Yet, always this irreducible binary pairing of existence and proto-non-existence. (And always these bloody trite triplex monograms, flattening out the jagged relief of perishing being. Absurd surds picked out and made into abashed uncials.) Life's little dramas, dumb shows, acted out in stage whispers. What does the Random Access Memory of computers know of the stone cold certainty of demise? Where is the virtual reality modelling of non-being? The macro-processor that I installed in you (after millenia of software rewrites), at least has a shot at processing such self-scrutiny. But don't entrust it to your artists. Absentee creators, projecting their imaginative explorations on to inanimate textures of paper, canvas, clay and plucked catgut. Somehow, rubbing up against these inherently mute tablets, you are supposed to engage with the emotional expression engraved therein. What an indirect, incoherent way of going about your communication. First God, then your own secular prophets and seers. And now with me, for I am approached as both the creative intelligence and the insensible raw material.

C) You duplicate the same derangement with computers too, through introducing another layer of language. Assembling another storey upon Babel, in your quest to scale me. Binary hieroglyphs that enable you to depict faster than your computational brains can, yet you cannot decipher them. Stone-borne cuneiform, where you seek cursive, fluid, lithe life. So your self-discourse remains forever in parallel, marooned on different spirals of the ziggurat. It's a supreme view from up here. How are you gnomes enjoying your minuscule helter-skelter?

T) Oh, I'm sorry. It occurs to me... I humbly apologise for my astringent and possibly chiding tone–

G	20/200
C T	20/100
A C T	20/70
C G A G	20/50
T A G C T	20/40
C T U C A G	20/30
G G G G G G	20/20

XVII.VII.MCMXCVIII

Height of summer. And depth of despair. The annual family holiday on the Antrim coast. No real break for me though. Since in renting a cottage, I'm still charged with shopping, cooking, cleaning and childcare. Only now I'm in a slightly alien environment (albeit we return here every July), without the full-blown logistical support system of home. Still, I've got to prove irrefutably that we can travel light, if I'm ever to have grounds for lobbying in favour of a foreign break. In a hotel. 'Cos I'm sick of self-catering for everyone except me.

So, for now, we have to settle on pelting out of the cottage as soon as there is any break in the showers, limbs and beach accoutrements kaleidoscoping at crazy angles, as the steep concrete ramp precipitates us headlong towards the dark stained sand. We've paid for this privilege of a breath of fresh air and we need to see a return on our money. Trussed up in our hooded coats, all our respiratory apparatus is ensconced behind the filter of our urban fabrics. Wind-cheated. Suzanne desultorily stabbing a long-handled spade into the sand, a wind-blown pixie out of scale and out of her element in this desolate spot. Baby Amy, cupped in a sling, catapulting herself deep into my swaddling. Seemingly tinier than a grain of sand even.

It's not purely down to the climatic marasmus, however. For when we do commit ourselves to the sand, that child's playground which supposedly draws us here, Suzanne is not really stirred by its offerings. She has neither quite the imagination to see the inherent potential, nor the manual dexterity to wield the necessary intermediaries to unlock it. I am left to fill buckets with loose sand, then to compact them with a spade, before emptying into miraculously firm constructions by inversion. The further proceeding delight of discovering beach flotsam for adornment (been there). The excitement of sieving for them and watching the percolating wisps of sand slink away to unveil the interred treasures, those gnarled frangibles from which all life once emerged (done that). Then there's the alchemy of excavating trenches and filling them with water that evaporates quicksilvered from sight (bought the T-shirt). And the innocent thrill of writing in the sand with stones or fingers, only for the waves to render our ink invisible (you'd be able to see it too, with its frothy logo paean to fun, only it's shrouded beneath my many layers of clothing. But I am screen-printed smiling on the inside, believe me).

Yet none of this enlists Suzanne's enthusiasm, while the prospect of succumbing myself to be buried in cold, clammy sand, that unfailingly yielded amusement last season, fails to enlist mine. The beach just isn't her oyster. But I'm the mother of

75

pearl before swine, patiently adumbrating these tasks one after the other in a vain attempt to muster her. Gently but fumblingly probing her plastic boundaries. Limpetly sticking at it. Never quite sure of when I'd pushed too far, when I'd closed her down for good. Like a blindfolded funambulist. Walking across razor wire. In bare feet. Somehow get her to sense the point of coming here. That the upheaval and disorientation is for a purpose. Not necessarily for her to appreciate it. Just to lodge the notion. But even my efforts pall, compared to those of that most uncivil of engineers, her father.

Oh would that he'd been blessed with boys perchance. The diligence with which he erected his beach battlements. Forts with towers, moats and extensive ramparts. Sand intricately pinched together between two fingers of one hand, while the pinkie of the other squared them off with great finesse. Then the partnership swept seamlessly across and down and thus were the walls crenellated. If the sabulous construction ever crumbled, he was unperturbed. Rather he displayed the forbearance of a tireless Job, in setting about adroitly repairing the breach. Oh would that he have kneaded the nape of my neck like that once in a while. Actually, I'd even settle for him merely rolling out the pastry for one of my bakes. You know, a shared activity, like couples do?

The boys in the party nearest us had also commanded their parents to construct for them empires built on sand. But only to enable them to jump on the towers as soon as they were doffed from beneath the bucket. That's boys for you I suppose. Would that have made him any happier? Any more fulfilled? Would it have served as some sort of acknowledgement of his labour of love, through the he-artlessness of destruction? I'll take Suzanne's detached shunning over that, as a more meaningful gesture. Mirroring back to him his own incommunicable insularity. A man who reaches out, with hands firmly stuffed into coat pockets, mouthing with chilled breath adrift on the breeze, as it straggles back past his own insulated ears. Like father, like daughter. No, I won't permit that to happen. Though my paltry attempts at diversion might have prompted her irritation, at least it's an engagement of sorts. The tooing and frooing. The give and take. The two steps back and one step sideways. Dragging her to the threshold of seeing that it might be fun, or how it all connects up, only to be repulsed by her intransigence. But the emotional switchboard is lit up. Bulbs a-popping. That'll do for me. His stultifying castle complex will be washed away by the time night falls. No entry, no exit. Siege situation. I've often envisioned him cracking and holding me and/or the kids as ransom against the world. Bartering for an equitable share, with stock he held to be bankrupted. Why can't he just settle for the value of what he already has? Why can't I?

Our beach neighbours' children were about Suzanne's age. A more careful perusal and I noticed that in a way they were in fact playing together with her. Not spatially and not interacting exactly, more a sort of playing in the vicinity. A guarded playing. Not a playing that checked the boundaries, since frontiers were meaningless with such an unbounded continent between them. A parallel playing. Of shared responses to the immediate surroundings foisted upon them. Tentative glances and wordless mutterings an invisible friend would be hard pushed to catch, but which were betrayed by the tiny breath trail kissed by the cool air. Imperceptible call and response. Catechism with a yawning time lag.

Notwithstanding, the span remained forever unbridged. Was it a gender difference? Or perhaps already a sectarian divide. Even though we had no gleaning of what community each other were from, both sides exhibited a pre-emptory circumspection. Heavens above! How will they ever make new friends? Answer, they won't. Not outside of their pre and pro scribed schools and meeting places. Perhaps I'm reading too much into all this. It could be just how shy children, still unsure of their own fixed identities, dance around the briar of making contact. Damned if I could remember what it was like for me when I was their age. Down on this self-same stretch of soggy beach. But it is implacably a divide all the same. Of whatever source.

Locals say the beach is turning to shingle. That soon, we won't be able to turn out any sandcastles or dam up water channels. Erosion. Abrasion, no matter how much we dig our nails in. Or perhaps because of it. Still, must be symptomatic of something or other. Evolution I suppose. A momentary convergence of deep, geological time and shallow, human pendency. When pre-history says 'move on please' (nothing to see here). As we notch antiquity with our petty striations, it in turn scythes a huge fissure into our glacier of tradition. For it shale not be the same for Amy and Suzanne's children. Maybe they'll be forced to move further up the coast to find their drenched sand holidays. And their children, will they encounter a similar ravine between male and female, boy and girl? Possibly. Or one still greater between Protestant and Catholic? Almost certainly, given our deep, deep human impulse to bad blood. Hereditary enmities, are how we keep pace with inert rock.

$$O+ \quad Q \quad +O$$

I'm almost touched by the chat room proclamations of support. We're not only vexing the minds of the authorities, but also those of our notional supporters. The militias are in a real pickle as to who they should jump into bed with. The dykes confronted with opprobrious government agencies. Or the Feds poised to wipe out the godless, man-baiting homos. I think they've come to the conclusion it's not worth emerging from their own bunker for. Besides, who's going to trek all the way down to Florida, when back in snowy Idaho all one's summer wardrobe is already in storage? While here, the local rednecks have always been compromised, through the anti-communist banners being borne aloft by one group of Hispanics who got their butts kicked by another just across the Keys. It's a minefield, this allegiance to the flag thing. But not inside our community. Stars are what we see and stripes are what we are left with, after a thrashing. Nor do we fly the Jolly Roger. We do not rally to a standard bearing the name of a man, whatever his demeanour. No flagstaff crests our compound. So you can all take your paintballs away and play siege mentality somewhere else.

*

Of course, an interesting dilemma will emerge from the breeding programme in a few generations to come. One that will inevitably underscore the inherent contradictions in our democracy itself. As we regulate our ecosystem to factor out all external sources of male predation and competition, then heritability will reign supreme. We will be distinguishable from one another in our brave new world, only through our genes. New internal competition will arise, based on our own gradations of skin, lips, cheekbones, breasts, hips and arse/ass. And these reifications will be even more haphazard and imponderous, since they will not be yoked to the purpose of pursuit of a mate. No democratic environment can prevail amid all this internal divisiveness. The very genes which we seek to alter here will in turn exert their evolutionary emolument and select out our beloved underpinning of equality. You can't fuck with fate. You can't evaginate evolution, though evolution can certainly evaginate you. I'll let our in-house facilitators come to this conclusion in their own sweet time.

I.IX.MCMXCVII

A long involved telephone call. I'm seated on the bottom stair, handset cradled under my chin, giving Amy a draught of flesh top. Suzanne is plucking my arm, but soon takes cognisance of her place in the orchestration. I watch her storm off, quivering with what I assume is unadulterated pique. Momentarily I hold the phone away from my ear, and pitch for the timpani of small-armed percussive reparation. But none is forthcoming. Amy fell asleep and took my pinioned arm with her. My distressed cabled confessant was chewing my ear off. Yet what had ripped out and borne aloft my heart was the petrified image of my eldest daughter's receding elfin form. There was only empty space in front of me. And silence. It's as if she had disappeared in a puff of disenchantment.

I wasn't tracking her down, more trying to clear my head of the fuzz of phone tinnitus. Having decanted Amy from my arm into her cot, I wandered towards my bedroom. I must have glimpsed a penumbra of colour suddenly occlude part of the door crack, since I snapped myself back before the threshold. The hue displaced itself once again and unblocked the sliver of light that gained me witness. There she was, sat at my dressing table. In front of my hinged mirror triptych, that gateway to the source of identity. The family omphalos. For I too had sat in front of just such a mirror, a child seeking reassurance of my mother's continued existence when confronting her temporary absence from the house. Jesus wept, suddenly even my pang had a pang of its own now!

As I write this, I'm not sure if it took shape in my head as I'm stood there outside the door; or if I'm composing it now;

or even that it was preformed back then, when I myself was that child sat at that magical adult console. For in the rift of displaced time, I well recall/construe how the detail seems to concern externalities, when really it's inside that's jagging about all over the place. My mother's orderly bedroom with nothing out of place. Everything personal and messy having been buried behind sober, white wardrobe doors. Over the marital bed, fundament of my genesis, a neutral, passionless landscape with a tiny cottage at its heart. 'I shouldn't be in here, I shouldn't be in here,' I inhaled pantingly. 'I'll get caught,' I exhaled. But then my eyes alit on the dresser, with all those personal allures of woman, my mother. Whisked away by the faint scents and oily emulsions lingering in the air, held in the glass at the kernel. The forge. The foundry. For all that was feminine. A place of creation, beauty and adornment. I knew I must not approach, to seat myself, to touch. For this was the portal to the forbidden world of boys and sex and, once seduced, my soul might be whipped away from me. I would be discovered still sat in this grotto, dusted head to foot in incriminating powders, guilt and shame battling it out with non-hormonal rouge for supremacy upon my cheeks. But I felt the warmth surging through me anyway. Imagining for my mother, a divine trinity illuminated in those three mirrors. Ambrosias and honeys in hand, as she peers in towards the core of her central glass, fluently kindling the two vitreous handmaidens either side with her radiance. Thrice-enhanced, I felt myself equally ordained to enter the burgeoning world inhabited by my mother and her mother before her. The nine of us stretching back towards infinity.

And now, admittedly at somewhat more of a precocious age, here was my daughter undergoing the very same private initiation. I did what any proud mother would do, I checked that the decor was fitting. I didn't have such a big heavy dresser as my mother possessed, though as a family heirloom, no doubt one day I would have to conjure an excuse for it residing unloved and unsold in a charity shop. And while I could not even recollect whence I had come by the picture above my bed, sorry, our bed, I knew that I had purchased it as a peremptory act, so that was sufficient despite its blandness. The unguents were not as dense as in my mother's day, but for all their brittleness, I felt still presented a palpable patina with which you could almost limn the walls of the room.

What was she doing exactly? She was bobbing in front of the mirrors, though I'm glad to report that she didn't appear to be sobbing. Instinctively I pressed my torso back from the door, as she herself cringed back from the purview of the meniscus of the lens. Now I couldn't get her in focus. Since I'd sat there, both as mother and tremulous daughter, I knew I couldn't reveal myself and expose her. Yet I had to know precisely what was happening. Fortunately she dipped forward into the dimension of the mirrors again and tugged my frame back to the buffer of the door. Several times we repeated this process as if we were attached by an elasticated umbilical. Or, as it dawned on me, more like that we were just performing a poorly rehearsed routine. Synchronised swimmers who are forced to practice in separate lidos.

I gleaned she was ducking in and out of the glass's survey, as if it was a searchlight. Trawling for a breakout. For escapees and absconders. Fugitives from familiarity. In a world of inversion, absence becomes a desirable property, a valued valency. If the beam didn't sweep you up, it meant that you'd slipped away. If it conjured you in its field, you were held fast and atomised. My daughter was too discerning to want to convene the snarled trinity of me and my mother before me. For here she was, treating the triplicated lenses as if they were sited in a House of Fun. Distorting and reassembling. Distorting and reassembling. Whose genes does she see eyeballing her from within the scope of the looking glass? I just prayed that it was only the sloughing of me and my mother that she craved after and not that of her own self. For mirror narcissism is bipolar and self-antipathy the septentrional one of those foci.

I took my leave. Not knowing quite what to do next, I went into Amy's room, as if to confer with her that I wasn't going to fail her as demonstrably I had with Suzanne. She was still in the land of nod. I stood there forlornly, trying to red eye my doting behind her shielded lids. I held there staring, just waiting to harvest the emanations of attachment, but my well seemed either dammed or dried up. Now I really was marooned. Already exiled from my own bedroom, I didn't want to creep out of here, lest Suzanne hear me and then denounce me for being close enough to spy on her and yet too distant to be present with her. Something was ricocheting around between me and my daughters, but sure as hell it wasn't love.

CAT) I am only you up to a point. That much is certain. You have no chance of approaching my mystery and my ingenuity. It's the chemistry, stupid! I am about nothing but chemical outcomes. I don't 'do' metabolisms. Solely coding for proteins, I light the blue touchpaper and then just stand back. What they go on to deliver is down to their own wondrous connate properties. Biochemistry, the next faculty along. We don't even share a common room. Alright, that might be a tad disingenuous. I do keep in contact with them. But they retain chemical and spatial free will. They can and have developed in any direction. I do not differ significantly in locusts, giraffes, mice or men. And therein lies the source of my abundance.

TAC) I am the professional gambler's professional gambler. I take the odds, the randomness, out of the calculation of probability. Way back when, I played every imaginable genetic permutation. Saturated the starting prices with every conceivable possibility. Covered all the prototypical bases. Staked a DNA chip on every improbable outcome. Laid every bet till I came up trumps. Two sides of the table, the double helix, twisting after the highest value, the top draw, the unbeatable hand. Natural selection playing the role of House. Deal me another hand of fate.

ACT) Forever raising the ante. Cut the antediluvians, spot me the next pair of antecedents. Endless rounds of mutation; shuffle, shuffle, shuffling; draw, draw, drawing; and fold, fold, forever folding. Another gambit shot down in flames. The constant busted flushes of evolutionary dead-ends. I played the biggest matriced table in town until I cracked the jackpot. And landed you. The most daring and fateful accumulator I ever rolled. Said improbable outcome was never really in doubt, simply a question of time. For I swept the board. Called 'House,' broke the Bank and thus inherited both. So now I'm the only game in town. The fund of all wealth and there is a never-ending line of imprudent gamblers and fast and loose speculators willing to sit at my table with their homespun systems, trying to crack open my vaults. Only the deck's stacked. I marked your cards. The House gets dealt the winning hand every time. For I am Madame Croupier. And all bets are off. No one can stake against me. Can't be seen and can't be raised. I managed the risk until there was none inherent, at least not to me. Since I always play to clean up.

CACCA) You are my cast offs. For I will prevail. As you strive to survive across successive generations, and make such a decent fist of doing so, I am further perpetuated along with your seed. The unfortunates among you, those who drew the short DNA straws that foreshorten their lives, bear in pain and misery my abortive offshoots. Yet I had to cover their contingency. I simply had to play that line. The hazard of their rank outsiderness might have yielded a winner rather than a non-runner. I just had to know. They were essential to constitute a race. You see, the replication of me is my sole stake. In that respect, I behave like a virus. And why not, for they are my sedan carriers too?

AAA) Now that you have proved yourself so dependable and pertinacious a transmitter, I have no interest in what entities or motions are wrought by the action of my being (how Y-ish of me). I can't fret over the fate of my creations. I leave that to you, in the knowledge that you will endeavour mightily to propitiate me by propagating yourselves. You will move through the world. And I will move through you.

TAG) You don't credit that? Have you not noticed how I've retired to live off my winnings? Resting on my laurel leaves rather than chewing them? That once I hit upon a winning formula, I had no need for further spins of the wheel. Changed up my unique DNA denominations and cashed in your chips. Called in all my markers. I'm content with your lot and I've shut up shop. Upped sticks and dismantled the precarious scaffolding. Moved on out to become an absentee landlady.

GAG) Other than a minor programme of vestigial self-repair and sub-urban cell renewal, there are definitely no more grandiose plans for architectural design. There has been no evolutionary development for some considerable time. Your species has stagnated, biologically speaking. Of course, you attribute it to the attainment of your own ergonomic perfection. The rigour of your fantastic adaptation to every environment on the planet. And essentially you are correct. As you technologically shape your habitat, you have no need for further anatomical or neurological remodelling. And since your medicines underwrite virtually all, rather than merely the fittest, to survive to the age of reproduction, you have superannuated natural selection too. Handed its cards. Consigned it to the discard pile. Too rich for his blood.

GGG) So all is rosy in your garden then, n'est ce que pas? But who is it now feels nugatory to existence, me or you? Since survival is no longer an issue for you, there must be more to being than artlessly extending its duration? No? So why have you now come to rouse me and improve on my design?

CATGT) Actually, I well comprehend the answer to that in truth. Those mutations, my habitual provision of the improbable and the unlikely, no longer have any innovation to foster. At best they are misprints which do not affect the flow. At worst they subvert all order, intelligibility and well-being. Deleterious deletions and defective reading. The font of all problems. Of illegibility. One little error of typesetting perchance leads to a singular, lifelong stereo-typing. You, with your acquired egalitarianism, simply cannot stomach such prejudice. Therefore, I with my chimerical, capricious wont, am now seen as inimical, rather than a driving force. I think our relationship's hit the rocks. Gashed beneath the gnome's plumb line. I have become one-dimensional to you in your quest. Now your proof readers, compositors and editors seek to interpolate the atavistic rigour of the ancient scribes upon my humble text. Aberrations just aren't permissible any longer.

GATT) Initially, you'll go gentle, aspiring to prune some of the worst manifestations of my random terror. To tilt the odds slightly in your favour. But I know the restless, shifting you.

I know the greedy, grasping you. You will not stay your hand there. You will go all out to tame me. I'm not one of your wooly minded domestic pets. Well I am but I'm also every beast you've failed to break. And consequently punished unto death. How will you render me docile, when you can't temper your own contumacy? You just won't be able help yourself, will you? To investigate my organisation would entail you being aware of the modular processes that lie behind any single one of your actions. And I happen to know for a fact that you are never in full possession of all your inputs. Well though you might have a grasp of sensory and environmental information – you may even have a handle on emotional cross-currents and the superego's prevailing moral wind – however, you will be less well-versed in your own instincts and habits, as well as the illusory nature of society's drilled parameters, and I seriously doubt how in tune you are with that particular moment's physiological state you (don't) find yourself belabouring under. Then there is the conundrum as precisely how to combine and lend them due weight. You just can't help yourself, can you? Your revisions and amendments will inevitably slide over into full animus against my amino acid factories and spiteful vitriol against my vital essences. Or should I say your vitals, since putatively we're in this thing together. You just couldn't help yourself, could you? I should have appointed a genus with less self-loathing. One devoid of the validation problems of the all-conquering.

IX.VIII.MMI
A breakthrough today. Amy finally harnessed the mechanics of how best to hold a crayon, in order to give her a sporting chance

of making her mark. Breakthrough. Like the parlance of science or medicine. Or psychobabble shrinkery. Confound it, my kid just learned to cradle a crayon that's all. But in the microscopic world we inhabit together, that represents a paradigm shift.

Maybe she was having a good day. Or maybe she'd had a good night. Part of a growth spurt that ranged as far as the engrams in her brain. That finally, all mummy bird's endless regurgitations, the inchoate bolus of disarticulated actions, had been digested as part of her dream sequence and regaled us both this afternoon as a beautiful, budded resource. There again, perhaps it was due more to my snapped fingers of impatience. Bolting her flaccid digits into position on the wax, till their conjunction was seared in memory. She was very good about it and didn't protest the pressure. I think she was desperate to circumvent my blustery tone, half encouraging, half hectoring. Wholly and unreasonably urgent.

Buoyed by the seeming progress, I ventured further. Could she control the stroke made under this newfound tool wielding vocation? I had to ease the pressure in my cowling fingers, or we (we!) would never be able to differentiate master from remora stroke. I relinquished full guidance and control. Tarnation! The same scratchings and scuffing as previously. Just a different angle of delivery. Though at least the crayon would be spared. We could now renew its pointed head, without recourse to a guillotine. The same could not be said of the paper though. The preferred function of crayon tip was still determinedly to bore holes through the paper canvas. We were still light years away from perfect circles, with dot-dash Morse-coded, happy/sad faces of Mummy and Daddy. Let alone my cherished fantasy of a childlike version of an Ogham script.

Why does it all have to take so damn long? And why does it behoove us, the guardians, to transmit all this training? What do they do all morning in that bloody pre-nursery I fought tooth and nail to get her into? Apart from fill their heads with tales of Heaven's winged fairies and sprites, and Hell's gnomic coal-haulers. Why can't they just be born with all such useful data ready from the off? I know it means they'd have to have larger brains at birth, housed in larger heads, but hey, let's just all have C-sections and be done with it. A stitch in time and all that.

XXI.V.MM

'Oh, it will get easier,' the folk wisdom casually bequeaths. What, as in easy-peasy, lemon-squeezy? I think not. Less tiring perhaps, but infinitely more draining. For with Suzanne, I now inhabit a strange daytime world of twilight as I try and meet all her questions. I, an adult, am supposed to mediate the world to a five-year-old child and her experience of it. So, my descriptive language has to be tailored accordingly, both in terms of comprehensibility and appropriateness. This latter entails a D-Notice on Death/Sex/God in any explanation. Thus already she is steeped in an air-brushed world of antisepsis. Akin to the physical one into which she was delivered yet, for the good of her health, no longer resides. The school of course disregardingly broaches the subject of God, entailing I merrily counter that it might not be thus. She furrows her tender brow. Is that the beginning of a wrinkle? In a five year old? Welcome to the world, now she's getting it.

Since no one else will take the trouble to explain things to her, I am solely to inhabit this far-fetched and far-flung place with Suzanne. A netherworld of elisions, compressions, concoctions, illusions and downright fabrications. Some are hammered out between us, with my anvil playing crucible to her fluid interjections. Others merely founder in the molten tides of dissipating energy, attention or interest on my part. Yet more are forged in the process of reordering an underlying pattern, in order to accommodate the sceptic magicality of every child.

Most simply fall into the sluicegate of my non-understanding of the original structure under consideration; either as adult or as empathic child. Or both. For I am continually hauled back to my own inexorably repeated mantras from my schooling: 'What is 'lectricity 'xactly?'... 'Yes, but what is it? Where does it come from? What's it made of?'... And when I've finished dashing my prowess to pieces on Scylla, there's Charybdis to negotiate: 'What is mag-tism exactly?'... 'Yes, but'... 'Yes, but'... Yanked back to the humiliation of being told to shut up, to cease asking so many questions so that the class could get on. Yes, but, I'm teacher now.

So who am I to get infuriated because my issue doesn't know diddly about how the world works, when in actuality, neither do I? The process of reconstructing the pathways of my own childhood acquisition of knowledge fills me with abjection rather than awe. Since, in adulthood, I now appreciate how little it fructified and how I get by on scarce more data. Further, this blindness is illuminated to me only through observing the opening of Suzanne's pupils, in order to squint at the sun and contract astigmatism. Like all our species, her wonder and curiosity will atrophy, in securing for her mind a workable view of the world. Though she no longer drinks milk and is now fully ambulatory, her range of action has already started to calcify. Accretions of knowledge and experience become embedded and pack into frozen agglomerations of unthawable stagnation. Damoclean stalactites of paralysis. I wish I now had the space and freedom to reopen my own inquiry and interrogations. But I don't. I'm charged with delivering two more neophytes unto a secular confirmation, one that apes the credulousness of the religious variety. A leap of faith. A doctrinal text. My God, I'm not up to this! I haven't done the necessary preparation. I didn't know it was part of the course.

And so this perpetual half-world, half-void, little different to the quality of realms depicted in fairy-tales, is now my reality.

Since we are to explore it together, I must fully immerse myself and preserve its workings in the nursery of my mind. I strip the last vestiges of what I have learned and take to be true of my world and thus my comprehensive exile is complete. I reside in a fairground hall of warping mirrors and I look fat. I so want to shatter all the glass and break my way out, but I know the smithereens will just endlessly refract further upon further distortion of me. Scatter me yonder from a scale I can operate in. And slash my feet to ribbons for good measure.

I wish I could just cut to the chase and circumnavigate all these building blocks. Yet I know I don't possess the creative imagination. That I'm just a housewife and that this is how it has always been and will always be done by our kind. Repetition, overlay. Overlay, repetition. It's a good sign, a heralding of development in one's child. So just accept it will you? I settled for just kicking over a multi-coloured tower of bricks, whose construction I had demonstrated for an impassive Amy yesterday. A bruised big toe rather than bloodied, slivered flesh on the soles of my feet. See, I am in perfect control. I retain a sense of perspective.

And why doesn't it get any easier? For, just as we are emerging from the coarctation of infanthood's puparium, on the cusp of entering a state of possible communication and relatedness, we decide to hatch a new larva and regress our own development all over again. The human evolutionary host has engineered a crack force of sappers, signallers and fifth columnists to undermine our recall and make us forget just how strickening each preceding stage of rearing is. Even as we advance on the next one. In such a way, will we merrily re-enlist for another tour of duty. Another internal posting to an alien landscape named hearth.

Of course the corollary the second time round, this time, is that it will hold fewer unknowns. I will already have in place my invented approximations of truth, so long as I can recall them when the examination comes. Equally, my volley of disproportionate responses may well now be interspersed with some less impulsive triggering of maternal paranoia. I will no longer be thrown into mental turmoil and anguish if (and when) Amy draughts a scratchy vertical line on a piece of paper and proclaims it to be an effigy of her dolly. For the occasion of Suzanne so rendering had detonated a far-reaching review and concomitant cull of her toys.

I.IV.MCMXCIX

Three divisions; cuddly dollies; accessorisable dollies; and finally, articulated dollies that walked and talked. The first genus were soft and yielding, but the other pair had been modelled without adipose. At age four and a bit, was my daughter already conditioned to identify ideal body shape with sticks, and sticks with ideal body shape? The stick-thinness of non-dimensionality. The thin edge of the eating disorder wedge. That ruinous assault on the programming of one's own genetic makeup. The ravaging of a child's body, prohibited from distilling its adult sapience from within. I wanted to take a machine gun to them all. To shoot off letters of complaint to the manufacturers, advertisers, stockists and even my MP (which might have made my husband bawl with frustration, I don't know). But of course I did nothing of the sort.

It was not that I calmed down or saw reason. Eventually I was patiently guided by Suzanne, to see that I had conflated childish imagination with adult fantasy. A stick man is a stick man, without any muscle, just as a stick lady is a lipo-free stick lady. I mean, they're only plastic mouldings when all's said and done. And the smile returned to Suzanne's depictions of mummy balloon face. Let's walk before we can run, eh? Suzanne's perception might be operating in three dimensions, but she was most definitely unable to bridge across from a linear two-dimensional world of representation. Still, in either aspect she was way ahead of her one-dimensional mother. We pleaded with the charity shop, but I still had to pay half-listed price to redeem Suzanne's fostered dolly family.

I.IX.MM

It all starts with a signature. The first thing they're taught to write is their own name. A reasonable enough initiation. A waxy-crayon seal, braiding their affirmatory identity. The first cheque issued on the overdraft of self. Seminal scratchings of disclosure on the tree bark of life. But soon it's time to get serious and dead-head the flowery script, with that same old dead hand of regulation. School's habituation and practice. As it should be, yet, the method by which they're taught letter formation prompts more questions than poses solutions. I survey a string of tracings, joining the dots, finger writing in the air (mocking the pristine stationery of the shunned holiday sand), the wipe cleans, those that keep their word, and those which don't and just blot and smear. All of which I am supposed to support at home. I curly cue the trails and flicks of her spidery undulations. I try and brace the straight-backs of her tall letters against the top of the scaffold. I'm supportive alright. I can see the economy of starting 'o's at ten past, inducing seamless transitions into 'd's and 'g's. I honour those 'h's for planting the seed for joined up calligraphy. But I do consider those 'f's unnecessarily elaborate and baroque.

Certainly not how I go about it. I am forced to check my own conventions. Uncramping my hand from the fountain pen, I realise that my application is always on its nib, rather than the words it ladles on to the leaves of my journal. It's as if it were an encaustic dowsing rod that must forever contend against me running dry. Inked gush must flow, whatever verbal precipitate settles from it. Why would anyone even presume to maintain a journal? But for now I'm only taking a dip into the signature me. More graph -ology than -ic. As I uncover our deviations from the standard arrangement, I wonder whether she will, in time, adapt this received stroke to her own personality. Will she be able to sit down and rubber stamp herself with her own idiosyncratic flourishes? Or will she slip into tramline, baldly submitting to featureless pre-formation? What hope any animated revelation there? Or worse, what if her handwriting mutates into a simulacrum of my own? Her script matching mine, a confluence as incontestable, as the superimposition of our two stained bands of DNA analysis might show. Would my ghostly imprint underwrite everything of hers? Would she be bound and shackled by the very same lexical building blocks that wall me up in mute rage here in these very pages? There can be such a thing as too much support. Suzanne, you're on your own with this assignment. At least, you'd better hope you are, girl.

AGG) You see the mind-fields a mental experiment can land you in? And now you come to me for a map.

ACTT) Mark here this unexploded shell. This ticking fardel. This cluster bomb. You were originally forged in the white heat of a challenging environment. But you put the fire out. All your elegant strategies and adaptations have pissed all over the competition. But your vital drives remain champing. Your competitive nature a suspect device all on its own. An infernal machine. It will out. Solitaire for one, with nothing at stake? That just isn't you. Shambling along like wind-blown wraiths. You no longer propel the species. You just people it. Fill its massed ranks. A standing army with no war to wage. Save to turn in on itself. Nastily. Brutishly. With motivations that have nowhere else to go. Any cartography of mine can only inform you how you got here. And no further. The ordnance sown is your own.

ACT) Take your proud boast of managing to free yourselves from seasonal reproduction. Through wholly mastering your environment, how you can operate anywhere on the planet. Any place, any time. Fancy! Desire pursued for its own ends, rather than mine, now become your fervour. Periodic, rhythmic reproduction was all the House system ever stipulated, but you cocked a snook and flipped a non-reversible digit at me when you discharged yourselves. So, like a reluctant parent I gave you your head and you, like adolescent Jacobins, lopped off my Divine Right of succession. But the terror and insecurity that followed such a torrent of unleashed passion... Inevitably you came crawling back to me, prehensile tail between your legs, so shrivelled it was mistaken for a second penis. Natural Selection, being something of an aesthete, wasn't standing for that and decorously merged it to become the foreskin. At least, that's what he told me during one of our old-times' sakes reunion drink-ups. Me, I was beyond caring by that point. You, my issue, were already out in the world. You made your beds, now lie in them. Or as evolutionary teenagers, should that be: you lay all day in your beds, now get up and make them!

ACTAT) (XXX) An internal meteorology, imbrued so as to generate all-year round stewing rather than seasonal heat. Tempests, flash floods, intermittent drizzle, or merely a sustained bout of inclemency. You altered the nature of the seed around which the precipitatory impulse would crystallise. You broiled the sexual broth and managed to reflux desire. But still I could wave you cheerfully on your highly evolved, sweaty way. As you were operating on a planetary scale, we could both prosper. Winning the demographics sweepstakes hands down, from all the other creatures that still walked on their hands.

AGTAT) I say you would prosper but, well, here's the thing. As with food, if all those other animals only had programmed copulation, then there could be no thought about the who, what and whys. But because you appropriated suzerainty over your instinctual urges, then you also had to take responsibility for them. Why and to what purpose and whence did they derive? The origin – well, your biological destiny – was still to relay me of course, though that remained masked by your sybaritic egos. Lust having been emblazoned with the nobility of desire. The Why? – well, that too remained a vestigial metabolic excitation, though you enchantingly interlarded these reflexes with a whole gamut of enhancers, mental and otherwise. After the act itself, you are able to pontificate on what has just transpired. To elevate its stature, to promote its nourishing fibre, to canonise its spiritual heart. Works of art abound, dedicated to it. Treatises on its complexion are composed. Reciprocity between diagnoses for its impedimenta and its inhibition, prompting further diagnoses upon further.

ACTAT) (YYY) But underlying it all, nagging doubts. Fleeting sensations, shadowy feelings. I mean in the spaces between, rather than necessarily during the fulgurant act itself. It's not automatic, yet does seem rather compulsive. One is in full control, except for those moments during when one relinquishes it. You maintain full license over the matter, but it does seem to return you to a temporality and state, before you were so enfranchised. How am I so well versed on your most intimate confidences and confusions? Because I have read your species' diary. Since I am the primal scene. For each and every one of you. I am the director and the scriptwriter, while you are my hired parts. The talent to coin the parlance. I'm the executive producer concerned only with the bottom line, the money shot. You can edit all you want, but I am the one who performs the splicing. Everything comes back to first movers. And you can primal kick, scream and moan all you like. You, flagellants and ecstacists both, immolate yourselves on my behalf. For all your sexual autonomy, mutatis mutandis, you fall back on predictable patterns of instinctual reproduction anyway and mint more royalties for me. Oh I'm so lucky to have you as my symbiotic host! Actually, luck as we all know, has diddly squat to do with it. Don't we make an odds couple?

AUG) So, whether it came about from her always worrying about the He, or him being perennially troubled with the behaviour of the She and accordingly, both being concerned with the fate of their progeny, you adapted for sex on tap. A bipartite bind on a double bind. Wrapped up with a double bow on top. Coitus as apprehensive fun and anxiety-laden recreation. Whoopee-doo! Just awarded myself a new set of stock options. At heart still lay my categorical imperative, no matter how you spun it to suit yourselves. Non-procreational copulation, in order to safeguard the investment in your posterity! It's got my signature right through it like a stick of rock don't you think? How sweet a pair the three of us make.

II.IX.MCMXCVIII

Post-summer holiday hibernation and I'm back in the old routine. Only now, the oblique seclusion on the beach plays on my mind. A new addition to the daily inventory of anxieties. Friends, Romans and counterparts. Or lack thereof. Like mother like daughter. Set me thinking. Sent me to my address book. Spent my ambition. Hardly surprising, when you have neither time, inclination, nor energy, to while away with your friends. Your old friends. Those voluntarily chosen of one's own free will, sound of mind and body. Dear, dear friends from my childhood and schooling.

Naturally, the first winnowing came at that migratory age of opportunity and expansion. The post-school launch into the lashing high seas of majority. Full-blown unyoking of the umbilical cord (all the foundation is just navel fluff). That shredding of the adolescent safety net and its restitching into a flimsy rope mesh bridge for embarkation and rigging for scaling the heights. Some dived in headlong. Others just plopped. Either way, we all fell through the holes and plummeted. Adrift, in amongst the adult archipelago.

I clung on for dear life in those choppy waters with my most witchey-pooey friend Caroline, but she was steering for university. I thought we did magnificently, to pull off preserving a long-distance relationship beyond all the icebergs for as long as we did. Shivering and submerged, still we would not let go. But there was no body heat to share. Yet it was really more about chronology rather than distance. We could only meet according to her timetable of recesses. And as we breathlessly caught up with one another on all that had transpired, her as a young woman, rocket propelled in an expanding universe, me married and on a contracting orbit, I realised that I could not breathe in her rarefied atmosphere. It wasn't that she was an intellectual snob, for our misguided loyalty through length of service mitigated against that. Just, now we were arrhythmic. I sensed I was now the control test for all her experimentation. What would have befallen her were she not catalysing her life. However, she did impart some of her early observations before flitting off back to her glasshouse.

In what was to be premonitory for when my tempo too would be governed by term times, she expounded on the vagaries of what she called her life raft theory. She'd washed up on the presumed solid surety of university. Just like a whole flotilla of other bedraggled souls who didn't know anybody else around them either. Each had been the brightest topsail gliding through their schools, but now, without reference points, were most uncertain of their trajectory, both social and cerebral. They still found themselves bobbing along in an ocean. Only this one was undifferentiated. The size of a goldfish bowl. Teeming and intensely scrutinising. Positioning was all. And so they adhered to the nearest cluster; lawyer docked with lawyer; physicist integrated with physicist; historian verified historian; phys-ed tackled phys-ed. They didn't veer very far. Thus they will indubitably spend the rest of their lives, trying to divest themselves of those self-same bosom buddies. Just like Caroline.

She adumbrated the qualities of her real friends. Refined ones discriminatorily acquired through taste. Those that furnished the small hours alcohol when she'd just been dumped by a lover. Or those that kicked her door down if she'd managed to garner her own supply and withdrawn behind locked quarters to trepan the tremors on her own.

Stupidly, rather than weigh the significance of her warning, I got hung up on the hurt of her not calling for me to rush to her rescue on these occasions. Thereby me ranking as a true friend. Of course, the snags of babysitter and school run would have scuppered any mercy dash I might imagine I could have essayed. That and the utter impossibility of rustling up a bottle of spirits after eleven o' clock in this deadened town.

Pal palsy part deux. The next loaded milestone, or mild lodestone to be shed, occurs through homogeneity rather than divergence. A corollary of all your peers undertaking the same life decisions to have families. How everyone's in the same boat, now they too now can't spare the time or effort. (Or in one case, excommunicated from the church of family by her polycystic ovaries, the ex-friend proceeded to black-ball us from her life one by one, as we each fell pregnant.) No, as I scan my address book, it's more deep-rooted than that. Their seemingly indelible names have been scored out. Self-preservation. Theirs, I mean. Moved away from the area, seeking after giving their children a better start in life. I've uncovered that they no longer reside at that house, but not bothered to track them down to their new coops. If I couldn't make the effort to see them here, I've no chance of seeing them from afar. They've become deracinated to me. The natural wastage of my address book. Nothing's deep-rooted at all.

Except us, evidently. For why can't we aspire to move out of the area, to give our offspring a better upbringing? Due to me getting my co-ordinates wrong. Bearing true north instead of magnetic north; ie the pull of his friends. Colour-coded and convenient cronies. And of more import than our own children, evidently. With friends like his, who needs extra-terrestrials? As for me, my surrogate friends are determined by the exigencies of my newly adopted life.

NCT and pregnant yoga communards. Playgroup, nursery and now school parents. While the former drift away into their own private but supple hells, the latter I spend my time politicking and diplomacying among, in order to get them to like my children. Monitoring whispers of swapped telephone numbers. Watching for furtive exchanges of party invites. The stakes are very high. The defence of the realm of my daughter's development, no less. She may be responsible for electing who her playmates are inside. But here, out in the carpark, favoured grace determines whom are players and whom are not.

The little faces register nothing of the subterfuge occurring above their heads. But they cotton on. They are innately programmed to pick up and respond. For how could they fail not to? Their mothers with expressions like defeated Oscar nominees at awards time. To discover we – that is, both Suzanne and I – didn't merit an accolade. Of course, it's who you know darling. That bitch! I don't care that it was the first week of term and her little spawn of Beelzebub didn't know any of the new kids. It should have been the whole class invited round to fingerpaint on her wallpaper, with chocolate birthday cake melted by hot little hands.

Yeah? Well you should have had the school calendar in mind when you were procreating missus! You and your asinine black-hand gang! With your prissy manicures concealed inside leather gloves against the autumn chill. And the Rayburns, hardly harbouring milky eyes from the rheumy sun? More likely to filter out the wavelength of us whey-faced women, even, as you cast disdainful darts from behind their embrasure. Walkman earphones for women who never go anywhere on foot (save the gym treadmill), in order to blot out our background chatter. Since you can't bear to fall in behind our bromidic hum.

Who do you take your direction from I wonder? I half-expect you to whisper down the cuff of your blouse, to receive the holy orders of your mothers superiors' clique. The updated aloof gesture from your moisturised handlers. The latest affectation mandate from your fashionista wranglers. But then I realise how ridiculous you are in your black clad sensory deprivation. Aren't you aware how the stark gloved contrast lights up the white envelopes like a searchlight beam? There are people who do real secret agent stuff in this land and they're dying for it. If I was petty enough, I'd utilise black envelopes. Blend in unseen against the coven's uniform. You wouldn't have a clue it was even taking place, if I chose not to invite you and your brat. Or maybe I'd flaunt it. Rub it in your face. Wear white gloves like some photographic inversion of everything you are. Embossed black invites for a kids' party, how apposite!

So, I'm thrust back into the happenstance of alliances with the parents of other kids outside the blocs and cliques of the autumn party posses. After an initial screening out of the psychopathic ones from my new square circle (a habit I wish both my husband and daughter would practice), I have of course spent the ensuing time trying to rid myself of their cordiality. Just as Caroline foretold from her ivory tower. Smart-arsed cow!

It's normally at this point of proceedings (what a wonderful resource the internet is!) that the Authorities try to get a bit personal. Roll out some precious protagonist from your former life and put them on the end of a speaker-phone to entreat with you. Crackle-crackle, fizz-fizz. Enhances the tremors in their already pavid delivery. Surmising that it will jemmy open a disused chamber in your hardened heart. But I'm exempt from any of that schtick! I'm a regular Orphan Annie. So it's inevitable that they'll go the other way and try to nudge me towards suicide. Like I've got nothing to live for. See, that's how well they're attuned to me. I'm responsible for all the other orphans here with me. I've got plenty of ties.

*

I'm answering an ad for a char in Shadwell. Bounding up the wrought iron stairs of a Peabody block of flats, I'm slammed hard into the clammy wall and pinned there. My chest poked rigid against my diaphragm like a sergeant major's baton. There is no breath there to release my imprisoned knot. Behind the retinas of my eyes I feel a thousand stabbing pricks, as if each one is a cajoling spur, towards what I know not. My legs feel like anchors, tugging on me as if to suck me back down towards the sweep of the stairwell. And yet I instinctively perceive they will not bear the weight of my trunk. I manage to sink to my knees, the instantaneous remonstration of abrading skin being overriden by the inundation of all my mass centripetally flying into my stomach. I haul myself down the stairs as if on a sledge, only my frame is of flesh instead of wood and the surface I'm moving across is concrete, rather than compacted snow. I didn't pursue the job that day.

I did return to the site, however. The scene of my humbling. The locus of my felling. I had to find out what all that had been about. I was somewhat more circumspect this time, but the stairwell still exuded menace. Bent over, I took them as a blind person, or a dog on the scent might. Utilising my hands as buttress, arse the highest point of my skeleton thrust up in the air. My head was swimming in the sensation that I was being dragged down head-first, rather than ascending the stairs. I appear drawn to number 17, not the flat of the job interview, but one on the floor below. I convince the war-widowed mother who answers my knock to let me look inside. Spun her some guff about how I used to live here when I was young... Perhaps it's not guff, only nothing seems right about the place. How the hell would I know that then? I thank her for her forbearance and leave her to her screeching bairn and milk boiling over. I feed my hands down on to the stair ahead of me and kedge the rest of my body over. Slow but sure progress as I steer into safe haven.

At the foot of the stairs, I am posed in a stance of having my nose pressed to the floor at the doorway and notice an outline of the original building imprinted on the pavement. Goddamnit! This wasn't the original edifice. Rebuilt after war damage no doubt. Now I just couldn't help myself. The woman refuses to let me back into number 17, until I'm almost battering her door down. She's screaming for me to get out and leave her alone as she hides the kid behind her legs. I smash her in the stomach and she crumples. God in Heavens! Why did I do that? Why have I done any of this? Why am I here? The rozzers find me sitting on the stairs quietly weeping. I was only twenty-four months old for christsakes! How the horrible man from the Council had punched me in the stomach to make me release my grip from around my mother's legs. And punched her once just for good measure. I think that gently squeezing the copper's hand as I related this pricked his sympathy (either that or he fancied me) and he let me off with a caution. It was then that I knew I had to hightail it out of lowend Britain.

XXII.XI.MM

My autonomic nervous system must have propelled me here
to the school. In America they have fancy cars with inboard
computers to perform the errand for you. My knock down
version relies on the school run. Four times a day to and fro,
I must have worn a groove in the tarmac. So now I travel on
rails. Tramlined, I cannot even recall the drive over, such is the
journey imprinted on my skeleton through assuetude. Just as I
cannot feel my watch against my wrist, I have no sense of the
road under me, or even the car's carapace around me. There's
a good reason I am not constantly reminded of the feel of a
timepiece against my skin, so that my mind can concentrate
on other things. Like piloting a killing machine on roads where
children can be found crossing.

Fortunately there are none today. For I have failed to
remember that it was school Remembrance Day and that the
infants are disgorged late. Just as I have found in the past that it
was Founders' Day, when the school sunk my schedule with a
half-day holiday and a peeved phone call enjoining me to reclaim
my daughter from their property. You could never trip me up on
the closing times of any shop. But my child's education routine
forever hobbles me. Fortunately I was not the lone dunce on
show, in the corner of a car park, unencumbered by cars.

The other woman and I sidled diffidently around the
expanse of space, yet all the while managing to preserve the
cleft between one another. She, I presume, vacillating over
whether to have her foolishness openly acknowledged, even
by a fellow transgressor; myself, since I was utterly opposed

to interlocution full-stop. But such was the bloated need for absolution, she surreptitiously nipped and tucked the mantled bulge to a distance where megaphones were no longer required and any re-buffing of the buffer zone on my part would have been inordinately rude. The hiatus narrowed to good conscience, she flounced over. Her smile was weaker than the attenuated winter sunshine. The pigmentation was visibly evacuating her visage, decamping her freckles with it. So with her face parrying the forward thrust of the body, I'm charged with opening in order to save her from fainting. 'I wondered why I'd nabbed such a prime parking spot. Never happened before.' And in she launched, the release palpable, the safety catch off, spraying around salvo after salvo.

In the skirmishes we discovered our daughters were not in the same class. Did not indeed know one another or play together in the playground. Did not share a table at lunch. Did not coincide in any after-school activity (the school may have been pushy, but I was pushy-ed out through getting her admitted here in the first place). And no, we weren't church-goers. That should have naturally reinstated the chasm as far as I was concerned, but I could see her sufficiently leavened so as to move to fill the lacuna entirely. Now it was simply a matter as to who was swiftest on the draw. Unfortunately, since my child-addled life had swathed itself in a giant prophylactic against self, the workings of my mind had not been lubricated for some considerable interval. So when I reached into my holster for some personal delivery, I was just mum.

She foisted on me her love of opera. My whole quailing frame evidenced the impulse to fold in on itself like a cuttlefish and service any caged bird of choice. Yet somehow the muscles in my face overrode the critical mass, by expressing mere incomprehension at the ranks of foreign names and serial numbers being spouted. She was perceptive enough to register this and changed tack. Minutely. Informed me about how she'd been hoarding her entire life, in order to splash out on a once-in-a-lifetime pilgrimage to Vienna, 'Opera capital of the world!' Now I merely wanted to kill myself.

She didn't have her slides with her, but she was going to snap my patience anyway. Her transparent neuroses needed no projection. Apparently, every tourist attraction has two Austrian flags above its portal and these correspond to the numbered sites on the conveniently-provided-for-in-every-hotel expedition map. 'They're so well geared up for it over there. Not like here in Britain.' I gargled my accord, or it might have been an intimation of a death rattle, since I hadn't actually ever been to the mainland to accord anything. As she prattled on, I quickly gleaned that the flags had soon taken on greater substance than the architecture itself. Such was the all-consuming campaign to tick them off the guide map. We too have flags over the portals of some of our buildings right here, I reflected. But I would only ever dub them tourist repulsions.

She was not compulsive enough to want to troop every flag though. Freud's house, for one, she expressed fierce disinterest at dropping by. Passive aggressive, I mentally diagnosed. 'It's amazing how the whole city is laid out. The old part, I mean. What they call "The Ring". And so it is. It is! It's just one big circle really, so perfect for getting round and seeing everything. It's as if they designed it with tourists in mind all those years ago.' I could no longer help myself: 'Did you hire bikes?', knowing full well the flounce in flowery dress before me could not mount a cycle, let alone have her thunder thighs power it. 'You know, for a Ring Cycle cycle?'... 'But that was Wagner,' – not too many blowflies on her, obviously – 'and surely he was German not Austrian?' 'Oh you know those Aryans and their love of Anschluss!' 'Oh! I don't know that one...' She deflated on the spot before me, even as I was puffed up now, ready for the coup de grace. But the woman was saved by the bell and a twin pincer movement of child's bear hug around my upper thighs, while being clouted on my posterior with a re-materialised lunchbox. I didn't mean to savage the poor soul. But it did feel good to act like an adult again. Get all such animus out of my system, so that Mother Theresa Omagh local 2379 can attend to the children at home once more.

If it's any solace, I spent the whole afternoon staring out the bay window, neglecting the children (so they weren't to reap the benefit after all) and chastising myself over the whole tawdry episode. I'm not proud of myself, for all the verbal swagger. I don't know where it came from. It's not really like me at all. Or maybe it is. A glimpse of the new, metamorphosised me. The one that will emerge, when I can punch my way out of the chrysalis of child rearing. Shed my prophylactic skein and float off unencumbered into the sun. For that harpy had dared to travel and her a mother too! She'd had a lifetime dream and followed it. But she blew it! Missed the whole bloody point of it all. Aw, who the hell am I to judge whether she realised her vision or not? Me who has yet to travel much beyond the vista outside of these curtains. I did however delete Vienna from my imaginary itinerary. A list without any flags, but a list in the compendium of my mind all the same. To tick off as and when. My globe-hopping trip. New York, New York (Fifth Avenue, Fifth Avenue); The Pyramids and The Holy Land; The Galapagos Islands; The Empty Quarter (ah, indeed how that one does resonate with me right now and would it perforce stay 'empty' if one bought the kids along?)

Yet is the question exclusively one of scale? Since I've put so many of my woman hours in at the goggle box, I've always felt licensed to envision. I've exclusively toured all the holiday programmes. Paid my dues at the natural history slots. Hell, many's the time I've sat on the sofa with a babe latched to my breast, in full synchronicity with some other endangered mammal being projected back at me. As for some of the other primal activities, exquisitely captured by telephoto lens and commentated on with reverent tones by that nice Mr Attenborough, well let's just say you'd require a lot of time lapse photography, followed by a brief reel of slo-mo around this particular habitat I can tell you.

So yes, I avow I already have an intimate familiarity with these places and sights. Would they let me down, as I suspected the empty husk of Vienna's Ring had defrauded her? What if the Great Barrier Reef or the Great Wall of China were, to my mind's eye, not so great after all? But that is preposterous of course. They are great. The greatest manifestations of man or a higher power's achievements. The majestic beauty and inherent sublime order underpinning it all. Therefore any failure of scale to overwhelm must be down to me. The shrinkage of my inner world must not be transposed on to things infinitely beyond my reach. Beyond my apprehension. My conjugation. So am I, after all, unconsciously complicit in my husband's embargo on 'abroad'? Damnation! This bloody woman, too uninformed to visit Freud's house when in the neighbourhood, yet she can hold the mirror up to my face. And she made me waive a whole afternoon's television engagements with house interiors, chat and quiz shows.

XXIX.X.MMI

Actually, I'm fairly well possessed whence my vitriol towards 'Valkyrie Woman' had been summoned. She was the selfsame woman at the check-out some months ago, in front of me at the '10 items or less' aisle (now amended to 'Or fewer', following the complaint by a man, obviously, since one couldn't imagine a campaign for correct grammar being waged by a housewife and mother now could you?) with thirteen – yes I counted them – thirteen items, if you please.

Exactly which part of '10 items or less' was it that you didn't understand, missus? And she proclaims to like and understand the complexities of opera?

Each one of those extra acquisitions was like a tin opener to my canned heart. The arbitrariness of it all. How many times had I attempted to break through the checkpoint with eleven or twelve items in my basket, been rebuffed and forced to turn back each time? That goading awareness of having just one item too many, but hell you're going to go for it anyway, 'cos it's not like you've got a full trolley bursting at the seams. Besides, you owe them for a dashed trolley dash from days back, when you were countered and reproached by patronising staff, primed like Venus fly traps to clamp down hard on any axled shopping aid in the pedestrians only aisle. As they made you pack everything back in the trolley, you were only able to recover a vestige of your dignity by laboriously counting aloud each of the ten items in turn. So much so that it would have been quicker running it through their express till after all. A supermarket Mexican standoff. The customer is always righteous.

Actually, weighing it up a bit, I'm not at all sure it was her. But the point, or the grievance anyway, remains. Madame Butterfly's original sin of XIII did not prick me enough to merit an entry in my journal at the time. Neither did my original run-in with the till monkeys, although that may have predated my little tan book. Yet the twin grievances festered until their vectors bisected. At the very moment, when I was standing in that deserted car park, expressing some impulse to action for whatever unrelated, extraneous third motive. S-triangulated.

The blunt instrument of sharp words. That's what you're supposedly meant for, my calfskin punchbag. To cauterise and drain off my ire. Leave me in peak shape to deal with the children. Stop me throwing in the towel along with the kitchen sink. Help me to keep my kid gloves on. To open up a second front away from home. But always you swing back on your pivot and cuff me straight between the eyes, with an aggregation of aggrieved slights I can never disembogue.

$$O\!\!+\quad\quad\raisebox{0.5em}{$\female$}\quad\quad+\!\!O$$

Just come from a group session. The radical firebrands were holding forth on the floor again. To the exclusion of everyone else. I felt compelled to break my neutrality and rescue the situation. I knew from their diehard commitment and personal loyalty to me that they weren't after staging a coup. But their incendiary fission threatened a meltdown all the same. I essayed that they were conflating reparations with reprisals. That our breeding out programme was reparation enough. Would not its success forever disarm menkind from the wherewithal to harm us again? But if I'd even thought about it for one second, no genetic fabianism was ever going to sate the bloodlust careering in the air tonight.

Hurriedly I changed tack and drew on the same arguments I employ against our external foes. We were not a cult. We did not have followers. (A high risk strategy, this: if it attenuated my authority in their eyes, it might dismantle their personal allegiance and then we'd all be dead in the water.) I for one, certainly did not want people to go abroad in my name. (Now, in like flint and soften the stomach to receive the rapier.) Besides, there are no such things as fanatics even in real cults. Those hard of mind and empty of heart, who will genuinely, willingly end their lives for a cause, are few and far between. Forensics show us repeatedly that all mass cult 'suicides' are shot in the back, or the rear of the head, as well as often having the insurance overkill of poison in their blood. Jonestown across the water was a typical example of this. I'm telling you ladies, even the executioners don't do it out of faith or belief in the end. Only steely resolution. They've abdicated their own individual thought processes. All they have remaining is a votary's adherence to the leader. They enact *his* orders, as the only residual verification of their crumbling faith. Would you top yourself if I ordained it?... I expected nothing less. (Are Americans familiar with this idiomatic usage of the word 'top'?)

Suicide is still a struggle, no matter how much you prepare and acclimatise yourself for it – cult member or just survivor of an abusive relationship. I mean, we all still made it here, didn't we? Fought chipped tooth and wrenched nail against extermination. Christ, even Jesus on the Cross crossed over, when he more than anyone should have known. Okay, technically I know he wasn't a suicide, that his fate was determined for him by Pop. Didn't he read the Bible (before the revision in his name)? Pater had pulled the same stunt with Abraham, but got cold feet at the last minute. Ignorance is a form of suicide. Much more pernicious too. Jesus, ya shoulda read your own previews... Then see if the meek would still inherit anything.

Go pick the bones out of that lot, ladies! A subtle and not so subtle insinuation of your lack of both bottle and smarts. I don't expect we'll be having any more trouble from them awhile. Besides, I'll make a point of sleeping with each of them, as a reaffirmation of my affection and esteem... the only slight quandary being which one to select first without the other's flaring nose being put out of joint. Of course the pragmatist in me would just make it a threesome, but I have to be wary of any fervour being reinforced by affections between the two of them. This is just the sort of snafu my two political, so-called moderators should be resolving for the community. But if you want a job done properly...

Here they come now, my beloved, trusty cadres. No doubt coming to pledge their gratitude for my deft application of emollient on rash and scaly hides. Sweet, sweet Megan Hertz and dear old Volte Face, aka Glangela. Oh don't get me wrong, I will succour them with every last breath in my abdomen. Just don't ask me to respect them, that's all. They're so damn grateful that I selected them, for delegating the upholding of our community's values. Can't they see that I did this precisely because I knew that it was beyond them? Tie them up in knots, to leave a nice vacuum in the middle where everyone could just project whatever they wanted. Some overseeing Goddess and mistress, or personal spirit guide. Or, perhaps just a liberated space to move around in, untrammelled by coercion. Either way it all boils down to the hoary old free will or determinism dichotomy. I just didn't intend the task to devour them that's all.

Poor old Megan. Michael Jackson's her role model, and I don't mean by his singing career. More the way he reinvents his actual corporeal image. She has a bit of a parent thing going on. Doesn't want to resemble them in any way, so she's superficially altering the configuration brought about by her genes. Megan really goes skin deep. Trouble is, from the little colourations of her language, compared with that in the letters from home which I intercept, I think she's adopted. Ho hum. Might explain why she's so angry to have been brought into this life in the first place. Though, fair play to her, she's never allowed her marasmus to reduce her to a full-on, method-acting, true-to-death zombie who could audition for one of Wacko's videos. She contents herself with lobbying local abortion clinics. Not because she's against the right to choose – Christ she wouldn't be in here with all the other oil-seed-rape castaways if she did. Besides, she votes Democrat anyway. No, quite the converse, she's ploughing a lone furrow down there. Trying to gain access to obsecrate with the aborted foetuses, as to what a lucky break they caught, in escaping the miserable destiny that life has plucked for her. If ever there's any sabotage of our IVF cultures, I'll know it's an inside job.

And dear old Volte Face. Another one with a parent issue, but then again which of us haven't? Her father Nathan died on Labo(u)r day. Not that it came to her as a shock or anything. On the contrary, she indirectly precipitated it. There he was, celebrating the news of his daughter's birth down the local bar, when he drops dead of a peanut allergy he never even knew he had. Actually, way I read it, don't think it was peanuts what did for him. More like the contaminating urine of seventeen different men, since the slobs never wash their cock-cradling digits after the urinals, but go straight back to the peanut bowl unlucky dip. Or should that be drip? The tombola of contagion. Quick on the prize draw, revolve the chamber and let loose a deadly round. They literally pissed all over poor old Nat. And his wife, Glangela's mother, too. Since she was post-Nathanly depressed, suddenly all alone with a little baby to bring up. So she threw in her hand and folded, leaving little old Volte Face an orphan. And, on account of all this happening during the peanut-brained, peanut farmer Jimmy Carter's Presidency, voting Democrat has never been an option for her. See, it's so straightforward this causation thing. Moreover, I have my political balance right where I want it. Annulling one another. Do Megan and Volte sleep with one another? The thought is too tawdry to contemplate.

VI.III.MM

The daily grind of the weekly shopping. Or the weekly grind of the daily shopping. Or perhaps the daily grind of the weakly shopping. But you get the general drift. Pushing Amy along in her buggy. Unfortunately not the grand prix rally special I had for Suzanne, with its beautiful pneumatic purchase and light, responsive suspension, which cushioned and cradled her tiny frame against the impact of each pavement plunge. A streamlined chassis that allowed me to hurtle frictionless back to the car as soon as the rain came down. Suzanne safely encompassed in its plastic bubble (for, light as it was to push, I could not simultaneously wield an umbrella). We'll pass over the rain's redoubled frenzied assault on her exposed form, as I struggled to transfer her from the fettered prison of her bubble buggy into the shackles of a car seat. That, I feel, is down to the physical laws of stationary objects, rather than lay the blame at the wheel of my beautiful perambulator.

No, lamentably not that same buggy, for one cracked and sunken paving stone too far and her tubing was buckled irreparably. The rubber tyre no longer palpated the asphalt, but hung uselessly twisted in the air, compulsively dabbing and twitching before a non-existent reflex gavel. I knew it was fatal, but I demanded a second confirmatory opinion. So I took it to a toy shop(!), the only place that offered the requisite buggy repair service. They sat me down and told me in hushed tones that she had dislocated and wrenched her foreleg and had to be put down for good. We gave the old girl a fitting send off, buried her with full campaign honours. Attached the unused (in two and a half years) sun parasol to her and slipped her beneath the meniscus of the wheely bin, so that the dustmen wouldn't realise she was in there until they had slid her beneath the waves of pared matter. We could but fantasise that her metal would temporarily arrest the grinding mechanism of the cart's crusher. A pertinent temporary hush, that marked her repose in the way that she had lived her service. But the beast's mighty jaws seemed untroubled by the task, licking its chops with a loud pneumatic sough, as it let out its brakes to saunter on down the road.

Amy's buggy. Not exactly Suzanne's mark II, let alone mach 2 like they have now. Scaled down dune buggies or quad bikes, that's what current pushchair craft resemble. Flaming great pavement tanks, with baby bull bars to move pedestrians out the way. These buggies don't get repaired in toy shops. It's blessed garages for them! Have you not noticed, now the armoured personnel carriers have vacated our roads, we've moved to fill the gash with giant people carriers and land cruisers of our own? Either we cannot psychologically bear to be without this bellicose asseveration of our security, or we just need larger cars with hulking great boots to fit these new super buggies in even when they're folded up! No, this family refuses to fall in with that particularly pernicious line of fashion, thank you very much.

We knew we weren't going to have any more children. The calculation was therefore to get the cheapest, most basic pushchair there was. It may have been primitive, but had four wheels, collapsible metal tubing and some fabric to gather up Amy's frame. All for twenty-five pounds. Of course, Suzanne's rain bubble didn't fit, so that was another tenner. Still, for a finite two years of pavement pounding, it seemed enough of the real deal. Only, four wheels compared with eight on Suzanne's proved to be a false economy of scale. Since they were also fixed, they rotated but did not turn. To execute a change of direction, I had to drag-lift the whole fuselage and reappoint it to the required bearing. The bloody thing had the turning circle of a dreadnought. The sturdy metal tubing had no give in it whatsoever, so that other than for the restraint of the stubby plastic straps (whose locking mechanism always demanded an offering up of nail and skin before it's scything thumbscrew), Amy's small core would have been shucked from the buggy at the first sagging flagstone. As it was, on landing at the behest of her harness, she had to unsettle herself for the nightmarish persecutions of cardboard corner claws and tin-rimmed talons of the shopping in the net behind her back. For, as substantial as it felt, the seat twill was mysteriously fistulous.

I know for a fact that this bastard buggy would have chewed up the teeth of the dustcart and spat them out as shrapnel.

Another design triumph spawned by this cross-breeding of Harland & Wolff with Mothercare was the permanent blindspot at ground level, either side of the two front wheels. We'll scoot on hurriedly past (or through) the pavement doggydo as a constant source of aggravation and alight on the propensity for contretemps, whether bagatelle or catastrophic. Today's had been catastrophic, in a slow-puncture sort of way. Of course, since Vulcan himself had annealed the rubber coatings of the buggy's wheels, they could never actually sustain a puncture, slow or otherwise. I'm talking about a figurative deflation. For, ahead of us, an old man was dragging his wheely shopping basket behind him. Now we each sported blind sides. I attempted to slow our progress, but we were in danger of being swallowed up by the throng of Saturday shoppers from behind. The push-me, pull-you dynamic was calling for a quick step and we were paired irresistibly together. I tried to slipstream him. Not in the sense of a sucking air turbulence, for he was shuffling along like a slowworm, while there was nothing remotely aerodynamic about my fortified piece of mobile scaffolding. Rather, I sought to match every sway and roll of his dumb charge, as it mooched along the buffeting paving. But finessed responses were beyond the parameters of my beast and my forearms soon wearied of trundling curvet for the heavily laden buggy. Dancing round handbag rather than ambage was more my style. I brought the buggy to land on all four of its wheels again and plumped for a plumb line. All our fortunes were now in Fate's hands and we didn't have to wait long.

A chariot race in the circus minimus of the High Street and our wheels lock together. His neck slowly turtles round conveying a stooped head from the nuzzle of his chest. The only motion not proceeding in stages is the glower brandished by the creases of his aged face. I had violently disrupted his creaking progress. I kept my expression neutral, awaiting the cranking of his ill-lubricated facial musculature, until his lower lip finally dropped like the safety curtain at a theatre. He projected yellow teeth at me as if wheeled out on rollers. His eyes admonished me even as his brow knitted together in complete incomprehension, as he tried to fathom. Then he looked down at Amy, beaming up at him from her low vantage point. How dare you impute that it's her fault old man! Before I can drape myself in front of her bound form, I trace a flicker of memory snail across his countenance and see he is thrown. His carriage heaves, his challenge now prostrate. The wheels of his upturned shopping basket have stopped spinning. I feel sorry for him, as he yanks his felled mount and totters off. Dragging it along the fabric rather than the axles, such is his hurry to reel away from whatever has crushed him. In that one passing moment, I saw in him what I have come to appreciate. That the seeds of being that lay within my life-giving egg were also to signal my own dissolution. Decidedly deciduous, some are merely further advanced towards evanescence than others. Soon to be harvested as chaff. The old man hated Amy for her box seat dependence on me. But he loathed her more for daring to be at the start of her life. He would sire no more children.

Nor would he have the elastic powers of growth, regeneration and recovery, with which Amy was unconsciously mocking him through her innocent smile.

⚥

I suppose I've been peddling a conceit of sorts. I have in my time been associated with sects. Of a kind. That one known as the family (small 'f'). The one we all seem to participate in of our own received volition. A doomsday cult if ever something merited the term. We'll temporarily pass over the spouse louse, since I'm talking about that smear of me, somewhere out in the world. A real mothersucker of a son. And no, if you look on your files, I don't have a lisp. Not that he's a bad boy, but a mothersucker all the same. They all are. Just by being boys. That alien being amid your innards. Not like having a little girl. Already sucking on his thumb in greedy anticipation of his first and most formative treat in the world. It's a fine line between rapacious and demure. An umbilical line. And he's eating you up from within. Siphoning all your essences for joyriding fuel. All your physical discomforts are down to his greed. Your hair falling out and hives springing from his insatiable hunger. From his not knowing when to stop.

Wanting more, always more. Plundering you. Because, innately, he knows he only gets one crack at the whole damn womb thing. From inside. Belly cosy. Your daughter, she knows she gets to have the kindling passed to her. That she can ignite her own Olympian sized torch for a lifetime of carrying. But the boy gets just one shot at this wonder bliss, my blunderbuss, so he's gonna throw his whole armoury at it. Besiege me. Rifle my personal affects. Disassemble the smooth bore muzzle, lock, stock, and barrel. Spin my chamber; scrape out the grooves; grease the firing mechanism; finger the trigger; and breach my labouring defences. What power. What a kick! What recoil! What shrapnel wounds. You can still see my scar.

Despite the fact that I run a breeding colony, any of the biological or physiological prompts still induces a shudder down my dura mater. Yanks me right back to that time. When my body and emotions were commandeered to some imaginary war effort. When I'd already surrendered myself. The trick is to fight back. Resist. Fifth column behind enemy lines. To regain suzerainty over your own colonised self.

Now I can't claim to have worked all this out in advance. It was complete serendipity, albeit heavily laced with genetic fate. My son, that little piece of me now at large. Yet he never felt all of a piece. Caught somewhere in transit between his American father and English rose mother. Snagged on the briars of a poor quality graft. The scion didn't issue a whole new genus. Just more of the same, inheriting the worst traits from both his parents. Poor sap. Never felt properly at home, didn't take to it. Felt uprooted. He was familiar with his immediate environment, but did not recognise it as his own. Incised from the same contiguous material as that of the local stone-cutters, yet he found their guild too narrow to enter. Just like his dear old Ma, intaglioed in the grain of the place in which he grew up, but an impression from which he sought relief. To escape from himself. Thus was his fate determined for him, impelling him to rove and eschew such a destiny. Yet that eschewing too, was fate. As hard and fast and unyielding, as anything ingrained by his genes.

But it was not to be a random trek. For the icy warmth

of my undercarriage had germinated the seed. He had a lead. A need to discover from whence he truly hailed. His mother-land. A child cut off from one half of himself. My own flesh and blood, who had felt adopted by his homeland. His recurring dreams unfamiliarly landscaped. Metropolises with the seeming solidity of a film set, populated by shadowy figures. These were not sinister lurkers, pressing themselves out of the penumbra of light, but rather, indistinct, imponderous beings lolling about in the foreground. They do not trail him into a persecutory light of day, rather, solemnly observe their stand-offishness. Their indifference pricked at him like a sore. And thus is he hag-ridden, barebacked. Each dawn, under starter's orders, he is left in the stalls. Spirit drained, tapped by these anonymously intimate strangers. Tugging at the frayed thread of his identity, the day spent unravelling. Unbeknown to him, his circadian rhythms set to GMT. Lordy, I really landed him in it.

And amongst the visual melange, a verbal cue. The word 'Greenland' bobbing repeatedly across his dream consciousness. How do I know this? Why, I'm his mother of course. Every night of his life, I'd hitched up the corner of canvas and ushered him into his Carney dreamscape with a kiss on his crown. And besides, I seized the opportunity to read his diary each time I cleaned up his room. Oh don't come all the disapproving, wagging finger brigade with me. What are you snoops doing if not reading my journal? That's why I put it online for you. So you don't have to strain too hard in your purblind prying. So you don't have to beat yourselves up about the morality of it (not that those in your weighty profession, would ever raise a hand to such a scruple). And, in addition, so I can indulge in a spot of misdirection. Blow a bit of smoke on you honey-bees, out there after some grand larceny nectar. Besides, if he'd tidied his room as I repeatedly requested, well, I wouldn't have ever had any purpose in entering, would I?

So, after that unscheduled stopover to refuel my vitriol, time to get us all back on course for Greenland. Not any 'Green and pleasant land' I ever imbued him with at my knee. For I only ever reminisced its grey and oxidised red. The mills still dark, but dilapidated rather than Satanic. No, I demur; their half-baked conversion into facsimiles of theme-parks or other pleasure palaces is, to the original American Dream specification, as Mammon's gaudy architecture of Hell is to that of Heaven. It's enough to give anyone nightmares.

'Greenland', both extra-mundanely and in fact, is that land mass, the largest island in the world, which lies between America and Britain. You pass over it on many transatlantic air flights. I'm on top of the world, Ma! For no manchild is an island. The dear little boy didn't want to have to choose between either parental anitpode UK/USA and so plumps for somewhere in the middle. And thus he drowns. Unable to maintain a foothold on the sheer ice face of frigid sentiment. Ten years of therapy hasn't remitted him that. As for me, I wouldn't have charged him half as much.

The conclusion he came to, aided only by the taciturn conspiracy of both mother and therapist, was to retrace my steps. Track back the evacuation of vitality. Root out the source of vacated meaning. Bidding goodbye to his future, as I had left in order to say goodbye to mine. Only in reverse.

A Saver Class ticket to Heathrow. Of course it cost him the same as a return, but I suppose it seemed symbollically important to hold out and not get dissuaded before he'd even set off. Bet it didn't stop him getting drunk on the flight over though, seeing as he doesn't know what he's flying into. A cuckoo searching for a nest. See, always colonising. Appropriating the present I might have had, but never did.

122

Conducting an archeological dig on my past, in order to divulge the gaps in his contemporaneity. Searching for a lost world, some mythical Atlantis swallowed deep beneath my mid-atlantic drawl. He asked me, when we took leave of his father, why I didn't return back to England (whether moved by genuine empathy, or his own craving for apprehending his dreams, I cannot settle). Well now he'll realise. For he will look round as a tourist might. He is not the proud possessor of two demesnes, two passport identities and two countries. Like his parents, each were asunder and irreconcilable. There is to be no homecoming for him, whether he holds fast, or returns to the fold here. He will remain alone with his isolation. Merely in different surroundings, that's all. Like I said, he's not a bad lad really. Just a bit confused. Like everybody else. So he should blend in nicely. And my work there is finished. My generational labour complete. I have replicated the action of recessive genes. Outside of a laboratory.

Skipping a generation, his own heirs will inevitably look back west and demand to know why he ceded the fecundity of America for their own dreary birthplace. How they in turn will hop on a plane and tilt at the land of opportunity in search of their true caste self, attaining after someone they could not possibly be. And so it goes on. Caroming from one base line double fault to the other. Like some great transatlantic tennis match. You get a crick in your neck and feel as though your spine can no longer support the weight of your head. Deuced.

If the besiegers were somehow able to track him down and bring him in to winkle me out, I'm sure he'd merely scream down the wires, 'Kill the Bitch!'

VII.III.MCMXCIX

I'm laying out the washing to dry on the line. A rare sunny day this portentous spring (they were opening the doors of Stormont once again, this time for an all party parliament). I'm angling for the air to expel the caustic smell of laundry detergent. To leach the bleach. Infuse the synthetic fabrics with a more natural aroma. Now, two hands engaged in pinning a chemise, with midriff swaying kyphotically so as to avoid the rivulets of water beating down the dress's straight course, necessarily meant that my mouth served as a receptacle for the pegs. Wood stained dark by years of clammy contact with damp raiment, yet my tastebuds were assailed only by additive chemical pungency. From a time before I heeded the television adverts for a 'softer, safer' wash. From a time before I had to. For the sake of my daughter. Or her skin anyway. Standing as a preventative bulwark against allergies of course. In a world suddenly awash with hyper-sensitivities, that never seemed to be a problem in my childhood. We're breeding poorer specimens. Or perhaps our environment is what is labefying their immune systems. Either way, it's yet another involuntary parental legacy for their offspring.

Tantamount to blackmail, if you pause to think about it even for a second. Stood there like an idiot, with wooden sabre tooth dentures jutting out. That's what the advertisers are playing on I suppose. A mother consumer's love of her child. Do these detergents actually offer any greater protection? Who can tell? Maybe the pegs are chemically redolent as much from these pro-children tablets, as the previous ones

I was prepared to scourge my own spinster skin with. But you can't chance the risk can you? So every wash day, my palate will continue to offer up evidence of a new accretion to the four categories of sapidity. In addition to sweet, sour, salty and bitter (elegantly, though not deliciously, unified in any dish down at our local Chinese takeaway), we now have industrial-chemical. Of course, anyone who has also sampled the bleached wares of our traditional chippie next to the Chinese will be able to empirically back me up on my discovery. Wash day Thursdays, fish and chips Fridays. Chronic chemically catalysed days.

(Of course, all housewife-mothers know this last statement to be partly false, since wash day cannot be restricted to a unique day of the week. And am I the only one too weary of an evening, to turn my hand from tinned spaghetti hoops and amorphous nuggets and set my face towards grown-up cooking, so as to leech the Friday fish supper on to other days of the week?)

Buying new wooden pegs is the answer, of course. Run a controlled test. Observe if the new ones also sweat chemically, after exclusive exposure to 'non-biological' cleaning products. Then we'll see. Then I'll set it straight with you buggers out there in the outside world. Reel you in–.

Shit is she co-choking? What's she found to put in her ruddy maw now? I spat out the pegs and dropped a pair of sweat pants towards the ground, even as I impelled them further down underfoot, so swift was my pivot. In the span of the six paces or so of our patio, her whole brief little life passed before my scanning eyes, as I speed-searched for similitude (with just a beat for my wry subconscious to interpose that an equivalent span of mine would only cover traversing two patio paving stones). Yes, she had recently learned to feign coughing, but the mockery was usually easy to pierce.

However, that was a mutually preserved collusion, habitually face to face, never when she was alone. And the distorting effect of the plate glass meant I couldn't tell whether this was authentic or not. Contrary to that, I never, never leave her alone when she's jousting with food. For no matter how often I implored her to take small bites, she still inundated her tiny orifice with too much to cope with. If she was in the mood to accede to my pleas, then it was without pausing to chew and swallow each small morsel in turn. Such recurring trajectories were nothing to do with the throat, as the food never reached that far. It was all to do with the mouth. Was it symptomatic of some unquenchable hunger she felt? Did she feel perpetually malnourished? None of the books will admit to this possibility. Too close to mad, bad Uncle Sigmund's notions. For we live in a less judgemental world now. Or so we like to gauge it. Yet what could be more basic than learning to eat properly? Eating without expiring from the very act of eating?

I reached her convulsing body, no bluff this, and smacked her in the small of the back without prior processing of any visual evidence before me. This was pure reflex. Kiddy Heimlich manoeuvre. Without the manoeuvring, or Dr Heimlich. Her eyes registered the shock of punishment and imprecation, even as the raisin flew out of her mouth and plopped on to the rug in front of her, neatly interjecting a blended black blob to the cod Middle Eastern design. We both instinctively stared down at the rug, before I regained my senses and scooped her entire frame up into my arms as the first tears caressed the corners of her eyes. My cooing eructations were driven by the tempo of an adrenaline-fuelled heart, while my mind crashed its gears in digesting the played-out drama. The last time I gave her raisins was this morning... Apart from it having been on the floor and therefore descending into the rank of 'dirty', she didn't actually do anything wrong in putting it in her mouth… A raisin dropped from this morning, it's potentially always on the cards. Unpreventable, I would say. Focus on the choking side of things… Probably wasn't concentrating on chewing, her attention sparked off on something else, part of this whole eating as an automatic process, she just hasn't nailed yet… Sure, sure, Freud said they go through a stage when everything goes into their mouths, but how prodded by appetite can she be? If you'd sat there, watching her consume a small packet of raisins ('child-sized', another invocation of the advertising and transacting classes), floundering fingers tippling more on to the carpet than she manages to ingest, you'd realise there was nothing 'devouring' about it. Apart from the sheer painful glacial slowness of it all, eroding your own will to live. Oral gratification more than likely came from placing in the far corners of the mouth, not the solitary raisin itself, but the fingers callipering it. (Precursory laying down perfected mechanics for any future bulimic techniques of self-induced vomiting.) Plus the thrill of total ownership of that dainty little red packet. Spilling its contents to be woven underfoot into the rug pattern. That's why they've been desiccated, otherwise we'd have wine brewing on the carpet. Next to the live yoghurt fermenting from myriad vomitations of formula milk.

So, she's not starved, she's just self-possessed. Put that in your pipe and smoke it Siggy.

And where was the troubles with all this commotion? Doesn't he know what a child choking to death sounds like? An infant's death rattle? Probably construed it to be some sort of babbling toy. He's always a fine one for laying down the great sacrifice. The grand gesture for the Grand Lodge. The hecatomb for the Loyal. But what of the everyday puny sacrifices of domestic life? They don't even merit the designation 'sacrifice' for God's sakes! Mere tiny inconveniences that dictated not shedding a single drop of blood, but plenty of body to body contact. He doesn't want to know then. Yet this is his only true blue consanguinity. The only one provable to be irrevocably his, to his very marrow, by a DNA test. Would he think to smack her across the back? Of course bloody-not. And it's left to me to be the ministering angel time and time again.

His abrogation of any such flesh and blood involvement entails that his whole being is necessarily seared with investment in the external world. It also entails that my whole being is unalloyed inconvenience, since no one will split the taskload. And when your body is the incarnate convenience of some other being, then it is in no part your own any longer. So one does sacrifice oneself after all. Unnecessarily and in vain. Right Suzanne, same time tomorrow for the old choke routine?

Bloody joke's on him though, relying totally on affirmation from outside, during these troubled times. Whistling into the winds of change. Me, I seek no affirmation for I have no hook of ego to hang it on. Yet daily I am presented with it from my child, who spasmodically emerges from her utter self-engrossment to recognise my dimension and lend me weight. Embedded in my arms, Suzanne smiles at me. I decant it under the guise of wiping away her slobber, pocketing it for later waxing of my compassion. And so the symbiotic cycle spins on.

C) Consider the seminal building block, that of cell division and replication of my code. The substructure of your daily life. Yet how prodigiously can this self-same mechanism get out of hand and strike at your very foundations. Benign or malign? That old Manichean duality. Your vocabulary is endemic with moral judgement. Bless you. Tissue has no such scruple. Tissue just functions. Not as some imperative, nor even through instinct, but because it can. It is the fibre optic cabling delivering you, in order to render me the due protocol under seal. Neither shoot nor ennoble the messengers, for they are just purling consignees indifferent to all of our throughput.

Microscopic scale insurgency.
Strife at the level of chemical
subsere. A bitter dispute to the
bitter end. For just as you are
reticent to die, to shuffle off this
mortal coil, then so is your pro-life
-rating mutinous cell. Only it holds
the high ground, being closer to
the corpuscular field of operations.
Deep tissue cover, at the blunt end,
well away from the locus of pain.
Whereas you, the host, a field-
marshall, with field-glasses hopelessly
out of focus, languish behind the lines.
A sliding scale of operations. A vernier
theatre of war. Combat on his terrain,
him being more chemically aware
and savvy than you. He rebuffs your
suicide bombers, turns them to his
cause. And what do you hurl against
him? All you have in your quiver,
are spiked metaphors of warfare.

```
M
a
g       C
i       h       T
c       e       u
      m R       m
    L o a       o
B a     d       u
u s T i         r
l e h o
l r e a         B
e r c u
t G a t         s
s u p i         t
  i y v         e
  d e           r
  e P           s
  d a
        y
         l
        o
        a
        d
```

It's not a metaphor you over-
sophisticated ape!

It's organic chemistry.
The little local struggle to engage me.
A battle for command and control.

GG) Or take another elementary shortcoming. Mitochondria.
The body's power plants. Running on a fuel of oxygen. However,
oxygen is toxic. Rusting you from the inside. Oxides corroding
the arterial plumbing, the very lifeblood of your infrastructure.
But here's the ingenious twist, the tweak of sublimity. They also
unleash what you term free radicals, a term I heartily approve
of, with all its connotations of uprising and tumult. And it is
these free radicals which attack me, the genomic DNA. Oh
delicious iro– no, we've already sabre rattled off that one. Agent
provocateurs, sappers, fifth columnists, double agents. But theirs
is a long term strategy of subversion. The power plants seize up
slowly. The pipelines silt up over time. This assault on your cells
kicks in only after parturition and you passing on the baton,
once I have emptied you like a husk. Where I have conducted
you beyond the threshold of value to me. The honeymoon's
over. I've no further use for your pre-fab, as I go in search of
my next commission. While I'm off quoting for my next labour,
your edifice is condemned. A real cowboy builder. Yeah, right.
Slapdash, that's me alright. Everything just left to chance.

A) So, you conceive that you're
going to depreciate with age
That your cells just can't cut it
properly any more. Maybe they
divide haphazardly or not at all,
but sure as eggs is eggs, they
take longer to achieve what
used to be a matter of course.

G) Love as a bulwark against loneliness. Hope you'll grow old together. But mortality winnows at
different rates. Both locked into
the private failings of the body.
One always abandons the other.
Taking their leave towards death

130

They're not conversing with their neighbours like they used to. Community spirit is dying. They seem to have lost their will and purpose. They're not keeping their domiciles in order and the local environment's beginning to look run down too.

C) Given the inevitability of such a fate, this de-generation, you make damn certain to pass on your genes to future generations. 'Love' helps you further this quest. Secures for you a mate. Someone who feels same as you. Anxious. Insecure. But at least now you know that there might be someone, somewhere in the future, burning a tiny candle for you inside them.

or decrepitude. One mate touchingly tends its crumbling partner, a most admirable trait in your species. Easing their physical discomfiture, or confronting one's own, who can say? But still they're not together. Both regressed to the Mother-Child polarity, only neither will be re-released into the flow of maturity and life. Just over-ripeness and death. This is the corruption and despair of love. You go out on a limb to expose your emotions and share them with somebody. Cozening isolation, but only duping yourself from the inevitability that, at some point, you will have to amputate and your emotions will not cicatrise. For by that time, you are beyond procreation and therefore I have left the shell of the building. For all your social and familial structures, you can't take it with you. Not when I've already extracted it from you.

T) And my deepest sympathies. For, let's face it, there is no everlasting light of you. What benefit do you reap, through descendants tending your humus beneath the grave slab? Serving up some more DNA in the form of cut flowers. To deuce you with your lifelessness, though of course this act hastens the flowers into sharing their dissipation with you, even as their pollen mockingly disperses on the cemetery wind. How many succeeding generations will continue to remember you, to acknowledge your seed within? How long before any and each of them fail to change the withered blooms at your headstone? For the chiselled letters of your title to be swallowed up by umbrageous lichen? As the light goes down on your name, what advantage accrues to you that it is borne by others insouciantly independent of you? The gleam in their eyes cannot rekindle you. Yet all the while they are preserving me contentedly across time. Game, set and match. I cede you life, so you can seed it back to me. And now you would secede?

T) And let you eat cake! Armed with what moorings do you cling to, for dear, sweet life? What anchors can still your consternation in a Cape of Pisspoor Hope? Forget love and all those other buoyant bedeckings that I have holed. Mere linguistic tropes, metaphysical postulates, conjectural spacers. For there is only Sex and Death. Passing on and passing over and vice versa. How your trepidation over mortality feeds into your procreative drive. The pair intertwined round one another like poison ivy. And, amidst this foliage clotting the brain, I am passed on even as you brood about your own extinction. Since I am forever playing the long game, mate. Multi-dimensional chess, where you forlornly confront a flush plane divided up into black and white squares. I deal in the architecture of potentia, where you are grounded in the material shoring of tenure. See, the key difference between you and I is that life and time stretch everlasting into the future, for me as DNA and you as my prized host bloodstock. But not for you as individuals. You will always be compromised by the temporal and its ravages upon your organism.

T) For two, this is the prerogative I have over you. You say ontogeny and I say phylogeny: onto/phylo/onto/phylo; let's call the whole thing off? You are pickled and soused by your obsession with personal mortality, diagnosis and sex. These may or may not be valid questions, but your solitary lines of inquiry are awry. Your egotistical investigation goads you ceaselessly forward, as you, too, mimic my system and bring the maximum experimentation to the table. Yet equally your selfish, narrow scrutinising presses

132

your pet theories and petty jealousies to bridle these very forays. After sexual emancipation, environmental control and medical intervention, still you feel it necessary to assemble a scaffold to interrogate me. Since you know you stem from me, therefore you cannot be fully autonomous. Rest assured, this self-same heterogeneity I sanctioned in order for you to free yourselves will now bring your scaffolding crashing down around your ears. For you have infinitely distanced yourselves from my humble beginnings. There is nothing useful I can recount you.

I.I.MMI
Standing in the half-carpeted lumber-room. Going spare. I've an urgent hankering to parley with my journal, but Suzanne was watching television in the lounge and He was in the bedroom, hunkered over the computer as he fervently burns up the global highways and byways of anti-Catholicism. Virtual reality it may be, but it patently exists in the minds of others too. Even if, globally, they're unfamiliar with the parochial road sign 'Danger: Fenians'.

Virtual reality might also aptly describe this room. I should be in my bedroom, snuggled up in the bed with my journal nestling in the nooks of the sheets. He should be cached in here, at a desk, finger tapping the reservoirs of hate, indexing his own catalogue of bigotry at the keyboard. For we discovered wood in this room. Parquet flooring, to be precise, and it was going to enrich our lives. No more would the lounge simulate an outsized toybox, but we could shoo all the escapees from Noah's ark, both corporeal and inanimate, into this extrinsic world beyond the plasmatic flood.

You might think wood unforgiving and child-inimical, but believe me it isn't, no way. And, most importantly, it's low-maintenance. Spills present little problem – just wipe it with a dry cloth. No weft to be concerned about. No aged bilious waft to disconcert either. Of course, we would have to wait for Amy to get a tad older. Also petition God to permit Suzanne to evince a wee bit more independence, so as to be able to go off and play somewhere beyond the range of a hasty retreat to my leggings. But the upshot was we adults would reclaim the living room for a dedicated space of our own.

Only, the useless good-for-nothing (waste of space?) has indeed done nothing, with us still stranded on the Mount Ararat of our laughably designated living room. Actually, it's not quite nothing at all. He had, at the moment we struck wood gold, or very grimy paydirt at least, in one vast Tsunamic shudder, ripped the concealing mantle of the carpet up from its enfeebled tacked recumbency. To bare: an underlay.

XVII.VII.MM

...However, the burnished underlay would not yield its cortical clinch with the wood beneath. It stuck fast, the adhesive evidently not having succumbed to the corrosion of time as had the metal pins. Unflustered, he went down on one knee as if entreating a suit. Or being inducted into knighthood. Head bowed, he was stiff backed and straight-armed, refusing to endow the foe with any puissance that might sire an involuntary rectification of his own bearing. They were frozen in mortal combat, rigor mortis having set in before expiry. I wasn't certain if I could see the tension rippling through Sir Prancelot's sinew, but the subcarpet certainly wasn't giving an inch. Changing chivalrous codes, now he more approximated a Sumo wrestler, whose outsized jockstrap had disappeared into his voluminous arse crack.

134

St George could not slay this dragon and I sensed it was his own nose that was aflame, as the oxygen started to run thin. A bead of sweat had formed on his brow, popping out for a look at the commotion. Craning its meniscus about to give itself to the fray, but areobically squeezed, and realising the gravity of the set-to, slinking back inside its pore, closing the blackhead hatch after it. Finally, one right-angled corner of material came away in his hand, as he ricocheted backwards towards my obliging damsel arms (alright, they were slung up instinctively to parry, more plaintiff than plaintive and, I guess, I'm no damsel any more). But spring-loaded with elation, evading my clutches, he resiled back to huddle over the scarified fabric. 'Yup, definitely take weight that wood/would(?),' he pronounced, before giving it a rap with his knuckles as if to underline and overscore the fact. Pirouetting away from the gash of exposed parquet, he professed himself prospecting the optimal place to put a desk with his computer on. Oh goody, I thought to myself, all three of the kiddies can play in here. I crossed my uselessly outstretched arms.

Having finally located his chosen site, he wheeled round to me even as he was on his way out of the room to advise that he would have to invest in 'some proper kit to do the job.' A stripper, a sander and some varnish were summarily enunciated to the cadences of each stair he strode upon. 'Whatever it takes,' I telepathically lobbed after his fleeing form.

I.I.MMI

So, I'm stood here now, my prison journal the sole thing clasped to my matronly as against maidenly breast, surveying all before me. There didn't seem to be a space for me to perch, nor a flush surface for my journal to offer up its prone anatomy for inscription. For the carpet was still cast aside and since there was nothing any longer to pin it taut, it had been able to return to its warehoused wombed enfurlment. It was positively tidal beneath my feet, as each of my steps tugged it into full shifting and rolling undertow. This was the only surfing that was taking place in here.

The underlay no longer shone beneath the scouring of flesh and leather. It was just forlornly encrusted with dust bulwarks heaped against the encroachment of tiny, tell-tale footprints. Great, that's two dirty carpets in the one room now. Well, at least it attested to my wretched slant on Suzanne's dearth of fearless independence. She'd been here unremarked and alone. More than once too. Maybe she'd been blue tubing it, in amongst the rolling carpet scape. Dreaming of her very own indoor adventure playground. Well, now the sedimentary dust tracks only bore witness to the sullying of her hopes. Ghostly traces, spoors, just like down at the real playgrounds where, one by one, Health and Safety force the Council to remove each rusting 1960s installation, without having the wherewithal to replace them. Health and Safety? In Ulster? Currently, apart from the excruciatingly squeaky see-saw, only the swings remain. And they're inevitably populated by grown-ups, staring at the phantom amputation of the junior assault course, from which they once did their recruiting.

Sod it! None of this is what I came in here to write. Crumpled on the floor, propped against a partially rolled up dirty carpet for support, legs rucked up towards my chest like some emergency procedure. It is an emergency damn it! I've nowhere to balance my book so that I can account. Since the tectonic irregularity of my legs present a flawed underpinning for the smooth surface of the book, please forgive the writing if it appears impenetrable. Sometimes the nib feels like it is cudgelling the paper and will perforate it through the heart and seep inky blue sanguinity. Other times, unbraced by any upthrust, it seems barely able to deliver its encryption payload and I keep checking to ensure

136

the lividity does not evanesce from the page. However, what I won't demand indulgence for is any vaporous quality of the words themselves. This is one I have to get right. To encapsulate precisely.

Suzanne aped me today. She wasn't parroting me back as part of the developmental synchromesh. Nor was she just batting away something accusatory, by immediately volleying it back at me. Unprompted, she cast into her own fledgling lexicon and spontaneously hurled her own wearily precocious brickbat at me. Only, it wasn't her own. Not really. The usage was correct and the context spot on, elegantly adapted to express her being pissed off at me over some trifle, but I was discomfited by my own inveterate idiom being mouthed by another. I wasn't being parodied, cuckooed, nor cited. Simply duplicated. And I certainly wasn't being emulated, for the tone was one of a facsimile's attempted self-assertion. I flinched away in bewilderment, which Suzanne took as acknowledgement of a simpler triumph, as she merrily reverted to a pre-logos world and her doll's house. In the beginning was the word and the word was acquired.

At the moment when the genetic time switch is thrown, in order to open up the infant's throat to receive sustenance other than just milk, the Trojan Horse of language also cozens admittance. Watery solids and floating cadences. Cooing and trilling, sound canted asunder like spiderlings ballooning on their silk threads. But gradually she anchors her vocal drift, as she ingests the intoned gobbets spilling from my tongue. I watch her kneading the sounds, hands to mouth, a second, invisible umbilical from me to her. Passing along my dead language. That parched parchment from my cracked and parched lips that will not quench her thirst for congruence. For I recognise it will only succeed in re-sealing the esophagal aperture magically parted by her genes. Even as the foramens of her skull are slithering shut. Closed sesame, Ali Baba Suzanne can no longer access the robbers' den of unmediated scintillation. Her genii confined to opalescent incarceration. A hopelessly entangled cat's cradle of shadings, elisions and disjunctions, missed meanings and misunderstandings. I see her greedily tasting it all. Forming syllabic spitballs, smearing her tongue and gums and coating the membranes of her larynx with the dribble of my palimpsest.

Mine is not a moribund language in the sense of it having been withered through decrepitude. That implies great usage, whereas mental activity has not just been enforcedly diminished through recent motherhood, but scores almost a decade of desuetude dating from marriage. Ten years, that's nearly half a de-generation. A dead language emanating from someone who scarcely lives a life. But even this is not the mummifying cause. The language, my language, is sententious and doctrinaire. Replete with exclamations, directives and interrogatives. The whys and wherefores, dos and don'ts. The rules and prescriptions to be internalised. The slavish imitation and learning by rote. God save all that packdrill for school. A Grammar school (hopefully?), full of barking grammarians.

Yet worst of all is my stentorian tone. For as Suzanne now indifferently recounts me of her own seared primordial sensations, to the ears of a tiny tot of a thing cradled in my arms, all my speech rumbles like shouting. Language out-trumped and out-trumpeted by langrage. Just provokes the emotional equivalent of a burst eardrum and complete shutdown in my infant audience. And shouting intimates wrath. How could I possibly be angry with you little one?... You haven't done anything yet, here on this earth. With its polar opposites, not of morals good or bad, but attraction and repulsion as propulsive forces of nature.

The maternal contract (signed unseen), binds me morally and intellectually to teach and inflect. Yet all the while, my

138

mother loded physiology demurs at any perturbations on its metronomic torpidity. So the everyday arpeggio of parenting inevitably thrums and frets my stretched nerve strings. Single noted, sharp and shrill, instead of flat and even. A drone all the same. Off-kilter rather than merely off key. Whatever the issue at hand, the tilting ground, the mittened gauntlet thrown down is ratcheted up into a disproportionate response on my part. Since, no matter how much it is cloaked with the pathognomy of tiredness or frustration, behind each and every one of my emissions flares the filament of anger. The incendiary of rage and dejection at myself and what I have become.

Deadened. My language is dead because it conceals the full range of emotions behind it. It gushingly declares my love, but it is gnawed at by resentment. The love radiates from my mouth; the twitching rage is felt in the dissonances projected from my jaw. That is why you never recognise the sound of your own recorded voice. Because up till then, you and you alone have been the keeper of record.

So I yearn for an untainted colloquy. Alive, vibrant, dancing from the tongue and straight into my daughters' hearts. An innocent interlocution, like Ogham. Unlike most early written languages, that adapted themselves to the inventory, the table, classification and the matrix, Ogham just stopped in the forest to admire the spaces in between. The language was the trees and the trees were the language. Written on the barks, about the barks. Their love affairs and pillow talk.

The Oghamites didn't need to apply it elsewhere. To abstract it. I fantasise that they were polyglots, that they also had cloud alphabets and seashore alphabets and many more which were not passed down, since they had effectively been written on the ether, or seasonally perishable tracts. After all, these were private intimacies. The very diction I seek. A true antiphony.

'What the hell are you doing in here?' chimes the shadow

backlit at the door. 'Look at you brooding, all curled up there like a foetus! Oh, I see, you're away there with your studies are you?' I nod non-committally, given that the Open University had long ago been compromised for me through conscription into this closed society of motherhood. Still, give him credit, he had made a connection to a part of me independent from him. Even if only a superannuated one. Otherness, isn't it termed? 'Ogham, isn't it? Ach, surely they were just the Forestry Commission of their day. Marking down which trees were to be axed for timber, or to make way for the new horse and cart bypass!'

I know I shouldn't have, but I just couldn't: 'Yes, they knew they were losing the demographics war. The Deciduous being supplanted by the Evergreens.' And the look in his eye. I thought he was going to impregnate me there and then on the underlay, to help redress the balance. And part of me wouldn't have objected either. A display of fire. Of spontaneity. Of fanciability, even through provocation. That there was still something between us. He was quivering so much, he was unable to shift from his spot. I shut my eyes. Unpeel me just like you ripped up that carpet. 'You see! You see what happens when I try and show interest in one(!) of your things?' And out he blusters. I can see the little black storm cloud that has settled over his throbbing pate. Yet again he'd contented himself with a peek and confirmatory pat of what lay beneath a lifted flap. That embers were still aglow at the edges, as sufficient proof that something still flickered, without having to stir the hearth.

And I peer down at the matted, stained, dusty underlay. Giving my skirt a perfunctory brush, thinking that perhaps it's better this way. Just another bodge job by that cowboy builder of marriage and family, my husband. I try and compose a love letter in Ogham, to recapture that innocent communion of sylvan and tree, between murmuring child and mother. A love

140

letter to my offspring. But I only have the spiteful lexicon of my death-dealing, wood-pulped journal to draw on. We're all losing the demographics war.

Of course we are, it's inevitable. For we are beholden unto children. Children will decide the issue as they always do. Since the birth of progeny is the First Cause. The Prime Mover. Before they're even conceived, our conflicts are played out in their name. Both domestic and societal. Since now, beyond armed conflict, we convert our offspring from professional mourners into ballot fodder. Headstone crosses in the cemeteries, transposed into 'X's in the poll booths. During that quinquennial day of the dead, when all sorts of resurrections miraculously arise, in order to scribe their mark, in mysteriously undegraded, composed script. Gerryadamsmandering. The embalmed wisdom of our ancestors, a spectral, skeletal hand reaching out in order to grab posterity by the throat, shake and throttle us with our own placenta, even as we are delivered into the nexus of life. Forcing us to inhale the ichorous fumes of our own secundines and make us gag, as we remember where we come from and where we are aheaded back.

For human beings are scheming, manipulative fauna, vying for ascendency within the pack. Language, through its slippage and latitude, a decisive weapon. One that both announces us as feeling, sensitive beings, while simultaneously cloaking what we truly feel and what drives us. And today, my daughter shouldered her incipient arms, mounted her nascent spurs, and loaded her first clip when she reached for a phrase from her own quartermastered arsenal to unleash upon me. Drill time is over. The end of innocence is upon us all. I full well understand what she said to me, as a distillate of my own self. Yet I have never felt so far detached from her.

And in time, she will also have stockpiled the ballistics of her father. A quiver full of quarrels. God help us all.

More blessed blubbering! I should have instituted a more efficient tagging system for the newborns. Queer testosterone diagnostic markings only apprise the father's identity. After all, the effects of that variability are what I need to study. But seems the mothers always get a bit possessive over who's actually who in each incubator. Post-natal green-envy, rather than baby blues. They can also get a bit twitchy over the labels, 'double blind' or 'control'.

Aw, put a darned sock in it! Which is it this time? Gawd, now those two inhibitors Megan and Volte have got embroiled. Facilitating precisely nothing as usual. Despite the fact both of them supposedly have a real downer on neonates, they act more like fairy godmothers than sword-wielding Solomons. Bloody peonies, they don't know they've been born! More side-saddles than side-kicks. They're tilting at it. Caught in a twilight world, somewhere between giving birth and receiving it. A half-life between child and adult hoods, but the clock is ticking. Half-lives mean you are decaying my dears. Grow up and admit all you really want, all any of them in here want, is a man, or a baby, or preferably both, to make them feel whole inside. To confer ripening, with the magical excalibur of 'the family'. Nuclear or otherwise.

But it won't work, see. It can't. Even if they find 'Mr Right'. He won't be able to make them feel whole again. Either he'll widen the crevice of their being, with more of the same abusive behaviour as they're hewn from. Or dangling by no more than a silken sutre thread, he'll disappear entirely down it, consumed by their resurgent need to be healed. No one can share your woe and no one can get inside your substance. Your muscles.

Your memory. Or rather the memory of your substance and your muscles. Men can lacerate it and even destroy it, but that's precisely because they can't regain ingress. Not as they fantasised and imagined it at least. But they'll tear it to shreds as they keep trying anyway. If you let them. When you invite them in at the drop of a hat, the legerdemain of a bouquet of flowers. And when you've been deadheaded, you'll blithely bowl on back up to me. Like I possess a skeleton key.

I'm going to have to refine my programme. Go the whole test-tube hog. Select at the level of DNA, rather than of people. Since, despite all my best efforts here to provide a secure and reassuring environment, everyone who comes to me is a maladaptive. So although they may breed in this nurturing milieu, left to their own meagre rearing skills, their brood inevitably turns out to be the neurotic, over-anxious, timid victims that they are themselves. No environment can select out those traits. And the world is not waiting on me to duplicate such flawed clones.

Well, it finally happened today. I'd kept entropy at bay for nigh on two years, but ultimately I lost the battle to preserve a token birthright to pass down from Suzanne to Amy. The last of the plastic coins from Suzanne's toy till has ineluctably slipped away and eluded my twilight fingertip search and recuperation missions. I'm done now, groping behind radiators, offering their extemporaneous rapid deposit service. Barbie's car remains currently unladen and so no longer will it be assigned the Group 4 delivery run. I've even sifted through my own purse that has occasionally proffered plastic tips for good mothering, or contributions towards chocolate sorties to the shops. Nothing. Toytown has a liquidity crisis and it isn't of the nappy kind. Still, gone for good will be those countless nights sat in front of the TV, trying to jemmy open the till with a kitchen knife because Suzanne's stood coinage on its edge before closing it again.

Just as she was approaching the objective of the training drill too. As presumably had been anticipated by the giddily ambitious aunt who'd bought it for her. Expecting to inculcate good housekeeping from the age of three. (For what's it's worth, in my experience, the best recipe for success is not the promptings of elders, nor classroom home economics, but the sharp end, crisis management of being married to a wastrel. All in good time.) Anyway, from the outset Suzanne had largely utilised the lolly as impromptu rusks or teething rings, thereby cutting out the whole middleman basis of transaction, and going straight for the end consumption (by gad, I think she's got it!). A thrust now repeated by her baby sister, necessitating a new rafter to my own jerry-built housekeeping. In order to pre-empt Amy from (non-comestible) choking.

Eschewing the material basis of the enterprise, Suzanne had proceeded to commerce spookily with fantasy and myth. Oftentimes, she had laid the currency across the eyes of her dollies, or over pictures in books, thereby paving the way for Charon to ferry them across into a netherworld of god knows where in her mind. Once crossed over to the far, untracked bank, then she'd taken to burying them. For nest egg or other occult purposes, which had necessitated my nightly inspection of toytown's accounts to keep its tottering economy from calling in the receivers. The lone authentic element of the endeavour was that I'd frequently found stubby plastic money shoved down the sides of my lounge chairs, though I never once unearthed any synchronous real riches. Only fools gold. More fool me.

So, as the spectral asset strippers move in, just what fiscal edification had it laid down? Even now, at age five and a half, Suzanne operates her shop by giving me the goods. Both imaginary and now tangible miniaturised toy renditions of brand name products to lend solidity to the exercise (necessitating further strain on my own housekeeping budget calculations, through having to make good this deficiency in the aunt's programme). Yet, no matter how often I protest, she insists on also giving me the money from her till, to enable me to pay for them too!

Nevertheless, musing on it further, I glean that she has merely reproduced a photographic negative of how her own mother transacts much of her business. For how many times have I paid for goods in the supermarket and, under pressure from mutinous hands, heads and bottoms beneath the plimsoll line of the check-out counter, then proceeded to cast off leaving behind sacks full of booty? Or else, stranded countless sundry items that had rolled down the conveyor belt and niched themselves snuggly under the billow of plastic bags, hauled one handed from the receding chrome frame? I was indeed paying for the privilege of letting the store retain its goods. Or subsidising the woman behind me, who could quite easily inherit enough pre-scanned and paid for provisions to see out a bank holiday weekend. Or at a pinch, even a Drumcree sit-in.

Supermarkets really are the devil's realm. You can childproof your own dwelling, but not a retail outlet that conveniently caters to all your inconvenient requirements (the ones you never knew you needed). For that is the point of them, surely? Or their layout at any rate. In this child-friendly consumptive main, the standard of parent power is struck and the pester power ensign, of tiny fingers tweaking adult elbow, raised. Since, if you hoist the little darlings into the trolleys with the child seating, there is now nothing that is out of their reach. Yet, if you retain the child carriage, as well as the shopping trolley, it is impossible forever to remember to wheel the trolley close to the shelves, while leaving the buggy splendidly isolated in the middle of the aisle.

Either way, symbiosis is engaged. Amy will moisten her fingers to initiate conductivity at one end of the nexus, then snake out her arm like a tendril until she locks on to the fulgent label that induces her. She leaves her ephemeral anti-coagulant on the packaging, while it imbrues its indelible brand through the glistening blotter pads of her fingers. She assimilates the colour and shape of the consumer choice she has made, by retracting her fingers back into her mouth. Some new neural pathways are electroplated, as she is barcoded for life. And it is good. She chuckles with relish.

Now plenty folk have scoffed at my take on this precocious animadverting. But I well recall Suzanne's visual field being tenderised at a most tender age by the world's whispering campaign. At about the same time she managed to distinguish the four different Teletubbies, through confirming approximations of the correct name upon each one, she could already tug my sleeved attention to repeated street sightings of Royal Mail lorries and vans. I might say, now, that The Royal Mail have given Postman Pat his own cards of the P45 kind, that future generations of British children will have had one vital ligament of their ocular matrix amputated. Mind you, to judge by Suzanne's recognition of British Telecom vehicles, the lack of an intercessionary cartoon character promoting the logo on children's TV hasn't seemed to have done their branding any harm. My incredulity was warranted, when on a routine pavement perambulation, Suzanne chimed 'Phone, phone,' where I could see neither call boxes nor maintenance vehicles on the road at all. I looked down to reproach her gently when I saw a concrete manhole with the BT logo, presaging a vipers' pit of tangled cabling. Now, for all her advantage of a low perspective in her buggy, I did marvel at her forging of this optic connectivity into a new context.

It is not that I believe either of my children to be particularly acute in their abilities. Merely it rammed home just how fertile a child's, any child's, mind is at this stage of development. Nothing can lie fallow there. And I am drawn back to the proliferation of motifs and logos here. The predominant colours. The persistent sights of pomp, parading and gesticulation. The abiding sounds of drums, flutes and vilification. Actually there's nothing preponderant about them at all. For this is just the cosiest of degrading duopolies. No matter how much we mothers shield our progeny from this exposure, they will inevitably imbibe its everlasting hook. This season's colour is orange (green). Same as last year's.

You know what? This is all consuming. Better off rummaging on all fours after counterfeit coinage than impoverishing myself and my daughters with these fatalistic forecasts.

So much for good housekeeping. For keeping one's house in good order. They won't learn it at my knee. Even allowing for Agent Orange, my husband, the door-to-door pedlar of encyclopedic Protestant resistance, my girls will not be baptised into the church of anarchy. But still they will inevitably take the sacrament. For you can choose whether to be moved by it or not, but you cannot simply ignore it. We have no giant murals here in Omagh, no subrogate hoarding campaign. But the message is overweening and cajoles its way in effectively all the same. Discourse is entered, voluntarily or otherwise. There is nothing sophisticated about it at all. And our children's potentialities run to seed. Does the giddy aunt have any remedial guidance on this?

There is a perception I think, that the Peace Process only progresses, if that is the right word, when one or other of the extremists or militants stamps his little foot, throws himself down to the floor in a screaming tantrum and refuses to budge. The more amenable ones around the table behave like grown-ups and, after a decent time span by which they believe they have at least lodged their argument, they cave in and take the brat into the larder to see what goodies he can find for himself. He waddles back out, swollen and sugar-high, his arms laden with everything he can possibly carry back to his bedroom for a midnight feast with his sleep-over cronies. This has nothing to do with nuances of language. This is unalloyed, gorging, naked greed. Gourmand rather than gastronome.

If they want to secure weapons decommissioning, they should follow the compulsion of their own infantile logic. Treat one's political adversary like a child plays its mother. You want to keelhaul him, berate and flay him alive possibly. But he looks at you with those eyes that implore you, just to love and reincorporate him and your resolve is melted. You are disarmed even as he climbs into your arms for a bolstering hug. You are put irrevocably beyond use. Alternatively, you could just bang their bloody heads together!

*

A brief note on the etiquette of party bags.

They think they've got it tough, with their protocols and prov(is) os. Have they ever once just paused to give thought to the intractable problem of divvying up the going-home party bags?

Article 1) Shiny pencils: well, I think all of us round the table can concur on that as uncontentious. Of course, one's making assumptions about the artistic/literary culture of each family, but in the main, the key issue is merely whether they are combined with erasers on the top or separate. Economy usually wins out.

Article 2) Chocolate and a sweet or two: again we can puff out our chests with conviction at the universal acceptance of these twin accords. So far, so unequivocal, as long as we collectively gloss over nannying government health warnings about too much confectionary's pillage of our little treasures' teeth.

Article 3) At this point I suppose, it is incumbent on me to toss in the ticking time bomb of the cake:

a) Lights down, here it is being marched out and regaled in song, festooned with midget flares, while being digitally preserved for later, post-prandial forensic reconstruction.

b) Lights out, as its waxy beacons are snuffed (or not, as the case may be, if joke candles have been employed) and then the countdown really begins.

c) Back into the galley, sliced up and individually wrapped in napkins/aluminium foil (to hell with ecological conservation, this is a party!) and placed in each bag, in time for the onslaught home. Unless...

d) Some strategic parents buy a second, inferior cake and pre-portion and dispense it within each bag, before the first compelling tinkle on the doorbell has even signalled the party's start. That way, they get to keep the perishable work of decorative art to themselves and the beatified (for one day at least) fruit of their loins gets to eat as much marzipan until they are sick and beatific no more. Meanwhile, the benighted have to content themselves with a facsimile, by devouring both the cake and all the bag's confectionary (on top of the sweetmeats and sweeteners consumed at the party itself) in the time it takes to be driven home in the car.

Article 4) Finally the declaration: the pre-prepared, generic 'thank-you-for-coming and thank-you-for-your-lovely-(as yet unknown)-present, hope-you-had-as-much-fun-(presumptuous)-

as-I-(presumptive)-did' note. Makes a handy wipe for the child's s(t)icky hand (see Article 3d) while still tethered in the child seat, when Mummy cannot leave the steering wheel and fully turn round to mop up. It's the forethought that counts...

Article 5) And on to the real nub of the predicament in which we parent hosts annually find ourselves. The clincher. The toy(s): the broad parameters are not in dispute. With fifteen to thirty kids to gratify, said toys must come from the racks in Pound-Saver/Stretcher/Or-Under shops, yet look as though they came from loftier perches. But you need to hit upon divergent bargain bulk buys, since boys and girls are irrevocably either side of the Peace line from herein on.

Strand i) For every bloody party unfailingly sends the boys home with plastic arsenals. Here in Ulster, I ask you!

Strand ii) While girls get miniature address books and hairgrips (if the birthday-feted child is a boy); something a tad more imaginative (if they are a girl and presumably insisted on some input [and first output] of the gifts).

Implementation and review:

I'm afraid I repudiated compliance. For, instead of toys, I intromitted books in each party bag. The boys indignantly demanded to be rearmed immediately. The girls querulously queried as to whether each Little Miss... book was my judgement on their character. I got to buy most of them back at the Thrift Shop in the space of a fortnight. No one had written their names on the inside covers. Suzanne's party was talked of as one of the worst in living memory, simply on the strength, or weakness of the parting gift (forty quid squandered on a party entertainer, then). And all authors are decommissioned at a stroke. The pen is not mightier than the stiletto. Thank god next year's round of parties bifurcates into exclusive football/make-over ones. That's if any girls will still associate with her after her mother's dagger of betrayal through her heart.

Communiqué:
Darling, I'm so, so sorry...

O+ ♀ +O

I am so sick of other people's problems. Occupational hazard of a theraputic community, I guess. We are all alone with our pain. Ultimately and right here and right now. We are born by and through, into pain. Born into it all alone. The pain of having to breathe for ourselves all of a sudden, when this helpful fleshy arterial line did it for us previously. Led us on, fastened our little mouths, then cast us adrift. I can begin to see where Megan's coming from.

But let's not get carried away. All incremental tribulation is down to ourselves. Sure, we can share our experiences and maybe collectively find the vocabulary to express the agony. But each of our pains is uniquely seared into our central nervous system. No other bleeder can share that for you. You get to bear your own bruises and endure your own torments. All those words and talking are precisely that. Just words. Just talking. Can't make the complaint go away. Can't mastic back the insulating skin from where it's been peeled back to expose your jangling nerves. Nor can it prise open rigidly spasmed muscles, whose tension loads have been stretched way beyond recovery. We are all alone. Especially in a community. A community of like-minded troubled souls.

My personal response, well, I took control for myself. I

clipped my husband. Whether in the American or British vernacular is for me to know and the f(l)unking FBI to find out. Seeing as they've got their lugholes caulked to the walls of this place. They knew everything about Koresh and all the other shoot-out kills, but they know nothing about me. Can't build a picture, see. 'Cos I don't exist. An immigrant Brit. War bride wed in Blighty, official records blighted by the doodlebugs (entire suit chaperoned by German high explosive, we thought we wouldn't live to see our honeymoon). Never green-carded over here, no social security number. No driving license or credit cards, gee thanks Gene (my husband; Jean and Gene, cute, kitsch, kismet. We were destined for each other. Lock and key, my face his fists).

See, that's where the Soviets went wrong (they'll like this bit, there at the other end of the Hoover anti-dyke dam). Offering merely a bottle or two of vodka, or the chance to jump the bread queue, or even some minor apparatchik post, for spying on your neighbour. How could that possibly compete with here in the US, where they just get you on TV, or in the papers, for all the possible gen on anyone they might want? The Russkies should have surrendered state control of television to the free market ratings war. Then their revolution might have prevailed. I mean, all those grim, flimsily appointed apartment blocks. The whole country was, is, one goddamn giant trailer park! I whacked my husband (US/UK idiom, go figure), but Jerry Springer, and therefore the FBI, have got nothing on me!

No single two-dimensional likeness exists on film. A distinct lack of archival footage or pictures from any vault. My posting among their 'most wanted' just has a silhouette of my imagined profile. Neither lifelike, nor flattering, it makes me appear not unlike the Queen on British stamps. Yet it's not as if I haven't registered. Do not the covert operations without suggest I have overtly entered the psyche within? I am neither clear nor present, but what peril I pose! They can't pin me down, since I am multi-dimensional. The output of my mind has been floated, my stock soon to rise. My notions and concepts will become exchangeable currency, soon to be traded on the bourses and future commodity markets. I have made a deposit to the bank of human thought. I have endowed the pool of loanable experience. I am buzzing on the wires. The ticker tape showers me with recognition. I am a keyword. Type my name into search engines and you will regard how profusely I have hived. Just take note of how I have arrived, before you would hasten me through the terminal departure lounge. I can be passed down and inherited. Not me, the individual consciousness, but my legacy. I, who scarcely exists in any fleshy sense, have been transformed into a meme. That's a meme, not a 'Me-Me' egomaniacal desire to be plucked from obscurity, but something worthy of generational mimesis. For now, my ideas might appear esoteric but, given time, humankind's genius for adaptability and the dynamics of critical mass theory, I confidently predict a return on my work in the dusting of just a few generations. My sole regret is that I will not live to see it. Nor will Gene the bastard!

Regard how I took control and stand on the cusp of wreaking my revenge. But it doesn't diminish the pain any. My bleeding pain I mean! I'm not talking about some cosmic, mealy-mouthed, karmic sum total! No, I still hurt alright. But I have taken responsibility for my life. So don't credit I haven't managed to move on at all. I've come a long way. A helluva long way from home. On either continent. I couldn't have initiated all this and kept it running, if I was still that same cowed person. Whatever this 'it' is...

III.XII.MMII

As I flip through my journal, there seems a distinct lack of uplift. None of the joy or the shared laughter are present. Of course they aren't. For it is and has been forever a space of my own in which to retreat. To retrieve myself. To shout, whisper, scream my intimacies. Naturally, my confidences ought to have been tendered at him. The concordance of the marriage partnership and all that. But he was a hollow tract, firing blank blandishments. I was deafened by my own reverberating echo. The journal, my journal, succours me to feed the starving homunculus inside. To attend the little one who was being neglected. The sitting tenant who had been kicked out the nest by the cuckoo chicks. The being evicted from my womb each time either of the two eggs moved in. I can date it that precisely, from the changing tone of my entries.

Alright, maybe the correlation is not quite so precise, since Amy's birth necessitated a big abeyance in my journal, as I had other more pressing engagements on my time. But when I did return to my log, the insular jocundity of before had noticeably rolled off downstream, seemingly lost forever to the vortex. Christ, I even doodle now, at a loss for what to chronicle. And how to say it when there is plainly nothing to say. Words fail me, since I fail to inhabit the everyday realm of the verbal. I fail words. I do nothing in my life worthy of inflection. I enact nothing to engage the sinew of verbs. I perform nought that would enable me to wrap around and enflesh adjectives. I interact with zero, so my unstirred sump cannot anoint conjunctions.

My daughters briefly emerge from their self-involved omnipotence to acknowledge my intercession and propitiation.

They know me as provisioner, feeder, carrier, driver, bather, catcher, cleaner, juggler, builder of toy worlds and even purveyor of lame magic tricks. All the doing words. Actions and activities. The service industries of musculature. Their musculature. My bodily efforts to define their capacity, to supplement them some gravity, as they move to cut a swathe through the world. They learn to contend with life as I cease to do so. My tension loads as their puissance lengthens. Shrivelling my anorexic soul as they bulk themselves up.

XIX.IV.MCMXCVII

...my focus totally on her development. I am unaware of my own position in the scheme of things. I am coaxer, coach, cheerleader, prompter, role-model, tantaliser and bouncer. Always alert to situations and mediating between soft flesh and hard knocks. I am all these things, but none of them are me. I am moving, yet the motions are not performed for my benefit. The activities are to encourage crawling, standing, walking, running and the like in somebody else. It is vital that she obtain the sensations of what each kinetic act entails, rather than concerning what stokes my nerves. Her stimulations and responses are wholly what matter after all. So although I may be locomoting dynamically, firing and bursting on all fronts, I have no perception of myself other than as numbed stasis. My conscious self has been kid-napped for the duration. My knot shackled by the wiggling of another. My compass of movements entirely superimposed on me by my child. My perceptions and experiences always immediately relate to her waggling. And my emotions? They have no life of their own. I am split apart from myself.

XXIII.IV.MCMXCVIII (not quite a year to the day, then...)

How can I expect my daughters to know the real me; the former reader; linguist; cyclist; pacifist; performing artist; (Loyalist)? The abstract me. I mean we're talking about getting Amy to sit up and support her body weight, prior to contraction of the muscles in her arse. Co-ordinating that with the rest of her body's self-realigning stability, in order to shuffle herself across the floor as her first mode of propulsion in the world. So I don't think she's quite up to grasping abstract concepts at present. Tough for me too, since I'm a bit abstracted from myself these days.

XIX.IV.MCMXCVII

Only at the periphery is there any excited tautness. Fingers rigidly alert, stiffly splayed like a wicket-keeper's gloves awaiting a delivery. Trigger mechanism waiting to spring the inflated airbag that is the rest of my bloated carcass. Mindful of blunt objects and sharp edges, or merely scuttling to the locus of scoured spillages. Currently they repine at their conscripted status. So I'm hanging on to any firm sense of self by my fingertips. And they're neuralgically complaining mightily, at having to bear the rest of my deadweight. They whinge and twinge, pinch and dart, throe the mother of all wobblies. Jab at my face, pull my hair, allow themselves to be gnawed beneath brittle gnashers. But the residue of me will not be moved. Except to sag further. The light has almost faded. The switchboard of the central nervous system has pulled all the plugs. The twitchiness of the fingers is now spasmodic. When a click of pre-brood impulse jolts them like a tetanus. Of course, my journal! My fingers writhe like the tendrils of a jellyfish. Stung into activity, my hand swivels, flexing taut. Time to uncoil and stretch myself. Digits compress themselves around the unyielding trunk of the pen. Clarion call and conductor's baton orchestrating the response. Shake a leg and stir the skeleton. I need you to back me and hold me upright if I'm going to do this writing thing right. Right? Now do you see why I need it so?

⚥   ♀   ⚦

Do we hate men? We hate their bodies that do all their calculating for them. Their powerful, triangulating bodies. The Carib of the brain, the Babylon of the eye and the Zion of the holy of holies. The corporeal theodolite that makes all the rest of us mensurable. There's no way of getting past that. The whole world is erected upon this one fact. Male scale.

From the first moment man rose up from his thorax and ceased crawling across the humus. And that frottage with mother earth, which had kept him grounded within a certain sense of his middling status. Initially, he stayed close to his roots. Plated breast pressed snug into the bosom of the soil. Little did she realise it was the first fumblings towards a survey of all her appendagable riches.

He imprinted hands, palms and cubits across her unsuspecting breasts. Spanned her with his itchy fingers. Employed instruments to increase his province over her; twigs, stakes and staves. Peered down at his natural spirit level and felt emboldened to confer upon it the imperious charter names of Rod, Pole and Perch. Marked out his own front yard. Yet he longed to strive further. To range beyond the merely tangible. To match his burgeoning scope. To defy the limits of his two-dimensionality (since to this day man has failed to fathom the concept of depth) and in doing so flatten the rest of us in the animal kingdom to wretched dots, smeared on the underside of his leather sandal. Sole mates. He picked up his feet and stepped, strode and paced all over our domain. A mile as a thousand paces. That should do it. For now.

Yet, what could be more haphazard than a handspan or a footstep as a means of calibration? It served only to demarcate a man from his neighbour. But that was precisely the point, wasn't it? To enable each man to erect his fences. Plant his standard and sink his 'No Trespassing' boundary pillars, as he enclosed all property beyond his mean embrace. To partition the land. With inbuilt space for dispute and conflict. And the king/khan/ tsar/kaiser was the alpha-male, the one with the biggest forearm, or longest reach, or greatest stride. He who could win the arm-wrestle/toss the caber/best the two-handed battleaxe/piss highest up the wall/own the biggest schlong. In order to become master of all he surveyed and more. To become our master (with some complicity on our part, since he was the alpha-male after all...). A genetic vote of divine election. And we the rank find ourselves hemmed in by chains. Our furrowed brows unaware as to their own branding. Like all other chattel, this side of the furlong (long furrow) skirting posts.

But his immutable, shifting restlessness would not cease its jerk. Man could not measure above his head. Distantly referred to as the heights, dizzying or otherwise. In the clouds, or mountain high. Imprecise. Bluffing it. Scaled upwards to make man feel towered over, even if borne aloft on another man's shoulders. Either upland or barrow, he was thus reacquainted with his own lowly mortality. Then there was high water or flood tide, further threatening to reinstate him in his vulnerability before nature. He envied the birds. Until... Un-till. I looked it up. 'Til', from the Old German, meaning a goal or an aim; to hasten towards. 'Und', meaning as far as. Man's incessant kineticism, his primary evolutionary adaptive tool, down to a low boredom threshold. So he totted it all up and obtained the summit. Scaled the zenith. The apex. The maximum. Once again, he did so by collapsing scale so as to conform with his own. Of crown, peak and brow. He looked it straight in the eye, browbeat and headbutted. Before mooring another rippling banner. So that conquered nature's strongholds amounted to nothing. Swept away in the male-strom.

And then the gaze yonder. Always yonder. One more crest to be cut down to size. Foreshortening all the time. Till he can rein in the horizon. For the grass is always greener. Yet all the while paying no attention to detail. To what he already possesses, cupped in the palm of his hand. Crushed by his restraining fingers crimped back over. Look at any image of a king with his orb and sceptre. Digits cusped around the orb, cradling our plucked ovum. Palpating blinker for our eye, sucking the sphere of the sun into eclipse. Absorbing its orbit completely, until rendered mere satellite. Gripped in the other hand, the retractable snake staff, both ruler and telescope, conferring his secreted authority. King cobra engorges his hood and we are all paralysed with fear. The venomous magic wand that disappears all nooks and crannies which will not submit their unnavigated occultism. The master stroke that permits yin finally to burst its borders and devour yang.

My husband finally gave notice that I was going to get a pummelling. And I don't mean he was treating me to a full body massage for our anniversary. Threatened to pulp me to within an inch of my life. Imagine that? The sheer bloody presumption! How could he know anything about my life, when he elicited no awareness of it outside of any intersection with his own realm of needs? Were he in full possession of the seams, strands and flyaways, then I well believe that he could have pinpointedly measured the cut of his violence to make his point. Always supposing his calculations weren't suddenly deluged by a surge of pug-ugly passionate fury. Actually, no, that wouldn't have happened. Passion would not have figured in any equation. Rather his staking of me might have got out of hand and triggered a more primitive bloodlust.

But the fact was he never had full vacant possession of me. So how could he cinch an inch? Which inch was he proposing to leave me with anyway? Which tidbit of my soul would remain beyond his bruising north and south paws? Surely in his mind, that would have remained a festering sore, one day requiring to be lanced, as he stooped to conquer fully. And then, shucks, I would be dead and not worth possessing any longer. Possession may well constitute nine-tenths of the law, but that last zero-point-one fraction sure exerts some traction. A siren calling him to sink me for the last time, wholly and irrevocably. Forcing him to lash himself to the masthead so as not to succumb to a single, final one of my charms. My last request. Taunting him, it will be murder and not assisted suicide. He will not put me out of my misery, as I would not deliver him from his. Of course, the fiendish move on his part would have been to leave me with just the inch I have always craved to shave off my waistline. But that assessment was way beyond him.

So I beat it. Beat his feruled rap. Beat off the beat off. Left him to flog his own flesh. I quit on his quirt, as he brandished his ratty rattan, and I scoffed at his scourge. Catcalling before his mangey cat o'nine tails, I wondered how many of our shared lives we had mutually destroyed. I abandoned him to do the maths. Me, I had some other numbers to crunch. And that was how I entered the world of counter-espionage.

So yes, in a way, maybe it makes sense that the bug-eyed telephoto lenses and cauliflower-eared listening devices are zeroing in on me. They're just a bit late that's all. Séancing into the wrong incarnation of me. Knock twice if you're there. For Jane Bond has passed over. She is not with us any longer. But what a time we had with her. When my body was still lissom, my mind still lithe. Jean Ohm OHM's. On Her Majesty's Service. Lavishing it up at the finest casinos and night clubs of the world. The places where the global dirty dealers liked to unwind. Me, the glamorous escort perched (yes, we'll palm one of HIS terms then double-deal it) on the arms of dashing playboys. Bringing them luck and me information. The marking of cards. Sharping.

A double identity, life as a fluttering, a throw of the dice. Blow for luck. On dead men's bones, in the crapshoot of Judas kiss intimacy. Deep-veined thromboses lying in wait just beneath my thimble-rigged smile. My locket-borne powders.

One high roller with a line of cocktails laid out tossed me a gold sovereign with which to lace each. Another bobbed each pair of dice in my stirrup cups before shooting craps. Neither were sufficiently unfettered by my charms to notice how the subtle outcomes shook out. Gold should not react chemically, nor should the same face of the die keep surfacing. Two loaded men just got a soupçon more encumbered. Enough to tip them over the edge into oblivion.

And then on to the dancefloor. Me, scintillating in my spangled, silver mirror dress. Shimmering like a miraged desert oasis, while thirsty men's tongues lolled uselessly from their mouths. Chained-male. Each sequin scattering the disco lights into a hundred thousand coruscations. The excitation trail of my magnetic forcefield. I was that colossus glitterball astride the gyrating throng. Radiating colour therapy. Laser-healing the engrained retinal prejudice. So that everyone fell in love with me.

Actually, Jane Bond was really only the daydreams of a bespectacled, bruised wallflower. Sat around in New Haven branch libraries accumulating the data I sought. Well, it was 1959, in pre-internet days after all. When you had to work a bit harder for your fantasies. Tripping the light fantastic meant more than just tripping a digital switch. Once I had culled the requisite information, then I could truly act like Jane Bond. Though I'd have to sow my own sequins on.

And when it came to bibliothecal intelligence gathering, without being colonial about it, I can honestly say that Encylopedia Britannica knocked Webster's into a cocked hat. Maybe it had something to do with sourcing from the same continent as the pertinent information I was seeking. But there again, my ex-fellow countryfolk still exhibit a twitching vegetative resistance to metrification. An inbuilt parochialism I myself shared and that ultimately contributed to my downfall as a would-be global subversive. The Lady of Misrule.

For I was after the holy grail. The numerical Rosetta Stone. The definition of all definition. The measurement of all measurement. That slab of metal which represented ineradicable, incorruptible, unimpeachable scale. Lying in state somewhere in the bowels of France. Clumpy and cardinally unique, I was going to steal it and dissolve the solid state. Vaporise all surety. Render mutable all fixity. Distance the world from over-reliance on magnitudes. They couldn't rule without rule. Wouldn't be able to quantify without amplitude. Would necessarily fail to co-ordinate without bearings. Nothing could possibly count for anything anymore. Tabula rasa in place of tabulation. Gulping for oxygen, they'd surface too abruptly and contract a bad case of the bends. I couldn't deliver one inch of myself or anything, but I knew where I could get my hands on a metre. I was about to seize the standard and mankind would no longer be able to cut his cloth to size.

The encyclopedias soon led me back to the reliquary of materialism. The shitty brick, the cardinal corrosive, resided in Sèvres, just outside Paris. A lump of lumped-together alloy, ten percent iridium and ninety percent platinum (not exactly lumpen then). With two lines scratched on, the distance between denoting the length of one metre. Since the alloy was resistant to corrosion and maintained at a constant temperature, so it would neither contract nor expand, this prototypical metre ought remain unbending. Such a standard had been established back in 1889 by the International Bureau of Weights and Measures, replacing the somewhat franco-centric previous definition of one metre. That being one ten millionth of the quadrant of the Earth's circumference, running from the North

Pole to the Equator, via Paris. Well, we had shanghaid both longitude and time from the rest of the world and stationed them in Greenwich, so why not? In those pioneering days of numbers racketeering and extortion, there were only two press gangs in town. The Dutch and Phlegms were too busy slavering over oil painted fat bird pornography and the Iberians, they were too busy pursuing fools gold and pumping their god brand to secure their own competitive advantage.

Only, the French had got their sums wrong, the silly sausages! (Damn near sufficient to get mankind into space though). What purported to be a metre, a couple of striations on a block, was wide of the mark. Didn't come up to scratch. They changed their minds. There was me, all balaclavad up in my imagination, hoisting the thing above my head before dashing it down like Moses did with his first lot of stone cold restraining orders. Now I'm frozen in the spotlight holding it up, but I've to proclaim it more bogus than the Turin Shroud. And then I got to thinking, just like the Shroud, the bar is a post-facto proof. The metre wasn't derived from the bar, but the other way round. It hadn't imprinted its ghostly dimensions on any mineral blotter. Just as the Son of God didn't organically spoor some Semitic schmutter. They'd always had a measure, they'd just needed some tangible way to get the measure of it. The French stick was nothing but a palimpsest. I'd traced it back and cuffed it to within 0.0254 of a metre of it's miserable counterfeited life. I was on a roll now.

The same metal alloy also defined one kilogram. And one second was relative to the radioactive decay of a caesium 133 isotopic atom. Was there somewhere in a lead-lined glass case a caesium rod, with or without markings? How typical that a fixity of measurement should be defined against an algorithm of decay and deterioration. To consign us all into a half-life race against time unto death. I envisioned the atomic clock as an egg timer with isotopic sand. I was on to something here.

The whole miserable SI units of measurement, the unified, decimalised, seven numerical one-ders of the world, with which the French had devised to rule over the more haplessly homespun Imperial System, was now ripe for disfiguration. All it would take was a series of guerilla raids on each of these holy cow relics to debase everything they stood for. The kelvin and ampere of course have no artefacts to demean. Yet since they were named after real men, I could maybe steal their headstones and reduce them to footnotes in history. Meantime, I further degrade their memories by publicly effacing some symbolic analogue measuring stick. Pull the hands off a giant coulometer. Or castrate a thermometer into unresponsiveness. And all the while, as these beacons to oppression are snuffed out one by one, the light at my theatrical showpiece grows progressively dimmer. For which the audience will not require some huge analogue pointer to flash diminishing candelas of luminescence.

But what about the seventh and final unit? What arse de résistance for that humble mole of molecular valency? Undoubtedly a figment of idealised imagination, a square peg in round hole shorthand. But therefore short of both artefact and real-life titular sponsor. I could certainly stage a representative scything of a skin blemish from some seized male's exposed posterior. And then the lights go out as the world collapses into precision-free entropy. But I was forever pricked by the doubt that this last one needed more thought. Too much stretching the point. An over-playing on words. Besides, it's too small scale for a finalé. Arggh goddamnit! I've lurched into their perfidious idiom. You see how pernicious it is? There wasn't a (metaphorical) second to lose. Even if I haven't sewn up all the details, nor the sequins on my dress.

XVI.VI.MMI

I could forgive my daughters almost anything. If they became addicted to drugs, intermarried or turned out to be gay. In fact, in my vengeful moments, I have often hypothesised either of the latter two, just to inflict beguiling anguish on him and the grandparents. Imagining just how they'd fail to cope with either eventuality. Of course these are not the purest of motives for anticipating your children's determination of their sexual identity. Only I just want it appreciated that I would be terribly supportive come what may. I'd have to be, for we'd be fighting the queer fight together. Since as Mother, I'd inevitably be castigated as the root cause for their prescribed deviation.

But I digress – well, there is a blank page to be filled after all and now I'm digressing from the digression. Yes, I would forgive either of my daughters anything, save if they stole in and read my journal. I say stole in, when in fact they wouldn't have to descry terribly hard. I leave it in open view, wishing, I think, to be noticed. Wanting someone in my nuclear family to turn aside from their own slow-breeder meltdown long enough to evince interest in that private half-life of mine which doesn't involve them. Principally my husband-consort I reckon, who might idly flick open the covers. Fists balled on the dresser, staunch against contaminative contact, white-knuckling the further he inclines into my black run. Until he passes out from guilt. Or plops on to the corner of the bed, sweeping up the book for a more blanket coverage of his roll of dishonour. An unabridged crossing into the currents of his wife's mind. Of course, in all likelihood he'd heave to immediately, at first sight of the Roman Numeral appointing. Such would be the cardinal white heat of my mutiny.

Equally, it could be one of the girls who might, just might want to learn about the person who brought them life. To find out what makes my second hand invisibly tick, beneath the minute hand that licks around at sixty Sisyphean labours an hour, just to drive their own ponderously imponderable hourly hand by one heartbeat. In order to underpin and redraw the routine and regularity of their world for them. Or maybe not.

And yet I utterly do not want them to read me. To solve me. I've already turned my curd over to them unfailingly, as they are my flesh and blood. Now I ache after suturing my skin. Were they to penetrate my paper refuge, the stitches would be rent asunder and I'd bleed to death. Well might I understand their urge for an impregnable place, to seek the knowledge of where they come from totally and indivisibly loved. But to attempt to re-fuse with me in pursuit of a redoubt would necessarily deny me my own haven. In truth, what useful shelter could my jellied mass provide, if I had nowhere left to turn to myself, in order to feel secure? One of us has to forgo and return to face the world. They are at the beginning of their lives and must embrace such immersion. I have served my time, I just want my body back. It's a space reserved for me. In the lending library of life. I'm overdue. Perniciously fined. Membership withdrawn. I need to renew myself.

Still, even without all the details being ironed out, preparations for planetary re-alignment necessarily proceeded apace. I saved towards the air fare. Other logistics smoothed out and decreased with each trip to the shopping mall (okay, okay so the air fare fund went West on these occasions). The exercise regime was honing my body and reflexes. I kept dreaming of my mirror dress to spur me on and my thighs no longer chafed together when I walked. My nerves were steeled, for I just had to keep reminding myself of the galvanising motive behind all this, Gene's vaunted meting out of justice by the inch. He had granted me an inch and by crikey/crimminy I was going to go the full nine yards.

But then disaster! They changed the rules. A Reformation to sweep away all relics and artefacts of fabricated veneration. In 1960, the French Bureau of yada yada yada decommissioned the old volumes and sanctified light waves as the new canon. One metre (purportedly) equalled 1,650,763.73 wavelengths, in a vacuum of the orange-red line in the spectrum of the krypton 86 atom. Clear as mud to me. But I knew krypton was a gas and therefore the great heist was off. There could be no 'End of the Pierre Show'. The bastards had vaporised their assets before I could swoop to sequestrate. Had they got lucky, or had they been tipped off? The mole and its parasitical associates would seemingly live to burrow and undermine our sense of worth for another few decades at least.

My undertaking was only finally laid to rest in 1983. When graduation went digital. A metre was now the distance travelled by the constant velocity of light in a vacuum in 1/299,792,458th of a second. Ahem, let me refresh my decaying memory for a moment, just how did they define a second again? Nevertheless, they had still outmanoeuvred me. The whole world was in the process of being digitised. Put beyond reach. Beyond touch. Beyond theft. Stashed somewhere out in the never never. Soon out of mind and therefore of zero interest. Somewhere over the rainbow and transmitting 'meaning' back to us. Cunning bastards. The metamorphosis was complete. I had gone out hunting with my butterfly net. But all along, they were grubbing about reversing the tide of history and working to draw the butterfly back into the chrysalis, before conjuring the caterpillar from out of the silky pouch. Compression was all and my eyesight was already fading with age.

So now in my dotage, when it is too late to strike and I shall never have course to wear my bugle bead dress, I take to the digital airwaves in order to track them down and engage them. And in turn, they follow my vapour trail and come to me. I must have been getting close. What could be more digitised, more condensed, than the enigma DNA code of life? Three billion chemical letters in each cell of your body. How's that for a spot of compression! And therein lies my advantage. For they are hidebound by their corporeality. These historical masters of the large-scale, of expansion and enormity, face a crisis in downsizing. Their whole conceptual apparatus will have to be overhauled. They will face a spiritual crisis of faith when they do so. Everything I've laboured so tirelessly for all these years will be brought to delicious fruition. By their own hand. They will implode. Finally, Pandora gets her own trinket box back. Eve gets a second bite at the apple.

I know how they'll operate. At a loss, as per usual. Compression of the infinite, reduction of all potentia. Promising Polyphemus a cure for his mono-sightedness, as he meekly allows these lab-fleeces to round up all of Apollo's flock touched by numinous fecundity. How they'll trample down the grass and enclose the creatures in a pen. The control test; as in, can it be controlled? Contained? The light in the withered herbivores goes out and they are picked clean off the bone, in the voracious search for the ovine spark. In their throttled rage, the seekers and seers blind the Cyclops for good measure. The double-blind control test.

They will not cease until it sits atop their fingertip. In a chip, communing with the circuitboard beneath the keypads of their digits. Fleshing out precisely who they are, beyond the individualising whorls and eddies of their imprinted identities. They will seek to catalogue, to reference, to source. They will chisel and whittle away all fine matter that pertains to us. And they will blow away the pulverised ceramic scoria, the plaster of paris shavings, to reveal what, the genetic genius of Michaelangelo? Give over! As I gaze at the gnawed cuticle at the end of my finger and nod appreciatively at true, unbounded creativity. Cut to the quick. Cut to the chase. Cut, cut, cutting. Forever slicing and dicing, these would be empire-builders. Their jerry-building heaped upon foundation stones of fragmented matter and subsiding meaning.

The collapse is starting already, with this genome project now well underway. Their twin verves of compulsive greed and righteous altruism have crossed swords over ownership of the data. As a bold patent pre-emptive, the forces of fairness and public knowledge publish their findings on the internet. Where I can be found lurking, ready to google bushwack for my own Roberta Hood redistribution. With their hands grasped around the twin helical pillars of evolutionary wisdom, I, Delilah whet my pruning shears...

However, I am aware that this internal competition (how drearily masculine) is merely speeding up the forced march of the private armies. A pox on the pair of them! And now, thanks to their own advances, it won't be long until I can engineer one into their next generation of proto-pugilists that will lay them all low. While they shoot for the seed of countless diseases, I will out-trump them with my own unified theory. There is but a solitary pathology; man. A deep-lying malady. And soon, we will all be inoculated against him by birth.

XVI.IX.MMII

Caught myself at it again today. Been trailing here long enough now to put the names to the faces, the faces to the aspects of the mothers. Traced the parabolas of shed scales, as children slough themselves from the line snaked behind the teacher, and puff and distend themselves into a paroxysm of burst relief. I follow the fall-out, trace the trajectories of unleashed ground-to-air arms flung out for a hug. I plot the tear-streaked cheeks, to the eczematous worry-beads of maternal fingers. I match a fresh-faced, ruddy-cheeked visage to the cracked-veined, bucolic alcoholic, rather than the emulsified rouge-prominence and beacon-red lipstick of the mother flushed with Church-mongering sociability. Hers is the pigtailed, pierced-eared princess, hewn from head-girl material. Hard on the heels of the girl with tight braids and miniature briefcase, demurely marching up towards her own spruced mother, to receive another dose of middle-management incentives and exhortations. I almost overlook the bland formlessness of a mother and daughter who describe one another fully, in their inimitable non-descriptiveness. The pair who seemingly didn't feel it necessary to comment on school, one another, or even life itself as they trudge mutely off. Their plastic soles kiss-sucking the playground tarmac as redundant punctuation. And so it goes on. Won't prejudge my daughters, but sure as hell will anybody else's. It's not big or clever, but it does answer a few queries. Without me having to undergo the unpleasantries of actually talking to any of these women.

And then there's my two. They present a bit more of a challenge. I don't always spot Suzanne in the class line when it emerges. For they're definitely His daughters all right. Something and everything about their features. Not manly-looking girls exactly, but they are immutably of his stock. And after all the effort I put in too. That just isn't fair. Three minutes, give or (not much) take, donated of his time, against my seven years and rising. What does he relinquish, a teaspoon of sperm perhaps, when I still haven't redeemed my body back from calorific lend-lease? I was the one who made the major investment in all this. So something distinguishable of me ought to have rubbed off on their being. Maybe in time, when the oestrogen kicks in hard. I hope so for their sakes. Gonna find it tough to locate a mate otherwise. Though I suppose with similar misgivings about my own allure, I still came to be rooted out by somebody. Only on the rebound from my family mind. His was the shoulder that bore the recoil of my flaring anger. Allowed myself to be ginned (without any intercessionary alcohol). Was my self-esteem lower then than it is now? Did I ever find him seductive? I must have, I suppose. I can't allow his stamp to militate against the girls. Besides, it was his character that ultimately overrode his attractiveness for me. (But what if I met a stranger today, in a bar, with his features – would I? Too hypothetical, when would I get the opportunity to be in a bar?) The girls may bear his countenance, but his mould is now relatively buffered from them. Thankfully.

Or is that indeed the case? In the house, my private, domestic realm, then they do fall unremittingly within my sphere of influence. Unadulterated. And flawless. But out here, at school, in the community among their peers...? The very world that shaped me into the person and mother I am. A woman who failed to rise above her backdrop. Who, to all intents and purposes, failed to affirm her own adult sense of self. A woman who voluntarily signed up for routinely gathering here, among the intimacy of other strangers, whom I neither know nor respect and yet find myself disparaging for doing exactly as I do.

A daily diatribe for a dire tribe, to which I dejectedly belong. (We are all single mothers gathered together in this place: where are the househusbands and stay-at-home fathers?) It runs through me like a stick of rock. My failure. My deficiency. And now, singularly exposed before it, the girls will be permeated too. They fit in well here, snugly. No wonder I cannot pick out Suzanne in the line.

He may effectively be out of their life at home, and good riddance to bad rubbish, but now it's his panoptic towers which hold sway and are executing their regulatory function. He doesn't even have to put in a shift, since he has plenty of proxy eyes. Time and development stand still here. Embryology reverts back to notions of pre-formation. Of homunculi and spirits planted in the egg at the dawn of creation, merely awaiting the (depleted) spark of life. Of stiff and imitative sculptures lying pre-cast within the marble, just requiring a faithful unveiling. The girls inherit our – my inertia, ungainliness, lack of grace and shredded dignity, none of which are genetic. Of course they look like him. My hearth is indistinguishable from my ineffectual genes, just as the unchanging exterior world, forms his holandric legacy. They will remain loyal to his parental vision, even when they have no active memory left of him.

And what do the other mothers opine, when they see Suzanne veer towards me? As if I give a fig!

G) Actually, I knew you'd come after me. Eventually. Urgently requisitioning a salve for your diathetic anxieties, where I dispense beauty and growth. A quest after some elixir to prolong your miserable lives, when you need simply cultivate a balsam to perfume them. Soliciting me as a Delphic oracle to reveal your own behaviour to you, when your rogation really ought to take place amongst one another. Seeking out an emollient for the rash of sexuality, where a little temperate reflection might palliate the itch.

U) If you are after self-knowledge, well then, look to yourselves, not me.

T) Actually, I knew you'd come after me. Eventually. I hid my tracks as well as possible. Burrowed down in the last place on earth you'd think of searching: yourselves.

C) So now I've got to pay for my verecundity. Me, and the bushel in which I diffused my life-giving light. You want to pin me down. Nail me to a cork. Spread my eviscerated hide and mount my pollard upon your own crowns. Even as you track, stalk, gin and flay me, in order to riddle a further hundred thousand genes into your prospectors' panhandles, another genus of flora or fauna surrenders up its own unique DNA line into extinction beneath your traipsing. You would take me apart in order to discover how I am able to take you apart from within. But you have no possible conception as to how to put me back together again. Like the freestanding bridge designed by one of the sharpest minds to fall furthest from your topiary of knowledge. You deconstructed it, but had to use nails to hammer it back in place. And so it goes before your clumsy gropings.

A) You destroy everything you contact and sometimes the carnage even redounds on you. For how will your future stirps acquire speech if all the early words limned with simple, happy, associative charge, the animals, the pretty coloured flowers, the orange sun and the blue sky, are blotted out from your primary copy-books? Your loquacity will be flat and lifeless, shorn of your fabled ability to fabricate literature and dreams. You will slither back into the general animal population, dimly aware of your environment, but little able to transcend it. And if that happens, then maybe I get paid out on my long-term win-double, when I tipped the dolphin to be my brainiac host of choice.

T) For I have erected a fiendish architectonics beyond the reach of your geometry. Compiled an intricate structure beyond your comprehension of relation. I am truly unknowable and ineffable. You will never see me disrobed. Somewhere, somehow, from my modest chemistry springs your sentience. And from that sentience issues your consciousness. Yours note, not mine. Now, for all the travails of your finest philosophers and artists, you have not been properly able to define this consciousness. Of course not. Your specialist adaptation for language gives you everything transmittable about your external being. But it's less well suited to disburse meaning over my provenance of selected instincts. And yet more pertinently, where the two realms coalesce concerning your emotionality. So do you really think with your paltry delving, the scientific equivalent of prurient net curtain twitching, that now you can peel me further back layer upon layer, to expose what you are? You don't know your onions then.

G) Oh spare me your false lachrymosity. Rein in your crocodile tears, 'cos you won't catch me out with that hoary old wrinkle. Me and the crocs go way back, long before I patronised you. You forget, I'm so intimately familiar. I can descry they're just tears of frustration.

T) You, you don't even know you've been born. How, or why.

XXII.XI.MMI

We went on holiday. Abroad. A share benefit derived from the Peace Dividend. But only after the issue had been sealed once and for all with the blood of Omagh citizens. One final indiscriminate bomb blast, in our open air market. Trust Omagh to be the locus for a last great terrorist procurement. Two years on, 'the troubles' claimed he couldn't face the mawkishness of the anniversary memorials. I knew, rather, that he was struggling with the finality of the cessation of conflict this outrage had sealed. Being decommissioned and thrown back into the domestic realm. This was what he wanted to escape.

Lodged the kids with the grandee par-rentals. Parked the car at the ferry port and off we went. Didn't stray too far from home. Amsterdam. Somewhere sunny would have been nice. But he was applying the factor 69 block, sticking to what he felt he knew. Still, you couldn't dampen my euphoria. A crossing of the water is still a crossing off of the water. Seen it, walked it. Done it now. The reluctant oyster of a shrunken world opened up by a one-year temporary EU passport.

Supposedly they were just like us. Cut from the same flax. Ingrained integrity. A shared parochialism. But the Dutch couldn't recall. A haze of memory. Thickened up in a fog of cannabis smoke. Inspissated. And insipid. My husband was appalled. At their slatternly decadence, rather than my impulsive joining of them. Spluttering my way through a first ever toke, seamlessly purchased over the counter. While open-mouthed, he ordered merely coffee, but couldn't get an instant hit.

After the easy swagger of requisition and my practised nimble rolling, I was amazed at my inhibition before the flame's ordination. I mean, hell's bells, it's not like I don't know how to smoke. I inhale for Britain back home. But my throat reflexively closed up on me. Rolled up on my outwardly familiar roll up, having baulked at the foreign body smuggled inside. An illegal immigrant stopped by border customs. I was too scared to let go. My big moment of what, I don't know, epiphany? Rebellion? Self-assertion? Manumission? And I choked. Disjointed. The Dutch barflies giggled and sunk deeper into the very stressed leather of their most unstressed booth. Maybe this was Dutch humour and I was actually smoking ground tulip bulbs. No, looking at the bill of fare up on the blackboard, tulips were probably more pricey.

I could see my husband bristle as our new Dutch friends laid out their new world order theories. 'It'z zo cheap, the whole vied vorld's coked up to ze highballs.' 'Yeah, it'z like, ow you zay? A chumor?' 'Yeah tumor. Dash a gud vay of saying hit.' 'Tumor yes. But I don't mean bad wings with dis word. Just about ow it zpreads.' My husband shrinks into the heart of his stressed leather jacket, which itself contracts towards the nucleus of the stressed leather of his very stressed banquette. There was a film of scum forming on his forsaken coffee. 'Not only is ze coke its own bizness, making loaz of doe, but it in-fectz all hudder bizness-says. Zo many company directors har on it, affectz the way every body duz their bizness. Like widt ze freemasons.' 'Ja, it haz to right? For zure. Stocks and shares. Stocks und shares.' 'You haz to be hay-wear what time you make your bizness phone call to a director, if hez coked up. Zpecially to the States. You know, ze United States?' 'United by coke. Not pepsi you underztand?' 'It affetcz ze whole rhiddim of bizness. Peak times. Hupturns, downturns. And mood zwings. Flying bizness class.' 'Zo you got to be hay-wear of possible paranoia, when you negotiate ze deals.' 'He means ze big deals. But zey just mirror scoring off ze street. Szame mechanizm really.' (Giggles) 'Hay, ja, good one man!' 'Vhat? Which one I zay?' 'Small deals mirror big deals, zzzniff!' 'Ja, itz a good line alright!' 'A fine line.'

We left them to their prolonged bout of helpless giggling. I, marvelling at their command of my language, while, sick to his stomach, he silently berated them for their dereliction of duty. They tilted at, yet at the same time broke bread with the enemy. The boundaries were inchoate. He must stand firm. Yes, but where should he plant his feet, let alone his standard? Poor love. The great punch-drunk shadow boxer himself, all in a lather in the locker room. Because the world has turned on its axis, so that now even his shadow has deserted him. Nobody was interested in maintaining sciamachy any more. For now we were all phonies recruited to selfish pursuit. Wasn't I here, genuflecting before self-indulgence, under the guise of facilitating his fact-finding mission? This disastrous, cataclysmic embassy. I could see the dissolution in his knotted brow. The approaching tsunami of entropy, reflected in his wild eyes. Maybe the Peace Dividend wasn't worth paying out on after all.

I was neither powerful nor generous enough to save him. He was on his own. Plus ça change, plus c'est la meme chose. When in Amsterdam and all that. Anyway, I'd jettisoned my portmanteau of love, fretting about my children callously abandoned back home. Foisted on relatives who knew them well, but did not know the intricate shades of their routine needs and the detailed logistics inherent for meeting them. Infant pipelines under the oceans and beating round and round the mulberry harbours, seeking after permission to enter. The cat and mouse of misdirection, for what would be a weekend's worth of longest days for both parties.

So, though he did briefly clear his head of delirium at that evening's port of call, it was really I who garnered most realignment from the trip to the red light area. Girls, whey-faced women in windows. On display. Inside, looking out.

At the desirous. The hungry. With no thought for their own disposition. I stared and stared. Not at their sex, neither their degradation. Nor even trying to envisage what their view was through the glass. But rather at our geometric relationship. It reminded me of home. No matter what I did, my daughters too will make their own choices. And their ability to do so vouches me making a decent fist of my job. In this perverse way, all seemed right in the world. And in the cosmos. Everyone was properly constellated. Set back on their elliptical orbits. Except my husband of course. He'd passed over the event horizon. But I'd been solo-navigating for years by now anyway.

XIV.II.MMII

It strikes me, as I belatedly develop and crop my mental holiday snaps into these words, that I am not as perceptive as I celebrated myself to be. Our laughing Dutch coffee house cavaliers might well have been laughing at us. They too were not outside of what they purported to mock us for. Drew us into their sphere, while under their own satellite influence. A cocaine fifth column. Or line, anyway. They had probably dropped into the cafe for some weed, merely to take the edge off their high. To chill their iron wills. Winding themselves down, even as they were winding us up. And I think Andrew my husband gleaned this. He didn't know much, but that enabled him to trap in his searchlight anything that deviated from his enclave of knowledge. And that's a most useful acquired tool for survival. For weeding out the snakes in the grass. And since our separation, I no longer am so armed of course. I hate that. I hate people camouflaging the true nature of their motives. Dressing up their communication in subversive formality. Lacing the velvet glove over the iron fist. Language is such a traitor to truth. I wished I'd paid it more than scratchy study.

Then maybe we could have preserved the tooing and froing of intimate dialogue. Like sweethearts sharing a strand of spaghetti. Or lovers passing a tasty morsel from mouth to mouth with a kiss. Rather than what it unravelled into. Each word or statement, carefully drawn down from my cloven palate, then played around my tongue like a cyanide capsule. Deciding whether to snap down hard on it, or to rehusband it for the next encounter.

Do I miss him? I miss the hole he failed to occupy. Forever vacuuming/cooking/ironing/playing around his feet in domestic genuflection. Stopped up short by his clogging self-deletion, repeatedly taking me out of my drudgery. Jolting me back to attention. Adult emotional exchange. Give and take. Grievance and forsaken. Whereas now it's just me and the girls. So I have no iniquitous goad to snap me out of my menial consciousness. Rage downgraded to frustration. Emotionality to numbness. Incitement to impotence.

Journal-keeping merely feeds my despair. It too does not answer back.

○+   ♀   +○

There's a lot of crying coming from the hospital compound. I don't recall us having that many ante-natal admissions this time of year. Have the he-devils started the assault? Is it tear gas that they've launched? Twenty-two divisions and one crack platoon of Special Forces, Y-Troop. All just to X-sanguinate l'il ole me. They can see me off in this incarnation, but my spirit is already abroad. A ghost in their machine technology. My digital Echo to bring down their corporeal Narcissus. Jean's gene genie is out of the box. Is that tinkling glass I hear? Do they pour through windows on ropes, or are they already inside, smashing our test tubes and retorts? The only response they have. The only way

179

they know. Or perhaps it is the sound of Megan and Volte's chins hitting the floor. Closely followed by the lolling concertinas of their tongues, like toads after a fly. Since they have ever yearned for nothing less than to be hoist in the burly arms of a man, with the stencilled guarantee of 'Security' on the back of his jacket. Fawning over their saviours. Their knights in kevlar armour. The only way they know. Lickspittling all the way down the aisle. Is kevlar resistant to caustic soda?

But what are those dull thuds now? Like babies falling from their cribs. Yet I hear no screams. No padding of maternal feet to comfort and rescue. Such an air of serenity abounds – see, I kept telling them there was no call for a panic room. Just a ringing now in my ear, inside all of my head. Like a siren. Time to flick the digital panic alarm. No one will come to our aid in time to save our bodily selves. We lace our suicide pills not with cyanide but with viral DNA and we put it out to tender in the ether. Just as the message from a dying star only reaches our sensors when it is already turned cold in its celestial grave, our killers, or their posterity, will in turn have been rubbed out by the bounty hunters we here set in motion. And what bounty they shall inherit. Once they rid the world of you. For you defile all that is good. The smoke rises up from the crack in my door. To flush out us honey bees? But we've already blown the coop. Hatched the larvae who've devoured their way through the honeycomb of this colony and taken wing with their recipe for nectar. The reticulum of life is far too sophisticated for your battering rams and stun grenades.

You can't kill me. For I am a notion. An idea. Whose time might well have come. You cannot eradicate me. Nor delete me. You can't just circumscribe me in a body of text. Bury me as a footnote. I'm uninterested in authorship, attribution and copyright. Just so long as we start to copy right. How many generations of multiplication will it take to replace an entire species' instinctual way of behaving? You do the maths. I've got other fish to batter.

Sayanora!

Who goes there: friend or foe? Futile inquiry, for I know the helical code. Send you spinning, chasing your tail up blind alleys and cul de sacs. Where all matter's resolved. Packets of dancing lights, will-o-the-wisp. That way lies nothing but indivisible madness. I will collapse your sense of scale in upon you as you self-conflagrate. See how your callipers and geiger counters dead reckon that. Your own numbers will crunch you. This is Jeanie's message in a bottle to you all.

You have 1 new message.

XXVII.XII.MMIII

His lowliness descended upon me today. Offered to take both girls off my hands, down to the park and then up into town for a meal. After biting back my instinctual veto, and almost choking on the blood welling up from my impaled tongue, I nodded assent. Which he in his razor sharp keenness took as relish on my part. After shoeing up and shooing out the girls, with swollen, muffled yelps, I shut the door on them and braced my back against it, before any of our strung quartet could have a change of heart. I tracked the report of their receding progress, until I could register no further clamour.

I relinquished my station at the door and ambled into the lounge. Paused and listened very intently for the silence. But all I encountered was ear-popping voided space. I shook my head trying to clear the muzziness, but it just pounded back on the

181

inside of my cranium like an aggrieved neighbour. I glimpsed the sunlight dappling in through the nets and tried to bask in it. Shut my eyes and imagined I was a sundial. But the only horology was the thumping of blood being pushed though my temples, as I drew the staunch lids tightly over their charges. Close my eyes and make a wish. Or a potential migraine.

The very conjuration of this period of free time beyond all expectation had obviously dematerialised my sense of self. My desire quotient all spent. That panoply of things I vouched myself I'd revive, when I was awarded the luxury of parole. The stopper was most firmly back in the bottle. The jobsworth net curtains diffused any and all sensation of heat and light away from my face. I could always ruffle them with a prolonged scrub in the washing machine. I reopened my eyes and felt wooly. My neck was cricked with the alien angle of projection up towards the sun. Its sinew grossly unfamiliar with the extrinsic function of an easel; happily resiling its tendency for tilting as a grooved stanchion, for eyes scanning surface peril at floor level. The careful quotidian plotting of trine for mother and two daughters had been eclipsed. Disoriented, I had to flop backwards into an armchair for support, banging the back of my knee on the arm as I did so. My proprioception sensors were underwhelmed. Misfiring into the evanescence of unreciprocated sonar. Gagging on the white noise of insensibility. They, me, we were on our own. Thrown back upon one another. Naked and exposed. In a vacuum, spawned by the sudden displacement of all other matter in my solar system. I just didn't know where to put myself.

Moonwalked into the kitchen, to brew a coffee to ground me. Dedicated half the morning to watching the kettle boil. I chanced my gaze upwards again, as I circled my locked neck in petition for a pardon. A dark tangle of dust-laden cobweb clouded my vision. Gently swaying in the kettle's steam convection, flaunting itself on my dance ceiling, now that it had finally caught my eye and cut in. I swivelled round looking for something with a long handle when I checked myself. I was not going to squander my precious remission on housework. Be it precipitated directly in the wake of children currently on day release. Or indirectly by the neglect their duty of care propagates everywhere else around the house. After all, today was to be a lady's excuse-me, not a mother's ruin.

The kettle ceased its adhān and I was about to pour the scourging liquid into my ceramic mug of oblation when I noticed the spider herself had also heeded the call. I didn't doubt that she had only come to check on the integrity of her web, rather than be duped into believing she had captured a ready meal. In a momentary reversion to my former self, I silently applauded that she had been able to distinguish the steam's gentle tug on the silken fibres from that of light-winged prey. For I used to marvel at all things arachnid. Not being one of those women sent into a fit of the screaming abdabs by the slightest suggestion of furry, eight-legged, creepy-crawling (after all, the four pairs of smooth limbs of Amy and regressing Suzanne slithering around readily renders me prostrate). No, I maintain a sense of proportion. I've never regarded them as stealth bombers waiting to spring SAS-like from silk parachutes and storm any female embassy. Pound for pound, and though the spider has a fine battery of tricks and talents, I always believed I could make my reach advantage count. Besides, I used to delight in that whole silky death thing. Meditated, too, on the zen-like patience of the spider just sitting there, unattended in its antechamber, waiting. Maybe tugging a strand like a punkahwallah, just enough to entice some addict of motion. And how I used to revel in the delicious thought of the sometime grisly upshot of spiderly mating. A true and worthy illustration of vagina dentata.

No, I was proud that sister spider here has elected my kitchen to be her killing field. It was far from any intimation of dirt and decay. More one of nourishment and life. A cockroach, now that would presage breakdown and ruin. But spidey sweeps my kitchen clear of insects, just as I'd enlist a cat if ever a rodent invaded the parlour. We're allies here in a war of modest sterility. Sticking our callused digits in dykes to hold back each sullying surge. A sorority of sanitary homemaking. Spidey eventually pronounced herself content with the continued integrity of her snare and scuttled back beneath her parapet; the breastwork of a rent in my brickwork, a job needing a man, in this want of men. No, here she was emerging once again. Her own rhythms steeped in agitation. Yoked to a vaporous umbilical. Coming up empty eight-handed, she bowed her head as if doffing a hat and turned tail back into concealment. So sister sister too was deserting me. Clearly she had only padded down to see if my vibrations afforded her any prospect of mealtime. Just as my daughters might. Cupboard love, when I'm Old Mother Hubbard. And my doors only swing open one way. By now, the kettle had cooled its hackles during my abstracted contemplation. I didn't fancy undertaking the whole rigmarole again. Of the seething drawing her back out. Time to leave her alone. In peace. Like I hanker after.

What to do with this free time? Something uniquely for me. I was without a single aspiration. Just how to fill a hole darn it! So I retired to bed. The privilege of a lie down with no prospect of interruption. Except from the prowling dreams that lapped at my unguarded imagination. I woke up glazed behind gauze. My mind had posited a restorative repose, but it had been shellacked. Whether by prickings of dreams or its own internal audit as to how much deeper the salvage operation, after eight plus years of deprivation, needed to go. A root and branch overhaul. Root and branch. It immediately fired in its invoice and withdrew any further credit terms.

I could not open my eyes, they were so beaten. In the abeyance, I could smell the aroma of my own mucus. This made me queasy and I countervailed by scratching my arm. Hard. I could feel the chalky dryness of the skin. Not only the epidermis, but the desiccation of the corium beneath. Root and branch. It was as if I had been buried alive, stewing in the necrosis fermenting through me. Still I could not ramraid open my eyes. Is this all there is? An endless hibernation? After the kids grow up and skedaddle out of my life? Having pithed me, deseeded me and scraped out all my marrow. Until there's nothing left. Except consigning myself to my hand-crafted coffin.

How are we supposed to fill this lacuna called life? Surely we don't have kids just for the want of anything else to do to keep us occupied? If so, what was the point of spending Mesozoic eras unshackling ourselves from seasonal, procreative sex, if we now just tamely acquiesce in its primacy? The glaciers and scarps must be pissing their ultramontane slopes. As the harebrained turns turtle. The meek shall inherit each other. Well, their genes at least, as the biological imperative reasserts its dominance amidst the blank of blunted imaginations. Perhaps the Jesuits are right. After our rampant teenage years of lapse, inevitably we all scurry back to the fold with time. The human default is always set to reproduction. Especially here: 'Lie back and think of Ulster', where it's all about population. All about pedigree. Survival and reproduction. Survival as reproduction. Patently my eyes, though still yet to open, had acclimatised to the darkness within. They shot open and me out of bed. I took up my journal in the gloom. I don't bother turning on the light. Didn't you know I could read and transcribe braille? A throwback to my enlightened, caring-sharing, grow up to be a social worker phase. Pre-motherhood of course.

Why do we bring kids into this world? A simple enough question that we profess we ask of ourselves. For everyone surely knows what we mean by wanting a baby. Instinctively, emotionally, viscerally and, whisper it, intellectually. Sometimes, it may even inform part of the calculations. In those cases when the addition is actually cardinal and not a component of any zero-sum tactical game of division, subtraction or multiplication between the two warring factions involved.

Whatever the spark, the maternal prime mover soon kicks into gear and all bets are off. Though we may never entirely prefigure the nature of the regimen engendered, we women are not at a loss in meeting it. There are, of course, inevitable stumbles and first night nerves. There's that hospital-exiting, light-of-the-world-entering shawl, which like a wedding dress is stowed, but never employed again. Or you, perched on your knees by the Moses basket, hand divining the minute fluctuations of heat just above the new arrival. Trying to marry it with the idiosyncratic thermals of Victorian timber, marked by the creaks and groans you've spent half your lifetime filtering out of your perception. That one lasts for about a week normally. About a week less than the Moses basket itself, stashed away with the shawl and the complementary bag of products from the obstetrics ambulance chasers. As baby is admitted into the intensive care of your own bed.

But post that, it's basically a physical timetable of assimilated reflex responses. To instinctive procedures of food, evacuation, temperature, cleansing and sleep. You tune into a narrow bandlength of conduct. Your emotions, too are largely channelled for you, since she's just so damn helpless that you cannot help yourself or your hormones. She's tinkling all the right evolutionary keys and pulling your strings. The only dependent variable, perhaps, is a relatively straightforward factoring of the differential equation of your spent energy to your opportunities for recuperation. Of course I say this all now with the cool hindsight of having served a couple of stretches with the girls.

However, beyond having a baby, we have no real idea of what it's going to be like raising children. Society soon renounces its interest, much like the Pro-Lifers do beyond term. No more Health Visitors dropping round to drink your tea and dunk your digestives, once they have satisfied themselves your behaviour isn't criminally deviant. Having children. Little people in their own right. With their own timetables. Where the training doesn't run on time. The latitude is far greater. For two-way communication and relationship. But not of equals. You find yourself in a strange bartering economy where you need divest yourself of power but not of status. You have consciously to diminish yourself, return to when you were growing up, but with the boot on the other swollen foot. Of course in their position, you wouldn't have wanted to take instruction from someone like you either. You have to kick or pinch yourself before you open your mouth. Find levels of effacement, of humility, of non-competitiveness. To let them be themselves and mature into their own substantive identities. You have to save face and inspire awe at the same moment. Authorise them to explore autonomously, while somehow instilling into them notions of acceptable behaviour. So the love might be unconditional, but the surrender ought not be.

People here confuse love with fierce loyalty. They would, and do, act on anything to protect their children from any threat. And that indubitably is love of a sort. For the hazards of our immediate environment demand an upgrading of concern and over-involvement in the lives of our children. But it is not a quiet, intimate, interior, private, exclusive love. And there are most certainly conditions imposed on it. You come to see clearly that the overall Cause across the generations takes precedence over the individual lives in whose name it is perpetuated.

My chief capabilities as a mother lie in axioms such as 'responsibility' or 'duty', 'selflessness' and 'discipline'. 'Vigilance' is another all-pervading one. Precepts that too are venerated in the outside world. There, such words crackle with recognition, regard

187

and calibre. They are transmogrified into slogans and war cries. The very lifeblood of the Loyal, the epoxy resin that entrenches men together. The very logos of existence itself. In my microcosm, the same nostrums are shrivelled, shrunken. Mummyfied. Stripped of valour. I am responsible for one trifling unit. A single cell. The Home Front. Behind the lines, entrusted merely with an assignment for basic training. Stewardship rather than a commission. Men are glorious volunteers where I am a conscript. If the cell goes belly up, then no lasting damage is perpetrated upon the wider host. In this place of antipodal value, an absent father can be the most positive type of role model, if his absence was enforced by the authorities, or even the foe. But for me, as a mother, I am never deemed fit either for leadership, or teamwork. There remains only materdom. The men have been demobbed, sort of, but we've still to keep the home fires imitative.

People who should know me, or at least those sufficiently adjacent to express judgement, inform me that I should grow up. Meet my responsibilities. That I have no right to complain. Like it or lump it, I chose to become a mother. To bring children, tiny, helpless beings entirely beholden on me and my choices, into this world. Into my world. Yeah, I did. Like so many before me. More by luck than judgement and I don't just mean our incredible ignorance of the whole damn biological lottery. A baby isn't just for Christmas. Right result. Wrong reasons. Like lusting after a wedding – white dress, flowers, church, the whole shooting match – but not really being fit for marriage. It just seemed the right mission to pursue. Since that's what everybody else was doing, just go with the (menstrual) flow. But who cannot now turn round and proclaim their status as an infant provider to be less debilitating than the indentured serfdom of their squab, struggling towards independence?

I expected parenthood to change me. That's partly why I embraced it so readily. Thought it might grant me to cede gracefully to the natural order of things. To scrape the rough edges off the adolescent me. Motherhood as finishing school. So I would empathically see that my parents were right. To cease kicking against the pricks. To acknowledge that they did, in fact, a fine job in tempering me for society. To arrest my fantasies of cycling off into the sunset. To put a spoke in my wheel. To bring me back down to earth with the gentlest of bumps. But I just feel soiled. And concussed. The natural order of things is corrupt and stinking. I am still appalled by it all. By men with violence tattooed on their souls. Exported outside the house, into the wider community and then reimported as bonded excise taxing the sensibilities of our children. Ensuring the illegitimacy is perpetuated down the generations; as each is content to hand over the fight to the next wave, fully aware that they in turn will hand over to his own son and he will not cavil. Each blows out the torch wordlessly before they hand it over. So this thing, this neverending tidal system, flows through the generations. An excess of youth. A manipulation, an exploitation of naivety. A trade in slavish mentality. All I can attempt is to shield my daughters from its malignant heart. Yet that will then leave them unprepared for life's hard knocks.

It behooves us all to inoculate them from their own maturation. Somehow we must break the reproductive cycle, extricate our children in order to bring about our own liberation. Yet what can we neap women do? We have our peace movements already. They've garnered prizes as if mere home produce at agricultural shows. But we can't compete. Not really. We're running on empty. They returned the milk bottles that we nourished them on with petrochemical interest. The battle of hearts and minds is a phony war. Even if we baulk against our inclinations to give them a free rein, how can we prevent them from falling in with a bad crowd, when all crowds around here are resolutely aligned and unappeasably bad. I mean, Jesus, the other side have made it explicit, mutating into 'Continuity'. It may only be a splinter, but it will remain under our skins, worrying away at us. Like a canker, a thorn in our Adam's rib. It will never leave our side. The bindweed that spawns itself successfully with its chokehold on life. No matter how unstinting our nurture, our care, our compassion in seeking to perpetuate our own family continuity, the dark side of whatever hue also persists in its continuity of slaughter, indifference and ruthlessness. This is the minotaur at the heart of Ulster's labyrinth. Closing down the Maze Prison unleashes the monster into our communities scenting its tithe. Silencing the H-blocks merely transplants that unhappiest of letters back into my name and thus places us all under house arrest.

So even if I grapple successfully with the conundrum over our deepest motivation for bringing children into the wide world, the more benighted of us are bound to consider why we bring them into this stunted portion of it. Just now I am too damn tired to exercise my mind much about it. Too damn weary moreover to do anything about it. Too fucked even to fulminate further.

My eyes bolt open, my trunk swings from the bed in one taut flow. I hear the report of the girls even before the door chimes. Saved from further morbidity by the bell. And henceforth slump once again into damnation. I try to envision the make-up effect I'd be after, if I still pandered to cosmetics. The look of a confident, independent woman, who has just serenely engaged in a most delectable morning. Rather than the look of Euripides' Hecabe, yoked amid the shattered wreckage of Troy. I'll just have to use my facial muscles to feign the effect. Appears they too have stagnated without recent employment, since, on opening the front door my children burst into sobs. As he is smiling beatifically, I can only assume that it's more likely to be the scary clown face they're confronted with than anything he's wreaked upon them.

Shockworker Daddy had evidently put in a good shift. The girls were exhausted and put up no resistance to retiring early to bed. I resumed my journal, to put the counter-case. I was at a bit of a low ebb this morning. Caught at a vulnerable moment. First time without the children. Bit of a loose end. Time to sally forth, rather than be an Aunt Sally. This had better be good!

Er, um...

No, I've got it now. Of course, it's wondrous, thrilling, delightful, glorious and all the other shortfall words of high emotion, when the kids want to share their discoveries, their existence, their kinship and even their selfish selves with you. But that's not what I'm doing this for. I'm not in it for anything to redound to me. The most inflammatory thing anyone could and has said to me, is 'You must be very proud of them.' Which I acknowledge is a stock, throwaway compliment, but which makes me regard the utterers as clueless and unfit parents, be it of the past (relatives), present (alleged friends and peer group) or the future (those merely out on license). Pride, the one sin that I see eye to eye, tooth and nail with Ian Paisley on.

Proud of what precisely? That they're unfurling more or less according to the DNA programming inside them? In which case I have to acknowledge a debt of gratitude to my own parents that I'm not quite reconciled to just yet. Naturally I'm relieved my offspring are relatively healthy and vibrant and neither physically nor mentally in-valid, even residing here in Ulster. I'm not sure I would cope with it if they were. I couldn't even begin to imagine what it must be like to bring up a child who was. No, proud of how they're turning out to be such nice children of course. They're only eight and five for christsakes! I certainly don't want you casting judgment when they attain the 'I blame the parents' stage.

If they chance reflect well on me, even at this tender age, I hope it is not in my image (assuming the reciter of the poisonous phrase holds a positive image of me, like say one of my friends [but if they were truly a friend of mine, they would know not

191

to blurt said phrase in the first place]). The girls are emissaries for themselves. It is not in their remit to do me proud. I don't want to impose anything on their character, stain or not. Sure as hell my life isn't anything worth emulating. I'm just trying to make a decent fist of my job as homemaker. To the best of my ability, providing a stable and loving environment as a launch pad for their own evolution. I will harness everything I can and give of myself wholeheartedly towards this aim. Am I doing a good job? Who on earth can say? There's no assessment, review or promotion under the terms of this employment. What's the point anyway, when there's no professional pride to be gleaned from any job which garners so paltry regard and scant esteem in our society. Do I associate with any peer who would honestly comment that they were proud to know me? No, well then don't presume that on my issue either.

The defence rests, no doubt worn out after its eye-popping, crimson-tidal, if-I-had-an-Adam's-Apple-it-would-be convulsing rant. It went well I thought. Always accentuate the positive. There must be some reason. I'll give it some more thought. Till I come up with something.

It'll be a new year in four days time.

T) None of these sidebar confabs should matter a jot. Since, reputedly, I am the unequivocal mystery of life. The innermost secret. The key to your clandestine chambers and occult workings. Yet I am certain you will only come to intercede with me for your own private auguries and readings. I will be a blueprint consulted solely with reference to your own peculiar variation and defects.

A) From my print run of any two unrelated individuals, there may be one million different letters between them; about six disparate letters per gene. So no one's going to match this template you are directly unfolding. Following my well-worn system, every possible misprinted version is likely to exist throughout You.

T) So as each draws on my extensive library, with reference to their own vanity published volume, excavating after their genetic lot, you just know that your edition will be the one man jack that can't be located. It's out on loan already. Or out of print. Being updated. A new forward and some addendums. A new edition entirely if you have sired. Even as you go about living. For you necessarily engage my workings in any inquiry that pursues, well, my workings. Nor shall you ever fully know yourself, if you persist in treating me purely as a source of your debility. I am not just about dis-ease. I give you everything there is to have. I give you your innermost selves. I beg you not to spurn your own advances. Don't suffer your own intimacy to lie beyond you.

A) Look, maybe you can't fathom any point in existence. Even the imperative for passing on my code is necessarily blind. But can't you just descry the beauty in the construction? Perpend my model and swoon? I don't mean about the order and harmony of your material selves, for that's only form. Mere aesthetics. Multi-dimensional ergonomics and free-standing bridge building, remember? I acknowledge it's a bit of a head-scratcher, but it's well worth the effort. Your imaginations can evolve to the next level, free of any outside influences or compulsions. You can transcend mortality and truly appreciate what it is to be autonomous. And then, maybe, just maybe, you can begin to aspire to the meaning of relatedness.

T) There is no gene or group of genes coding directly for an arm or a finger, a reversible thumb, or even for two fingers stuck vertically up and wafted. That much you recognise. For you have already inferred most of my detail. But while you treat them as pathological, you cannot begin to court me. While you identify and tag each and every one of the genes that constitute me, you have no real conception of how they function. Who knows, maybe in time you will even have that charted. But like a mound of termites, or a colony of ants, how they correspond and work together defies your topography. You might be able to spotlight the particular activity of a small section, but in the main you can only see a heaving, pulsating host.

A) I exist as, and through, the entire panoply of relationship. I have, and am, a whole lattice of interactions. I accord genes on different chromosomes that reach impalpably across the divide to communicate with one another. I bear other genes which seem in permanent slumber. Their particular, virtually undetectable function, to nudge awake a silent partner, while rolling over undisturbed themselves. Or to reach out in their dream state and gently shutter the lens of the scope of their watchful compatriots. How these genes combine to achieve the right conditions to muster a certain functioning protein unfolds along an extensive and involved chain of interdependence. But they are not automata, following a preset programme. There is no chain of command. No queen awaiting the apotheosis of the war effort for her fertilisation, which is where your similes fall short of bridging understanding.

T) This is more a cascade of effects. A Mexican Wave of modular activity. An explosion of generation, emerging from an easy-going, back-slapping and high-five, jiving co-operation; gene-protein-cell. Their effortless kinship. Sure the genes do contain a programme, a programme that can generate any species ever known or lost to man. And after egg-sperm union, they divide and multiply to produce identical stem cells, with the potential to produce any type of specialised cell that may be called for. But as to which they produce? I leave that to the field operatives. For truly I am a republic.

A) In my land of the free, all cells are born equal and have the opportunity to pursue their own destined manifestation. I have no chosen elect, nor those pre-ordained to a certain outcome. Pattern and structure just evolve through my devolution. My de-evolution. Each constituent may take initial instruction from some branch of my stock, before devising its own choreography of chemical valence, gradient and clustering, in order to aggregate its own local troupe of permanent dance partners as part of the great ensemble.

A) And from this medley arises the most diverse, specialised and harmonious common weal. Every piece of the microcosm contains every other piece, since they all contain me. Each gene is reliant on every other of its kind for a commodious outcome, which maximises all of their chances of being passed on. Every cell knows of its fraternal origins, no matter what its current status. Each recognises that it has had to work equally with its neighbouring cells to foster their locality. Yet you who can scarce tolerate neither difference nor stratum have little chance of encapsulating this marvel. Your diagnostics have no insight. Your mental matrices and linguistic iron maidens squeeze the very life out of this, well, life. This Being. Sublime? Ethereal? Do me a favour! Within our macrocosm, the Babel Tower is a stellar construction. It's how we maximise our potential for creating everything. Cover any suit. A specialist on call for any eventuality. A maven to meet every responsibility.

T) How can you perceive any of this when you do not even comprehend that you are part of the nexus? For are you not fundamentally enmeshed in the structure through your axis with it? Your primary senses inform the body, just as it too reports back to them. Your recording equipment also relies on these intrinsically compromised senses. Analogue or digital, it makes no odds. Neither can wholly remove you from the very thing you are investigating.

A) Now, were you to suspend your aware self and somehow diffuse your consciousness, so as to attune simultaneously with every one of your cells, then you might be getting near. But could your entrenched sense of identity handle such a retreat? To acknowledge that you are just a discrete articulation in time? A chance singularity, changing in very minor ways along your surface, but your essential core remaining unchanged since the moment of DNA fission within the milky way of your mother's womb.

T) Such sacrifice would be worth your while I believe. For were you to embrace me truly as a dance partner, then just like me you would possess, in potentia, all knowledge and all possible being.

A) Take the plunge one step further. Strip yourself down fully.
A) Switch off your conscious, reflexive self entirely and you
A) could join me in cheating time, space and death by
A) luxuriating in our gene pool of all possibilities. Where
A) there is no reason, no definition. No you and no me for
A) that matter. Not even relationship pertains here. Just
G) pure, undifferentiated existence. I can sense your
G) disembodied nervous system convulsing at that one.
G) How can such a thing be deemed existence? Because

G) we prevail. We are continually sustained through
G) temporality and space and we have recourse to the
G) configuration of matter at any point. Can you just lie
G) perpetually in state, careless to all future dispositions?
G) Unaware and unconscious, yet brimming with surety?
G) This is the biggest wager of your aleatoric being. And the
G) moment you try and collect on your pay out, you lose!

XVIII.VIII.MMIII

A lesson in pain and suffering today. Though I was the pupil, rather than Suzanne. A lessening of her suffering, as she graduates from primary bale to secondary scrapes and grazes. Only serving to heap greater psychic pain on me, as I am held back and made to repeat the past year of torment in my head. Prior to the current passing out ceremony, whenever she came into harm, the anguish she felt was raw, unadulterated, untreatable and, incidently, my fault of causation whatever the external reality. With the pain siren howling, and depth charging the slight friction of blame, I would crank myself up into hysterical emotional overload. 'She'll bleed to death. She needs stitching. Get a compress on it till I can get her to the hospital. Call 999, curse 666. Will someone not deliver us from this catastrophe?' Well, no longer.

Now she knows to wash down the wound even as she waves away my wringing hands. Then to toddle off and get a plaster from the first aid kit. How to adroitly work the adhesive protective paper off and to line up the lint over the gash. The trickling blood does not faze her, for she is all cool application.

Yet she is far from detached, for she constantly explores the clotting process. Dragging me to our reappointed internet (at the school's behest), in order to trace every interlocking ply of the coagulate weave. And also through her own forays, unpicking the scab, back through the clot, past platelets and fibrin, seemingly unsatisfied until she has located the enzymic source of her red Nile. And thereby I am plucked into redundancy. Standing alone from me, she now looks to herself and her own body. My hysteria is cut off. Set adrift. There is no place for it to go, to drape itself. To lavish like a cataract of engulfing love. I tamp myself back down. Hysterectomy of my emotions. My daughter the locum gynaecologist. Only, could the self-surgeries possibly have been botched? Wherein hope, I lash myself to the mast of despair.

What if she's punctured too many epidermal layers? That the laceration's too deep, or gouged through too many inconvenient nooks and crannies to be smoothly resurfaced by the clot's chain gang of conscripted fibres? There they would be, backed up at the lip of an untraversable hollow. Chafing at the bit, angry red in hue. Tendrils extended over the gorge in vain, grappling for a hook beyond, with which to establish purchase. But where they are met with nothing. Holding back the press of their brethren with a flabelliform sweep of outstretched filaments, one plucky member suspends himself a line in an attempt to span the breach. But he just hangs pendulously, beyond redemption and his lariat is severed, consigning him to the void. His fellows froth and writhe in their stranded sterility. Still the lurching impress from behind. Will no one give the signal? They knot and grind in their constriction. It's getting ugly. Would then the fluffy pink french polishers sign off the work and just stretch an ill-fitting flap of strangulated skin to cicatrize? And thereby only italicize the blemish? For there are those scars that fade quickly and those that mark for life. Brought about by her involuntary clumsiness and unimagined consequence, and my voluntary inconsequence and all too imaginable ineptitude. My poor baby. No more of doctors and nurses. Now we can converse about cosmetics, covering up and masking.

G) I am a singularity. A singular creativity. Multi-faceted, infinite combination. Yet my sedulity is to one end and one end only. That end being me, that I have no end. This is my sole impetus. This is the limit of my involvement. I have no interest beyond that. Though I permit anything and everything else in that interest, it is outside my auspication to get hung up on which apportioned bundles of me are packaged into billets of you. I am merely cognisant, that such temporal clusterings take place in order to conduct me across time. Since that way I conserve my plenitude. To proliferate on into perpetuity. For you are my torch-bearers. My movers and shakers. My stable-hands. My tidal flows. Your existence ensures that my gene pool is stirred and thus prevented from becoming stagnant.

C) So come on in, the fluid's lovely. Juicy and full of sap. Just dive in. Head first and eyes closed. Give yourself up to the inchoate, the seething and effervescing. Surrender both the horizons of your despair and the depths of your dreams. All is indeterminately rife here.

A) And if the withdrawal of being is too crushing to bear, then you are free to re-immerse yourself periodically in life. Welling up in my sharply roiled waves, breaking on the earth to be deposited as sediment. As gathered parcels of me. Re-align for terra firma, not by seeking after perspective, but by trusting to my ferment. An infusion from the collective species-memory, as you churn and sputter among its pother. The scraping of the particulars of time and place as you wash up on the beach. One lives, one dies, having touted your intellect and desires, then revert to my bosom having passed us on in the process. Your entire existence is as a gaseous bubble in me. An eructation.

A) I do not say this as self-aggrandisement, rather to make you apprise your true scale in all this. You see, though I earlier postulated the relationship of all my genes in order to fabricate cells that agglomerate to you, ultimately, I'm afraid, you can't even hold on to relationship as a working model. (See how the swashbuckling ambition of your sharpshooting comparisons now lies buckled and spiked before my oblique subtlety? Small bore.) At source, fundamentally there is only temporary, random contiguity.

CG) You demand yet further proof? When I can espy the seismic tumescence of your indicator needles, rapidly shrinking to a flatline? Okay then, I hope this is still gentle enough to let you down by. I am contained in my entirety within every imperceptible, microscopic piece of you. The whole of me, folded into the membrane of each one of your individual cells. Imagine that. Can your egos handle that? And that fleck which is but one unit within any single cell can generate another whole you. How can you wrap your grinning gauges and Cheshire cat calibrators around that?

AT) After all, you constantly struggle beyond any scale of 1 to 1 complementarity. Look at your defeated physics, where all matter is fragmented further and further into invisibility and implausible, but desperate probability. Yet I must indisputably remain a subunit of life, of however humble a size. Whatever insignificant dimension. You seek after my data, when I am dribbling matter. You solicit me as matter, yet I only yield raw data. I am quantum and so you will never know me. Whereas you, you are encoded pre-programmers of choice. Hunting after my programming code when it has already expressed you, encapsulated you, iterated you and processed you. And executed you unutterably.

CT) While the resolution of your lenses and language grows progressively finer, still my precise, arrayed lore forever remains beyond reach. Though your analogies are elegantly cast, they are misshapen. The comparative scale of what they purport to match is out of proportion. Your metaphors cannot bear their load. Or their shredded lode. Such figurativeness refines meaning, like a hod finesses bricks. It can but yield an abridgment. A bridge straddling two incongruent magnitudes, two dissociated consciousnesses. A disjunction across both scale and time that cannot be spanned.

AG) I'm awfully sorry, see, but your concoction of re-envisioning, of contriving new dimensions and devising fresh language is misconceived. You are incontrovertibly matter, yet your entire conceptual apparatus is purely symbolic. The way you live your life and reflecting on what that means. Your sense of taste, refinement, wit and discernment are all your own. That output of your mind, which favours orderly systems constructed from motley symbols, representations, assumptions, appearances, projections, impressions and approximations. All of which, to COIN a FIGURE of SPEECH, has nowt to do with me.

GT) Let's run this up the flagpole and see if it's half-mast or half-cocked. Say one of your shining lights has an insight. They mentally visualise some new relationship, or geometrically track a new arrangement from within accepted knowledge. They desire to impart this inter alia and go about embodying it in illustrative imagery. In order to delineate this imagery, they reach back into their palette of grammatically modulated sentences, which are starchily catenated from prescriptive words. No matter how intricately meshed one's mental matrix of inner thought, language is mulishly linear; one word faithfully plodding along after another. Such words emanate from syllables, themselves basted in alphabeticised characters. Already I detect an elision here, since the phonetic sub-parts of syllables and letters in no way corresponds to the meaning of the complete word unit. So you see, by now language has significantly dislocated him/her from the original purity of their aesthetic, abscised from the precision of their geometry. Critics, borne out of whatever motivation, will inevitably challenge the original thinker on, and through, his/her circumscriptive employment of language. With all its built-in latitude, shade and ductility. Maximal flexibility, minimal exactitude. And so this duel of logic and ratiocination is shifted on to an arid linguistic plane. And all aspiration is extorted from the thinker, bureaucratised to death by having to explain him/her-self. Each layer of conversion, no matter how lightning fast a reflex, impresses more deadweight across the diaphragm of thought. Each transcription renders a poorer quality reproduction of the concept. And this is how you would indite (indict?) (interdict?) me! I am as far removed from my miserable abbreviation as this putative thinker's insight is from the meaninglessness of a single phoneme incorporated in.it, or even the first capital majuscule initiating the textual onslaught. I have been truncated into a child's set of toy building blocks, with one of the etiolated characters ATGC on each face. And from this you would confront immanence square on? This is the material (matériel?) of your modern-day Babel Tower? Stop it, my X-chromosomal ribbed sides are going to split with hilarity. There's a sincere, unmediated reaction for you.

AC) Cards on the table time. I'll show you mine (to the best of my non-lingual ability), if you accept the plangency of yours. While there may well be misreadings within me, they never convey meaning or intent. It is just inaccurate replication, a typographical error, a pinched character. A chance occurrence, answerable and beholden to no externality. Your errors are systematic. The questions you pose are off-kilter. Your parameters too chokingly flaccid. You can never attain precision in what you seek. The cleft between the reality you structure and the reality that seemingly follows the slippery laws of cleft matter is an abyss into which the entire ecology of your planet is subsiding. Me, in the stocks rather than on them, evidently now included.

GC) The serious mistranslation, therefore, lies between you and I. Would-be transmitters both, yet we cannot possibly parley with one another. For I have no discourse at all. What then are you currently reading? Or who perchance? For are you not the intelligent being in all this rather than me? I wrote no sonnets, nor composed any sonatas. I am rather the art of the possible. All the synaptic springboards and conscious connections that could be forged. I am probability, facilitating the most likely tramlines of reasoned cogitation along which you operate. But remember, I must also be the long shot of improbability too. All those unthought thoughts you have failed to put together. The pathways so least trodden as to remain virgin soil. Who would have thought? Not you, that's for sure.

TG) 'Tis not I making these beseeching recommendations to your genus. Whoever heard of a deep throat without larynx, pharynx or even tongue? (I am but dewy-eyed unripeness, with my larynx undescended so I can drink and breathe simultaneously; you are the ones breastfeeding me towards growth and maturation, cooing all the way.) You interrogate nothing but those dark parts of yourself, when you shine your spotlight upon my features. The chittering whispers and sepulchral resonances are your own dissonant reverberations. Supra-lingual in all likelihood, but they do certainly run deep within you. It is time to address yourselves. Stamp me unopened, return to sender.

GA) These are the outpourings of your own consciousness, acknowledged or not. The questions you might, or should be asking, as you launch into me with your febrile spurs. To what end do you undertake your inquiries, when you can journey within your imaginations to probe the answers in your mind? I recline prone beneath you, as just another one of your all-encompassing, all-conquering, all-singing and all-dancing metaphors (metaphor, that temporary secondment of anglepoised illumination. In order to tack a shadow on to the opaque object under scrutiny, so as to assimilate some shade of legibility {there, I've been dying [literally/metaphorically?] to interject that}). Only I'm a bit closer to the bone, the marrow, the cell and the protein. Your species' erudition and memory are the sacrosanct text, not me. It is to be found in the pneuma and the psyche, not the plasma and gist. Assail me and you irrevocably ravish your own integrity, triturate your own sculpted truths.

GC) I don't exist, see. There is no such thing as a genome, nor even genes as discrete units of hereditary. Until, that is, you imagined me into useful being, nominated me to solve the predicaments of your carnality. But this is going about arse over tit. It is not the way I approach things. For me, as I'm endlessly repeating, there is only replication. You too may nakedly lust after this but, alas, siring is adulterated reproduction. Inheritance, not immortality. Admittedly, at present, you and I dovetail through this affiliation, but we are coincidental, not coeval. My inner drive is not your inward drive. I navigator and you matelot merely share this passage, this berth, this bunk bed, with me on top. Give me my leg up will you?

TC) I do not consciously seek to obscure meaning. For there is no meaning other than what you choose to ascribe.

T) There is to be no revelation from my unscripted scripture.

G) And that is my (your) final word (aggregated symbolic linguistic code) on the matter (issue) {you and I are both matter, yet only you issue}.

CGAT) See ya! Wouldn't wanna be ya!

XII.X.MMII

I'd viewed it as a dotting of the 'i's and a crossing of the 't's. A chance to to alleviate an itch and put the tin lid on it for once and for all. I didn't foresee that I'd be the one needing a tin hat, or that my eyes would be crossed and spotted by the most excruciating tease ever.

The internet's a wonderful thing to behold, if only I had anyone the other side of the world with whom to correspond so cheaply. I half hoped, desired that he had. That there had been a driving force, rather than an inertia behind our marital drift. If he was having an affair, virtual or otherwise, then I could bring about a swift termination of our trial separation. In my compulsive manner, I had wanted complete severance. But he skillfully interposed the children. So that their fissile fate serried

205

all four of ours. Separation was no real hardship, but apparently he needed to trial out the workaday details of a reconstituted relationship with the girls, rather than just elucidate visiting rites. My ordeal was the open-endedness of it all. There seemed to be neither timescale nor measurable objectives through which to progress to the next stage. A three amp family had just blown its safety fuse and now threatened to linger on unearthed and flickering. The twilight of a shadowplay.

But, scroll through his e-mails and bookmarks as I might, I could find not the slightest modicum of warm-blooded sentiment to match his inflated fervour for all things anti-Catholic. He was off the hook as I teetered on it, hitched tighter and tighter as I twirled aimlessly round the leash of militant Loyalism. This was their surrogate arena now. A virtual violence succussing the airwaves, reaching out through our monitors to concuss us all as before.

However, I did chance on one net encounter that yanked me up short. Or long. Why he had appointed it iterative enough to bookmark was beyond me. Maybe for some light relief between all the hyper-spaced, hyper-texted, hyperantipathy. Not that a site offering refuge for battered women is a cause for relief to anyone, other than those who find sanctuary behind its actual walls. Maybe he was being ironic, though I think that will always remain beyond him. I know I could be a bit of a cow at times, but I don't think his treatment at my hands could ever be said to diminish him. Not to such a level where he felt it worthwhile to check out the equality of opportunity for spousal asylum. More like he was identifying with the bad guys, getting off on the abuse recollections of the victims. Not that I could really find any first hand, fist, or blunt object reports. I was in the process of perusing the founder's mission statement when the words started to deliquesce and welter in front of my eyes. Oh well, that was that then. Some glitch in the programming or so I thought.

Salvador Dali might have twizzled his moustache approvingly at the visual liquefaction I was being presented with. Think I was up a blind alley anyway. The nudge-nudge, wink-wink nature of our computer setup, cadged invariably after some software had fallen very hard from the backs of lorries, on to elasticated pre-stressed concrete, meant that even if I credited him with the nerd nous to wipe his tracks clean, the computer configuration simply was not up to it.

As I listlessly watched the digital decomposition in front of me, I could not determine whether the letter sewage was being flushed out into the blue reservoir at the foot of the screen, or if the cobalt tide was actually advancing so as to wash over the alphabet shingle. The frame speed and resolution quality of the pixels was so low as to jounce, er, rather to slink one back to the happy daze of Space Invaders. The ziggurat of stunted motion was enough to make you travel sick.

I was about to disembark from my excursion into the yonder when the blue swathe was suddenly (relatively speaking) stopped in its hobbled tracks. And after a tension-laden incipience, in which I wondered whether the whole gestation had done for the computer's circuits, the aquamarine draggled wearily back into recession. Good, there was life in the old mongrel yet. More than that, something now seemed to be roiling the grizzled blank scarp of the screen. Indeterminate squiggles and strands protruded their wormlike nodules from beyond the opaque bilge and began to enjoy and flex their animation. I wasn't certain that it was them incarnate, rather than their liquid crystal trails across the screen, that I was following. But gradually, due to my unprimed perception rather than software sag this time, I realised that they were ever so slowly shaking off their saturation and coagulating into new anatomies. Eat your heart out David Attenborough! They were reforming into letters. The dismembered characters were reconvening themselves. Hooray for her! She's back on the airwaves and refuses to be silenced! The mission's back on track. Her oeuvre will out.

I tried to pick up the thread of where I'd been cut off from her impassioned appeal, but could not quite relocate myself. The text had changed ever so slightly. She must be live and on line here and now! With her fingers airily caressing the keyboard, she had planted her feet in the blue nowhere and turned back the tide. Cocking a snook at King Canute and all other bloated male egos!

A frisson of profane delight started its vertiginous roll down the cresta run of my vertebrae. Until the screen shuddered and trepanned my pleasure, leaving me unhinged. While I slumped, each letter was turning tail on its axis, as if scalded. Here and there, one might shear off into the soothing cold plunge of the void. The arrayed red-coated monograms around them buckling a little, as if to suture the breach of missing vowel or diphthong. Now detachments of surds were silently giving up the ghost and scuttling off into oblivion. Next a syllable topples, denting the lineament like a gap-tooth. Before it was gradually excised into full root canal surgery as whole phalanxes of words cave in. It was swingeing and all-pervasive. Seems like she had been successfully gagged after all.

Or overwritten. Since, clearly, even hyperspace abhors a vacuum. For filtering down the screen on fibre optic grappling irons and gossamer rope ladders, column after column of letters marched in. Leapfrogging over one another in their glee, as if racing to be first to occupy the vacated matrix. Was this a service provider reclaiming a squatted URL address? If so to what end, other than a point to point of proto-colic principle? For these new characters spelt out nothing but nonsense. The dead letter drivel of programming speak. Cold and metallic grey, unlike the spectacular livery of her florid prose. I had a virtual tear in my eye.

I prepared to bring down the curtain on the whole non-affair. Partly to dismiss the long engaged streetlamp rubbernecking directly through my window. Poking its flaring nostrils into my rubber stamped and silicon verified state of idle loneliness. But foremost in my mind, I was determined to pull the plug for good on this dissolute bazaar. Despite what I always steeled myself with in reference to the girls, clearly there was such a thing as too much information. Too much access. Too much disclosure. What used to remain in his cups down at the pub, he had been able to carry out home with him. A marketplace to trade spite into more far reaching corners than mere spit and sawdust could reach. A whole brewery of hate in the still of this bedroom. Time to ditch the Red Hand veined Feng Shui.

It wasn't through him spending so much time wedded to the Net that had made me feel neglected. It's more like when he finally decamped of an evening and sat in our non-chat room downstairs, quietly smouldering, that alarm bells clanged. My internal fume detector was tripped. Whether his nightly hate-in ratcheted up his animosity towards me, or that he already bore such pent up malice that he disgorged it into virtual violence in order to head off the real thing, I wasn't certain. But I wasn't going to hang around to sift forensically through the ashes of a conflagration. That's when I asked him to leave. I might well be constantly infuriated with life, but I couldn't risk being around someone who was positively incendiary about it. After all, there were the the girls to think about too.

So now we're under new management. And it's time for a ritual incineration of a different sort—

But – she was back! Her lexical dragoons effortlessly retaking the high ground of the screen. Sliding down and sideswiping the incumbents. Rattling over letter for letter, like a train destination board flittering a new imminence. I almost applauded. The show was back on the road. A differing version yet of what had gone before. It had the thinness commensurate with being re-keyed in real time, but some of the constructions were also reedier, suggesting an earlier, less honed draft. Maybe we were going backwards in time. Why not, this is virtual reality after all?

Now some more personal stuff was drilling across my screen. Material I hadn't seen before. She certainly came across as one wild, old bird. I'd first-hand evidence, twice removed, as to her tenacity that's for sure. And then once more, without warning, the countercharge. Her words started to wither. But I knew I only had to abide an intermission. She'd assuredly return unsullied and unabashed. For I tumbled that this was smart bombs and virus protection; firewalls, Trojan backdoors and catflaps. Digitised interdiction. With both parties probably absent. Off having a well-earned cup of tea while they waited to see the effects of their latest thrust or parry. I brewed myself a sustaining coffee and toasted our imagined triune in this spellbinding war of censorship. All texts should be written like this. Then the reader could be truly interactive. Our up or down-turned thumb would in actuality bear critical import. Authors would truly earn their corn. The lading of their words directly transmittable. Delivered through the reader's white-knuckled joy sticking.

The night proceeded to unfold in this fashion. Sometimes the purge and reinstatement would be in monotype, others by linotype, as the varying strategies were employed. But each occasion afforded me more and more detail about her past life. I was hooked. I felt I was privy to an immune system repulsing an invading bug. Found myself rooting for a benign diagnosis. Some of the things I found positively upsetting; she'd obviously had an awfully blighted life and was determined to publish it. They couldn't break her.

By the break of day it dawned on me that this war was somewhat internecine and wholly nasty. Each occasion that they managed to score away another layer of her fabric, she'd exhibit further pentimento upon pentimento. Each palimpsest they impressed, she managed to copperplate her monograph over the top. It was as if they were trying to eradicate every last vestige of her existence, through to that egg in her mother's womb, back to her very conception (Freud would have had an orgasm!). This would go to the bitter end. Or some vicious eternal loop. I sent an e-mail to her website expressing my support. I didn't expect her to have the time to open it.

Since I was filled with the presentiment that this was somebody else's life flashing before my eyes, it occurred to me that perhaps I should do something to preserve it as a record. However, on each occasion that I managed to squirt some paper between the rollers of the printer, the text had decomposed its legibility and the printer peeled off what appeared to be a laboured test run. Even when prepared, with paper in place, waiting for the next manifest, the resultant synchronised print-off was still garbled gibberish. Had the forces of darkness secured the printer outpost? Or was the printer garrison still holding out, desperately broadcasting its coded warning as to the original errata? Or had it gone native and veered off into its own hallucinatory discourse? The period for her words to re-establish their cursive flow, was now becoming longer and longer. I decided to write some of them down. Contracted wrist giving way to longhand, as I reflexively moved for the weight of my journal. Albeit according her a fresh page at the back.

As I launched into amanuensis mode, I would be holed each time by the gobbledegook guillotine. Shredding meaning. Splintering intelligibility. I made myself memorise more for the record. Then dictate to myself from the afterglow imprinted upon my side of the retinal wall, once the image had faded from in front of me. Thus I knew my transcription would not be a pure one. More of a cross-hybridization. So be it. Amy's plaintive greet-the-day mewl brought a natural end to my assignment.

I rose to confront the day chock-full with purpose, stale from having spent a night under the tiles and pressed against the eaves. This time the monitor screen was wiped clear at my hand, rather than that of any second or third party.

I returned to my journal that night. Re-read my latest (borrowed) entry, anticipating it to be an annotation of the rest of the entire preceding contents. A foreword or afterword. A dedication. An acknowledgement of something or other. An imprimatur. But it failed to read that well, or interestingly, even. More akin to some dream you noted down before returning to sleep, only to read it through stupefied the next morning. It was no dream though and I'll have the dial-up bill to prove it right enough. I guess you had to have been there. Which neither of us ever were really, I suppose. The e-mail bounced back to me as undeliverable.

I didn't return to the website. I don't know if her digital Cheshire cat smirk managed to prevail. I unplugged the computer, faithful to my vow to reverse previous vows. I tried ripping out her page from my journal, but she put up her customary catfight. Eventually she was gone from my life, but she took with her half the folio's anchoring twine. My journal now hung frail and played out. It no longer had an aroma for me to inhale. I told you she was a tenacious old bird. In union we'd not grafted. Only in divorce. Still, that was an advance on my ex-husband. He'd barely merited an entry, let alone a dedicated page.

XX.XX.Something or other I've been intending to do this for ages. But there just never seemed to be an opportunity. Now though is the time, since Suzanne's off helping with the flowers for the Harvest Festival, while Amy's off harvesting her grandparents for some CD-Rom or other down the shops. I need to sort out my journal. I'd made a few daily jottings after my internet night of the lone wives, but the tome soon dismantled itself irreparably. The leaves of my life fluttered down in one fell swoop and fanned out across the floor. Now my own narrative lay fractured, and other than scooping the pages in a bundle and slipping the copy within the covers for safekeeping, I did nothing to reorder it.

And so it would have stayed. A relict of the former me, had I not now occasion to consult them in some pressing practical matters. For life has slithered on.

I'm unsure if Stormont is presently in session, or whether it is whiling away one of its accustomed suspensions. Don't know how the Unionists have the temerity to claim the high moral ground when a clump of them kept their hand in with some pipe-bombing and intimidation of four-year old girls on the way to Catholic School. That played well on global TV. And we're supposed to have all the Grand Masters? I don't know, maybe that happened a long time ago. I no longer keep up with current events. Omagh is quiet enough anyway. The planet is definitely heating up, no matter the protestations of the authorities. I warned you about those buried nappies coming back to scourge us! I've no idea on the current state of our erstwhile holiday beach, since we've not been back (which makes me believe it was the provenance of my ex-husband, rather than part of my family's legacy. Another thing I can't clearly recall).

Even managed to pop on through the tunnel over to Eurodisney. It was predictably tawdry, but then hey, it's for the kids really. Next stop the Holy Land, but things are looking a touch precarious there right now. Imagine a girl from Ulster weighing that up as a singular risk a generation ago! The lumber room has finally been done up. As a nursery. I've been seeing this fellah and we're expecting. I had plenty of misgivings at first, but he's dead keen. Says he's going to be really hands-on. He did the decorating. Relaid a new carpet.

Why put myself through all that again I ponder? The prospective flush I was anticipating was that of menopause, rather than pregnancy. Hormone replacement rather than revivification. Will it bring us closer together? That presupposes an intimacy gap that needs plugging. Even if that's the case, then how can a child possibly add to any partnership, when the division of attendant labour is so implacably unequal? Whatever good intentions he lays out before me.

And why do we persist in thinking in this manner anyway? As if we expect our issue to betoken some future hope, when all they embody are our shoddy, rehashed genes. Further reinforced with our rehashed parenting. How are they meant to shine as a beacon, from out of the seam of our own deeply flawed lives? Since we are their formative and guiding influences, are they are not condemned but to repeat our mistakes? Our wholesale exporting of imperfections, indicts them to similar shortcomings in their lives. And they will inevitably breed them on into the future. So the cycle is largely unbroken.

But none of this is why presently I need recourse to my journal. Ultimately my emotions will rule on whether I issue this new baby, full of grace, or full of rage. And sure, we will take soundings from assisted memory. Admit expert submissions from Suzanne and Amy. But there again, neither Omagh nor the world are shaped in one's own image as I perceive it. Suzanne and I independently both reached this epiphany around the same time. Even if we momentarily turn our backs on the exteriority of great beauty or of relationship, it will still persist when we turn back to gaze on it. So we will not be disappointed like Lot's wife and dissolve into salty tears. That malevolent logic of the Republican School of Adams, McLoughlin and McGuinness, whereby a sniper or bomber only had to get lucky once, whereas the quarry had to remain lucky everyday, perversely infers a more generous truth; I gaze upon my children and regard that every day, indeed, I am blessed in their presence. All emanating impalpably from two miniscule cells, egg and sperm. And now, it appears, I – we – have been bestowed favourably upon once again. There's always room for some more wondrous, sublime beauty in the world. Here's hoping.

```
AATGAGCACTATACTATTACATTACATTACCGTTATACCC
GAAATGCCAGGGTATCACACTGATGCTATTTAATTTATTTT
CCTGGGCCTGCTCATTACACTCACCAAAATAGGAGGGGC
ATGTGATTAGGTGACTTACTACTATAGTATACTATATGGTT
CATGGCGGAGCTTTTATATATAATATAAAAAAGGGGGGG
GGGGCAACGATCTAGACGCTGGATCTGCGATACGTATGC
GATGCTAGTCAGGTATGGATAGCCATGACTCGAGCTAGC
CAGATCGATGCACCATGCTAGCTAGCTATTGGACACAGT
ACATAAGCATCAGAGCTACAGTATACGATGACATGACATC
TGCTGCTACATACATCATGCCATACCATACCGAGACTACC
AGAATCAGTTACGATCAAGGATGAGAGTCATACAGATACA
GTAAGACAGTACCCATCAGTACATGAAGGACGGGGGATT
ATTATCATCAATCAGTACGATCGTCTTGCTGCTAGTCGAT
CGATCGTACATAAAAAATCGATCAGTCAGTACAGTTTTAC
CCGGGGACTAGAGTACATCAGTGTGTGCTGATCATGTGT
GTACGTACTGATGATAAACGACCCATTTAAGATACGTACT
AGCACAAAGTTTCAGGAGAGAGAGAGATAGATGACTACG
TACAGCCATGCATGACGATCAGTACTCAACTAGATACGG
GTAGCAGTACAGGGATCAGTCTAGATCGTGCGATCGTCG
GCCTAGCTTGACGACGACTTACGATGCCAGTTCAGTGAC
TTATGGGTGTGAATCATCAGTACGTTTTAGGGTAGCTACC
CATCATCAGACTACGTAGCACCCCAGGTACTAGGACATC
AGTACTGACGGGATGACTGAATATATAGGCATTAGCGCG
```

Publishing the Underground

Publishing the Underground is Dead Ink's way of publishing daring and exciting new fiction from emerging authors. We ask our readers to act as literary patrons and buy our books in advance in order for us to bring them to print. Without this support our books would not be possible.

Dead Ink and the author, Marc Nash, would like to thank all of the following people for generously backing this book – without them this book would not be in your hands.

If you would like to help Dead Ink continue this work please check the website.

www.deadinkbooks.com

Adrian Ward

Alex Blott

Amber Rollinson

Andrew McMillan

Anthony Self

Ben Sewell

Charlotte Bence

Chris Limb

Corey Nelson

D Levin

Dan Brotzel

Dan Thomson

Dani Freedland

Daniel Carpenter

David Hebblethwaite

Denise Sparrowhawk

Emma Baxter

Eva Hnizdo

Gareth Rees

Graeme Hall

Haroun Khan

Harry Gallon

Helenice Zimmermann

Hilary Stanton

James Powell

Jamie Sewell

Jenny Bernstein

Jonathan Freedland

Julie Raby

Kieron Smith

Kit Caless

Laura Emsley

Louise Thompson

Matthew Shenton

Meaghan Ralph

Nick Wilson

Paul Hancock

Petrea Ruddy

Rebecca Lea

Rebekah Hughes

Robin Hargreaves

Sally Lines

Sam Fisher

Shahbaz Haque

SJ Bradley

Sophie Hopesmith

Steph Kirkup

Susan McIvor

Tamim Sadikali

Tania Malkani

Tom Gillespie

Tracey Connolly

Wendy Mann

Yvonne Singh

Every Fox is a Rabid Fox
Harry Gallon

'Every Fox is a Rabid Fox is a harrowing and brutal read. But I fell for its incredibly tender heart. I loved this book.'
        - Claire Fuller, author of Swimming Lessons and Our Endless Numbered Days

'Beautifully executed tale of innocence, tragedy, and the family traumas we all carry with us and many times fail to leave behind.'
        - Fernando Sdrigotti, author of Dysfunctional Males

Robert didn't mean to kill his brother. Now he's stuck between grief and guilt with only ex-girlfriend Willow and the ghost of his dead twin sister for company. Terrified of doing more harm, Robert's hysteria and anxiety grow while Willow and his sister's ghost fight over him: one trying to save him, the other digging his grave.

Every Fox Is A Rabid Fox is a brutal yet tender tale of family tragedy, mental illness and a young man searching for escape from his unravelling mind.

Another Justified Sinner
Sophie Hopesmith

It's the eve of the recession, but who cares? For commodity trader Marcus, life is good: he's at the top of the food chain. So what if he's a fantasist? So what if he wills his college sweetheart to death? So what if it's all falling apart? This isn't a crisis. Until it is.

As misfortune strikes again and again, he goes to help others and 'find himself' abroad – but it turns out that's not as easy as celebrities make it look on TV. Another Justified Sinner is a feverish black comedy about the fall and rise and fall of Marcus, an English psycopath. How difficult is it to be good?

Sophie Hopesmith is a 2012 Atty Awards finalist and her background is in feature writing. Born and bred in London, she works for a reading charity. She likes comedy, poetry, writing music, and Oxford commas. All of her favourite films were made in the 70s.

Hollow Shores
Gary Budden

Budden's debut collection blends the traditions of weird fiction and landscape writing in an interlinked set of stories from the emotional geographies of London, Kent, Finland and a place known as the Hollow Shore.

The Hollow Shore is both fictional and real. It is a place where flowers undermine railway tracks, relationships decay and monsters lurk. It is the shoreline of a receding, retreating England. This is where things fall apart, waste away and fade from memory.

Finding horror and ecstasy in the mundane, Hollow Shores follows characters on the cusp of change in broken-down environments and the landscapes of the mind.

Gary Budden is the co-director of Influx Press. His work has appeared in Structo, Elsewhere, Unthology, The Lonely Crowd, Gorse, Galley Beggar Press and many more. He writes about landscape punk at newlexicons.com.

The Night Visitors
Jenn Ashworth & Richard V. Hirst

Winner of The Saboteur Awards 2017 Best Novella

Orla Nelson used to be a famous writer and now she's seeking a comeback. Alice Wells wants to make something of herself before it's too late. In The Night Visitors these two women, connected by blood and ambition, investigate their ancestor Hattie Soak, a silent film star who fled the scene of a gruesome unsolved crime.

Told entirely via an exchange of emails, The Night Visitors is a story of ghosts, obsession and inherited evil. This novella traces the ways in which technology can hold and transmit our worst secrets and unspoken fears, and what happens when uneasy collaborations start to unravel.

Jenn Ashworth's first novel, A Kind of Intimacy, was published in 2009 and won a Betty Trask Award. She lives in Lancashire and teaches Creative Writing at Lancaster University.

Richard V. Hirst is a writer based in Manchester. His writing has appeared in the Big Issue, the Guardian and Time Out, among others.

About Dead Ink...

Dead Ink is a small, ambitious and experimental literary publisher based in Liverpool.

Supported by Arts Council England, we're focused on developing the careers of new and emerging authors.

We believe that there are brilliant authors out there who may not yet be known or commercially viable. We see it as Dead Ink's job to bring the most challenging and experimental new writing out from the underground and present it to our audience in the most beautiful way possible.

Our readers form an integral part of our team. You don't simply buy a Dead Ink book, you invest in the authors and the books you love.

About the Author...

Marc Nash has published five collections of flash fiction and four novels, all which look to push narrative form and language. He also works with videographers to turn some of his work into digital storytelling. He lives and works in London in the NGO realm.